Hunt on Dark Waters

Hunt on Dark Waters

KATEE ROBERT

BERKLEY ROMANCE
New York

BERKLEY ROMANCE
Published by Berkley
An imprint of Penguin Random House LLC
penguinrandomhouse.com

Library of Congress Cataloging-in-Publication Data

Names: Robert, Katee, author.
Title: Hunt on dark waters / Katee Robert.
Description: First edition. | New York: Berkley Romance, 2023. |
Series: Crimson Sails; 1
Identifiers: LCCN 2023022191 (print) | LCCN 2023022192 (ebook) |
ISBN 9780593639085 (trade paperback) | ISBN 9780593639092 (ebook)
Subjects: LCGFT: Romance fiction. | Fantasy fiction. | Novels.
Classification: LCC PS3618.O31537 H85 2023 (print) |
LCC PS3618.O31537 (ebook) | DDC 813/.6—dc23/eng/20230526
LC record available at https://lccn.loc.gov/2023022191
LC ebook record available at https://lccn.loc.gov/2023022192

First Edition: November 2023

Printed in the United States of America
1st Printing

Book design by Daniel Brount

*To Tim. This book wouldn't exist if you hadn't told me
to send that email I was waffling over. Love you!*

Hunt on Dark Waters

Evelyn

MY GRANDMOTHER TAUGHT ME EVERYTHING I KNOW. She was a withered old crone when my mother died, leaving me alone at the ripe old age of six. Bunny, as she insisted I call her, pulled up in an ancient car, took one look at me, and tsked. "Look just like her, don't you? Get in, little bird. No point in standing around with your thumb up your ass."

She didn't have much respect for laws—human or otherwise—but Bunny had an endless list of rules that were nearly impossible to keep track of. Don't do spell work during an eclipse. If you're going to lie, make it a good one. It doesn't matter what path you tread in life as long as it's the right one for you.

And stay the fuck away from vampires.

Bunny is probably rolling in her grave right now. Or she would be if I'd buried her when she died, the day after I turned eighteen. Our kind don't like graves—another thing she taught me. We prefer to be scattered with the elements, our ashes little bits of stardust going back to the earth and sea and air and fire. She held on to this life until she was no longer needed, and then she moved on to walk paths I can't follow.

It's just as well she's not around anymore to see what I've become.

Case in point: the gorgeous vampire leaning against the bar at my side. Lizzie isn't my girlfriend. She doesn't do labels, and I'm too much Bunny's child to *date* a vampire.

Sleeping with one, though?

I've always liked to play things too close to the edge. Hopefully this time won't kick me in the ass. My track record says otherwise, but hey, I'm a slow learner when there's fun to be had. It's not like I spend much time with Lizzie. We met six months ago, and after spending a glorious two weeks in bed that I wasn't sure I'd survive, we've been asteroids pinging into each other before flying away to commit destruction elsewhere.

I didn't even know she was back in town until I got a text two hours ago with a time and place. Imagine my surprise when I show up to a hole-in-the-wall bar filled with an equal mix of humans and paranormal folk. Most of the time us magical people avoid regular humans. They don't know we exist, and we prefer to keep it that way. But there are places that are exceptions to that rule, and this bar is one of them.

It doesn't seem like Lizzie's speed, but what do I know? It's not like we spend our time together *talking*.

"What about that one?"

I follow Lizzie's chin jerk to the pretty, petite woman sitting by herself at the end of the bar. It's considered rude to scan other paranormals, so I don't risk it, but she gives off a human vibe.

Which means Lizzie wants to play. We've done it a few times, picked up a human at a bar and taken her to the nearest hotel to have a night of sex and, occasionally, magic. As a bloodline vampire, Lizzie's bite is orgasmic, which paves the way for a whole lot of fun.

I'm not in the mood tonight. I shouldn't have answered Lizzie's text at all, or at least I should have begged off. It's the twenty-third of April, which means I turned twenty-five yesterday.

It also means Bunny's been dead for seven years as of today. A lucky number, but it doesn't feel lucky right now. Grief is a strange thing. Most days, I get by on the warmth of doing spells Bunny taught me, or cleaning with the particular concoction of kitchen-witch magic shit that she swore warded away negative emotions.

On the bad days, I go through a whole systematic process of remembering her. Cleaning and spell work and baking her favorite cookies, cumulating in a tearful trip through the box of photos I keep tucked away in my closet. She'd whack me upside the back of my head if she saw me on those days, would remind me that the dead aren't gone for good and there's no point in wasting my living years mourning someone who's stepped through a door to the next part of this grand journey we call existence.

On the good days, I believe her. On the bad days? Not so much. And the anniversary of her death is always a bad day.

"Evelyn." Lizzie's voice is cold, but that's nothing new. She might be downright sizzling when we're in bed, but she doesn't fuck around with the warmer emotions outside of it.

I sigh and try to focus. Giving her any less than one hundred percent of my attention is dangerous, which is exactly why I shouldn't have come out tonight. I look at the human woman again. She's rubbing her straw against her bottom lip in a really enticing way as she watches us . . . watches Lizzie. "She's pretty."

"Do you have another choice?"

I glance half-heartedly around the room. Nearly everyone is watching Lizzie, though most of them aren't doing it overtly. I can't blame them. She's a sight to behold, a lean white woman with a tight ponytail of dark hair and a penchant for athleisure. Her leggings and fitted long-sleeved shirt *should* make her look like a soccer mom who wandered into this dingy bar on accident.

Like prey.

Lizzie, being a bloodline vampire from the family that possesses the magic to control the blood in a person's body, money beyond comprehension, and an orgasmic bite, has never been prey in her life.

The other predators in the room know it, too. I catch sight of a female werewolf hauling her partner out the front door, and there's a demon with a wickedly skillful glamour in the corner who's motioning for his tab.

Clearing the way for Lizzie to hunt.

Too bad I'm not in the mood tonight. I knock back my third—fourth? fifth?—tequila shot and set the glass on the bar, trying to ignore the stickiness of the counter. "Whatever you want. She's fine." Any other night, I'd be sidling up to the woman at the end of the bar and giving her my best charming smile as I buy her a drink and lead her back to Lizzie. Tonight, it feels like too much work.

"Getting jealous, Evelyn?"

Even if I was—and I'm not—I know better than to say as much. Lizzie might like fucking me, but I'm not foolish enough to think she'd ever let orgasms get in the way of murdering me if the mood strikes.

Really, Bunny was right. I'm a damned fool. It's the only explanation for the way I jump into bed with Lizzie over and over again, part of me thrilled to be dancing right up to the edge of ruin.

It's that desire that has me leaning into Lizzie. I can have fun tonight. I'll *make* myself have fun tonight, even if it kills me. I don't have a death wish, normally, but nothing's normal on April twenty-third. Not anymore.

"Maybe I'll take her home instead of roping her in for you." I grin up at Lizzie. "Want to make it a wager?"

She studies me with her eerie dark eyes. "Are you drunk?"

"No. Probably not. Okay, maybe a little." I'm just being sentimental and letting it get the best of me. Not that Lizzie would know that yesterday was my birthday or that today marks Bunny being gone seven years. That's not the kind of relationship we have. What we have can't even be called a relationship. It's a . . . what do my mortal peers call it? A situationship.

"If you're not drunk, then what's wrong with you? You never act like this."

If I were a different person, if *we* were different people, this would be the turning point for us. I would confess why I'm so down, and she'd do something to comfort me. That's the stuff of romantic movies, though. Not real life. "I don't want to talk about it."

"Evelyn."

"It's fine. *I'm* fine." I lift my hand to flag down the bartender for another shot, but Lizzie catches my wrist. "Don't bother. We're leaving."

I blink. "Excuse me?"

"I'm not in the habit of repeating myself." She drops a wad of money on the bar and drags me toward the door. She's moving fast enough that I can barely keep my feet. I catch sight of the woman at the end of the bar and her disappointed look, and then we're at the door. No one moves to help me, though I'm not exactly in danger.

At least, I don't think I am?

"Lizzie?" I almost knock my hip into one of the tables, but somehow Lizzie senses it and jerks me to the side at the last moment. I hiss out a breath. "Where's the fire?"

"You're walking wounded right now. Every predator in that building was about to come sniffing."

I blink, but my response is lost as she hauls me through the door and the cold nighttime air slaps me in the face. It *should* sober me right up, but somehow it makes me realize exactly how drunk I am. I weave on my feet and jerk my arm out of Lizzie's grasp. Or I try. All I get for my trouble is what will probably be an outstanding bruise tomorrow. "Let go."

She ignores me. "If I put you in a cab, are you going to go home and sleep this off?"

Ten minutes ago, that's all I wanted to do. Now, I dig in my heels, buoyed on by the promise tequila whispers through my blood of a good night that couldn't possibly end in ruin. "It's early."

"Evelyn."

"Lizzie." I mimic her tone. "You wanted the pretty lady. Let's go get her."

"I'm not in the mood to babysit a melancholy drunk."

"That's rude. I'm not melancholy. Melancholy is for poets and people writing the Next Great American Novel. I'm *happy*. Fun. A riotous good time."

"Mmm." We reach the curb and she lifts her hand, I'm assuming to flag down a cab. But the car that pulls up is dark and without a single identifying thing on it. I'm not even sure of the make and model.

I peer at it. "Is this one of those expensive black-car experiences? Because I might pay my bills just fine, but I do that by not wasting money on shit like this. It's ostentatious, Lizzie. Honestly, just wasteful."

She looks at me, and I could almost swear I see her considering whether or not to rip my throat out and just be done with this mess. She finally shakes her head. "Get in the car, Evelyn, or I will make you get in the car."

"If you—"

Apparently we've reached the end of Lizzie's patience. She pulls a move that I might be impressed with if I weren't so damn irritated, jerking me forward with one hand and grabbing me by the back of the neck at the same time that she opens the door. I barely have the opportunity to curse when she's shoving me into the back seat.

"Stop treating me like I'm a threat!"

"You're not a threat. You're a liability." She slides in behind me and slams the door. I reach for the handle of the other door, but the car pulls away from the curb fast enough to throw me back against the seat.

She just . . . She honestly just . . . I spin around and look at the driver. A quick scan—it's rude, but I don't care—tells me they're a vampire. *Damn it.* I lean forward and knock on the back of the driver's seat. "Excuse me, I'm being kidnapped."

Lizzie rolls her eyes. "You're not being kidnapped. I'm saving you from yourself. You're welcome."

"No, I'm definitely being kidnapped. Stop the car."

The driver doesn't answer, but I honestly didn't expect them to. They're one of Lizzie's minions, a bitten vampire who serves a bloodline vampire. Funny how vampire culture mimics capitalism so thoroughly, but she's never appreciated it when I point it out. Bunny was really onto something with her rule about staying away from vampires.

"I'm not a liability," I mutter. "And I don't need saving."

"Sure." She snorts. "Whatever you say, Evelyn."

I slump back against the seat, my brain sloshing about inside my skull. "I think I hate you."

"No, you don't."

No, I don't. I slide over and lay my head on her shoulder. "Fine. I don't hate you."

"I know."

I poke her arm. Just when I'm sure Lizzie has no sense of humor to speak of, she lets little glimpses of it out. I'm nearly certain she's making fun of me right now, but when I look up at her gorgeous face, there's only a small smile curving her lips. In the darkness of the back seat, I can almost convince myself that her eyes have warmed a little, too. "I guess I should thank you for saving me from myself. Will orgasms work in payment?"

"Evelyn." There's fond exasperation in her tone. "Close your eyes and rest."

I don't know if it's vampire magic or alcohol, but my eyes slide shut despite my best efforts to keep them open. Sleep flickers and flirts, finally sweeping me away into its dark embrace. It's almost enough to convince myself I feel Lizzie's fingers stroking soothingly through my hair.

CHAPTER 2

Evelyn

WAKE UP, EVELYN."

I lift my head from the pillow and blink at Lizzie. My head pounds in time with my heartbeat and my mouth tastes . . . well, best not to think too hard about how bad my mouth tastes. "I need a toothbrush." I look around, recognition rolling over me in waves. I've been here only a few times; I recognize the large bed with its absurdly high thread count and nice down comforter. I'm still not even sure if vampires sleep, but Lizzie does nothing halfway. The bedroom is a luxurious dark oasis. Too luxurious for my tastes. Too dark. But I can appreciate it in small doses.

"Why am I in your bed?" I sit up and have to press my lips together to keep from being sick. "Why did you bring me here? You should have just sent me home." I have a vague memory of her carrying me into the house and tucking me in with her usual capable briskness. It might warm my heart if I didn't feel so nauseous.

Of course, then she promptly ruins it. "So you could choke on your own vomit and die alone? I don't think so." She waves a hand. "It doesn't matter now. There's no time. You need to go." Her expression is cold and her voice remote, not even a hint of the warmth I've gotten used to. There's definitely none of the softness she showed me last night.

Silly to miss something I'm half-sure I imagined in the first place. I shove my hair out of my face and try to focus past the hangover making me want to burrow back into the bed and not move for another few hours. "Why? What's going on?"

"This thing between us ends. Right now." She looks away, her skin so pale it's almost translucent in the moonlight streaming in from the open window. "I just received word that my mother is on her way. She'll be here soon."

Suddenly, I'm not worried about my hangover. Lizzie might have a soft spot for me, but her mother has an even more fearsome reputation than she does. If she finds out her daughter has been sleeping with a lowly witch, she's liable to yank every drop of blood from my body.

Damn it, Bunny was right. I never should have messed with vampires.

I happen to like my blood right where it is, so I jump up. My stomach sloshes in a worrying way, but I don't have time to be sick right now. I start throwing my clothes on. "How long do I have?"

"Not long." She sounds almost bored. Like I've been a fun toy she's amused herself with, and now it's time for that toy to be discarded.

No reason for that to sting. I knew what this was when I let her seduce me in that club all those months ago. Silly me for getting sentimental. But last night felt . . . different. Or maybe that was the tequila making me silly and sentimental. Lizzie brought me back here because I was making a fool of myself—not because she actually cares.

If she cared, she wouldn't be standing idly by while my death approaches.

Gods, but I'm a fool. I actually started to fall for her. I yank on my boots and tie them quickly. "If you'd just let me go home, this wouldn't be an issue."

"Just another mistake in a long line of them."

Well, fuck, that *definitely* stings. I drag in a breath, trying to think past all the emotions swirling with leftover tequila in my system. I can focus on my bruised heart later. If I don't get away, Lizzie's mother might rip it right out of my chest. "You have to get me out." Lizzie has the same powers as her mother—as the rest of her family. She can protect me long enough for me to run for my life.

"I don't have time. I have to meet her when she arrives." She drags off her clothes from last night—from earlier tonight?—and sets about dressing in a clean outfit. Fool that I am, I can't stop myself from mourning each inch of skin covered by her plain button-up dress. I've never had a lover quite as physically perfect as Lizzie, and what she can do with blood heightens every sexual encounter we've had.

And she . . . took care of me last night? Even though I know better, I can't help thinking about that soft moment in the car. I didn't imagine it. I swear I didn't. I hesitate, my heart pounding. Maybe I was wrong about this being nothing. Maybe . . . "Come with me," I blurt.

Lizzie lifts a brow. "Evelyn."

I know better than to fight a losing battle, but my foolish heart has run away with my mouth. "Please, Lizzie. You're more than the weapon they use you for. You could be so much more." I don't want to change her. Never that. But what could she be if she was actually free of her family's shackles? I never would have dared ask if I wasn't scared for my life.

She crosses to me and catches my chin lightly. Her dark eyes are fathomless. "I honestly can't tell if you're trying to manipulate me or if you actually believe that." She shakes her head slowly. "Either way, it won't work. I have no need to be more than a weapon. I *enjoy* being a weapon." Her grip goes tight and for several beats I think she might do something truly shocking, like kiss me. Even though I know better, I go a little soft in response.

Then she pushes me away. "Get out."

I don't have a heart left to break. Life is cruel and merciless at the best of times, and people even more so. I know that. Of course I know that. It doesn't change the fact that it *hurts* to have the woman I've spent six months sleeping with basically admit that she doesn't care if I live or die.

On the heels of the emotional turmoil from last night, there's a part of me that wants to curl up and just let what will happen happen.

The impulse doesn't last long, but it shames me nonetheless.

I watch Lizzie walk out of the room, her stride long and predatory. She's not even going to stick around to ensure I make it to an exit before her mother comes calling. *That's all I'm worth to her. Less than nothing.*

The thought is at least a little bit a lie, but somehow that just makes it hurt worse. She *does* care about me, but not enough to stand between me and her family. Not enough to save my life. "You are such a *bitch* sometimes, Lizzie."

I'm not going down like this.

I go to my knees and reach under the bed to pull out the pack I stashed there the second time Lizzie brought me to her house. As Bunny used to say, always have an exit route or six planned. It pays to be prepared for any eventuality in normal life, and sleeping with a vampire makes that doubly true. You never know when you'll run into your not-girlfriend's murderous mother.

I sling the backpack on and turn to the window. We're on the second floor facing the front of the house, so that exit is out of the question. No reason to present a target. There's a staircase used by the human servants near the back of the house; a door there will get me out. It means hiking through the forest that surrounds the estate, but it's a small price to pay.

I start for the door, but pause in front of the dresser with the big antique mirror attached to it. Lizzie doesn't wear jewelry as a general rule, but there's a bowl of it just sitting there for the taking. Bracelets, necklaces, rings, and brooches, all studded with jewels. Many of the pieces look like they're hundreds of years old. This kind of haul could set me up for years . . . or at least a few months of lavish living.

I don't make a habit of stealing from friends or lovers, but Lizzie's just proven that she's neither. That makes this jewelry fair game. I cast one furious look at the door and then shrug out of my backpack to dump the jewelry into it. The satisfaction I feel at the thought of her rage when she finds it gone . . .

I'm being petty and I don't give a fuck.

The hallway is blessedly empty and I don't bother to be quiet as I sprint toward the stairs. It's not like I can effectively hide from a vampire of Lizzie's family. Their magic is even more blood-based than normal bloodline vampires. In addition to a whole host of tricks, they can sense any creature with blood in their bodies within a certain range.

Makes for a quick game of hide-and-seek, I imagine.

I take the staircase down, moving so fast, I almost trip. I'd love to say all the sex with Lizzie has improved my cardio, but the truth is that I only run when jobs go bad, and my jobs rarely go bad. *If you have to run, you're already fucked.*

Each breath feels like a knife in my lungs, but I can't afford to slow down. Not a single person appears as I burst out of the doorway at the bottom of the stairs. Where's the door? I clocked it when I explored the house, but adrenaline and my hangover make my head buzz and muddy my memory. There are dozens of doors dotting this hallway. Servants' quarters? Was the exit four doors down or five?

A shiver shoots down my spine as my sensing ward around the house pings the presence of . . . Five. Ten. Twenty-five. Oh fuck, that's a lot of vampires. What is this, a family reunion?

I yank open the fourth door and rush through. Right into a dusty sitting room. I stop short. "What the fuck?" I was sure this was the way out. A moth-eaten couch squats against one wall, directly across from two equally decaying chairs. There's a dresser that appears one sneeze away from collapsing and a large swivel mirror on a stand that seems completely out of place.

Hushed voices sound in the hallway, accompanied by the sound of quick footsteps. I scan them without thinking. Humans, but that doesn't mean I want to get caught. I pull the door shut softly behind me and hold my breath as I wait for them to move past.

Except they don't.

They stop a few feet away from my door and continue speaking in soft, harried tones. I could wait them out, but I have mere minutes before the vampires reach the house.

The window it is.

I head for the window, scrunching my nose as each step sends up clouds of dust. Why don't the maids clean this room? Every other part of this house I've explored has been pristine. I shove the curtains aside and instantly regret it when a sneeze threatens. It doesn't matter. I just have to get the window open . . .

It's painted shut.

"You have *got* to be kidding me." I don't have time to cut the damn thing open. Surely there's another exit somewhere. I take a few steps toward the door but pause when the mirror in the room flickers oddly. Even knowing I don't have time to explore, curiosity takes hold. It will take only a moment to investigate. I move to it and send a flicker of my magic at it. What I find makes me grin.

"Lizzie, you've been keeping secrets." She's got a *portal* in her house. No wonder this room is forbidden to the staff. Having them fall through a portal when they try to clean the mirror would be a nightmare to deal with.

Where does it go, though?

I glance at the door and bite my lip. Trying to find the exit is still a good plan, but I can't move as fast as the vampires outside, and if Lizzie figures out I stole from her, she'll come after me. And not in a fun way.

But the portal? I can go through it and ensure no one can

follow. It won't stop her from hunting me, but I've spent my entire life learning to lose myself. I can stay ahead of her long enough for her mother to send her off to do some murderous shit or for Lizzie to find some other poor soul to torment.

Easy peasy.

The words feel like a lie, so I ignore them.

It takes two precious minutes to cut my thumb and carve a quick spell onto the mirror frame. Once I trigger it, it will explode in thirty seconds, closing the portal behind me. A risk, but giving Lizzie a direct way to follow me is riskier.

I hope.

There's no time to hesitate. I pull my shirt open a bit more to reveal the network of tattoos on my chest. Each is a prepped spell, just waiting for a bit of blood to activate it. I press my bleeding finger to the one in the center of my chest, drawing a shield around me. It will only hold as long as my concentration and power do, but I don't know what I'm walking into.

The door flies open as I take one step into the portal. Lizzie rushes into the room. "What the fuck are you doing?"

"Escaping." I just have to trigger the spell to destroy the mirror after I step through. Damn it, I'm going to have to time this right.

My backpack clinks as I shift farther into the mirror. She narrows her eyes. "You didn't."

"Don't know what you're talking about." My heart is beating so fast, she has to be able to sense the lie. I need to go and I need to go now.

I thought all warmth was gone from Lizzie. Turns out I was wrong. The last bit of softness disappears and she bares her fangs at me. "Drop the bag right now, Evelyn."

It's the smart thing to do, but I haven't been doing the smart thing for a long time. No reason to start now. "Nope." One last deep breath and I trigger the spell on the mirror frame.

Lizzie lunges for me, but it's too late. The last thing I see is her furious face as she screams. "I'm going to fucking *kill* you!" Then the mirror explodes, cutting us off from each other.

I realize my mistake the moment it does. This isn't a direct portal at all. Of course it's not. I should have known Lizzie wouldn't keep an open door to somewhere else in her house.

Darkness presses close, thick and syrupy. I can't see a single thing, can't breathe, can't think. Oh gods, please tell me I didn't flee from Lizzie only to die in this space of nothingness.

Damn it, *no.* Instinct gets me moving, despite the difficulty it is to take one step and then another. The only other option is holding still and suffocating, and I'm not going out like that. Panic flutters in my chest, screaming through my mind. I've heard drowning is a peaceful way to die, but there's no peace in this. Just terror.

Keep going. Keep moving. One foot in front of the other. You still have strength, and you're going to fucking use it.

Step after step after step. It feels like the abyss is swallowing me whole, but I'm walking on *something*, even if I can't see it. There has to be a way out. There *has* to be. I just need to find it.

But nothing has changed by the time my lungs start screaming for air. In desperation, I pick up my pace. I don't have much time left. Hard to say if black dots are dancing across my vision when I can't see anything at all. The very non-air seeming to fight against me, trying to hold me still and slow me down.

Fuck you.

I'm running now, pumping my arms as fast as I can while

my lungs shriek. I clamp my lips together to keep from gasping, but I'm seconds away from my body taking over.

I'm moving so fast, I don't realize the ground beneath my feet is gone until I'm falling.

Between one blink and the next, the darkness is replaced by pale dawn light. I drag in one glorious salty breath . . . and then hit something hard enough that everything goes black.

CHAPTER 3

Bowen

MERMAID OFF THE STARBOARD SIDE!"

The call brings me out of my cabin. We're not in mermaid waters, but if the sighting is correct, we have one bastard of a fight on our hands. I grab a spear from the rack, noting that my quartermaster, Miles, has the spelled net already in his hands.

We meet on the starboard side and I narrow my eyes against the glare of the sun on the choppy water. How the lookout saw anything at all is a damned miracle. "Where?"

Miles is a head shorter than me and built lean, his skin covered in fine green scales like a reptile. He shields his eyes and looks up to the crow's nest where Sarah is perched. I can barely see her blond hair from here, but it's obvious she's communicating with him using her air magic. A few moments later, he points. "There."

I follow his finger to see a figure in the water less than ten yards away. I tense, half raising the spear, before I register what I'm seeing. Pale skin. Long hair that's *hair* and not water weeds.

A face that is decidedly more human than the merfolk I've come across in my years hunting with the Cŵn Annwn. "Not a mermaid."

Miles shrugs. "Then leave them. The sea will take care of it."

He always does this. If there's a change of plan, Miles would rather run it over than bend to adapt to new circumstances. I swear he's started doing it solely to undermine me. If I say we go north, he starts arguing that south is a better route. Every. Single. Time.

To his view, allowing the sea to take this person instead of bringing them on board and triggering the decision between death and joining the crew would be less of a headache. There are others among the Cŵn Annwn who would agree with him and continue sailing.

But I am captain of this ship and that's not how we do things on the *Crimson Hag*. I have enough blood on my hands to last lifetimes. I try to avoid adding more whenever possible.

I pass over the spear. "We're not leaving them to the sea. They might be a local."

"No local is going to be out *here*." He shakes his head, the move too sharp to be strictly human. "We haven't seen another ship in days, and there's been no storms to sweep one down, let alone to bring a survivor into our path. They're a Threshold trespasser."

Probably. Likely, even.

That doesn't mean I'm going to let the sea take them without checking, and then offering them their choice. The whole purpose of the Cŵn Annwn is to protect Threshold and all the realms connected to it by portals on the islands scattered across the vast sea. Not all the islands contain portals, though, and there *are* citizens of the realm who are supposed to fall under our protection as well.

Not that all of our people remember that. At least, not when it doesn't suit them.

I wait for the *Crimson Hag* to sail a little closer to the person. I could dive in and retrieve them, but there's no reason to go through those theatrics. Instead, I focus my power and extend it, scooping the person out of the water and bringing them carefully over to the deck.

The crew eyes these goings-on with some interest. It's not every day we haul people out of the sea, and it's even rarer that they're still alive when we do.

I crouch next to our catch and take a better look at them. A woman, human or from one of the realms where they're more humanoid than not. She's wearing clothing that looks unfamiliar, a bag strapped to her back, so it takes me a moment to place the pants. Denim. Jeans. That narrows down the options of her origin considerably. They cling to a body that's lush: thick thighs, broad hips, soft stomach. Her black shirt hugs her torso, hinting at small breasts.

I jerk my gaze up to her face, determined not to stand here ogling an unconscious woman, but there's no relief to be found. She has round cheeks, a full mouth, and wide-set eyes. Her skin is pale enough that I want to get her under cover before the sun has its way with her, and her hair color is hard to determine while wet, but I think it is a few shades lighter than my own.

A spear flashes into view. I throw out my hand to stop it, but I'm too slow. "Fuck!" I tense, but it hovers in the air, its point a mere inch from her chest. A flare of violet magic surges and then disappears and the spear clatters to the deck.

I spin on Miles. "What the fuck are you doing?"

"My job," he says flatly. "She's not one of ours."

No, she certainly isn't. I don't recognize the magic, but based on her human looks, I'd wager she's a witch. No reason for that to intrigue me. It just means she'd be an asset if we turn her. "Our *job* is to offer a choice."

"The Cŵn Annwn have no use for women like her."

I open my mouth to tell him where he can fuck right off to, but her eyes fly open, stalling me. She takes us in with a single look and then slams her hand to her chest. Magic rises in a wave that pushes me back a full yard before I get my magic up in a shield. Several of my people aren't so lucky. Splashes sound, quickly followed by the call, "Man overboard!"

Miles goes for the spear, but she flicks it away before he can get his hands on it. "Where the hell am I?" Her voice is hoarse, as if she had been in the sea longer than I realized.

"You, don't move." I point at her and then turn my glare on Miles. "Get our people out of the water. Now."

For a moment, I think he might argue, but he finally gives a sharp nod and starts snapping commands to the crew. Within a few minutes, we've fished out the fallen crew and ensured there was no permanent damage done to the ship itself.

While I've been dealing with this, the woman has done some looking of her own. She surveys my ship in a way that makes my skin tight, like she's assessing every inch visible for value. I know what that look means.

Thief.

Sure enough, she has something in her hand that she's fiddling with. I recognize it instantly, and my hand goes to my hip where my flask usually is. Gone now, taken by her quick hands while I assumed she was unconscious.

Maybe Miles is right about her.

I shake my head sharply. That's dangerous thinking. A choice. We always offer a choice. It's the very essence of what separates us from the monsters we hunt. *Their* victims are not offered anything resembling mercy.

She catches me watching her play with the flask and grins, completely unrepentant. "Should I call you Captain?" Her voice is throaty, and she puts enough innuendo into the question to sink the *Hag*.

I take a step toward her before I catch myself. This woman is no siren—they're all but extinct, thank the gods—but she has a pull all her own. "You're aboard the *Crimson Hag*, a vessel of the Cŵn Annwn."

Interest sharpens her eyes. I belatedly realize they're a green that makes me think of magic and lush forests. She leans closer and makes a show of looking me up and down. "Funny, but you don't look like a hound."

"A hound," I repeat.

"Mmm." Her gaze snags on my chest and stays there. "Hounds of Annwn, the Wild Hunt, and all that. I know my Welsh myths."

I have nothing to say to that. We aren't a myth. We never were. But history has a way of becoming myth if given enough time and distance. There are stories about the Cŵn Annwn in a lot of realms. As long as there's been Threshold acting as its given name between the realms, there have been the Cŵn

Annwn, protecting it. If the originals occasionally shifted forms and hunted in other realms . . .

Well, we try not to draw attention from the originals for a reason.

The rest of us who make up the fleet of ships that sail under crimson banners are mortal enough. Even the Council, who squat back in Lyari, ruling Threshold in the originals' absence, tend to be only slightly more long-lived.

Not that I'm about to give this stranger a history lesson on my people. "You have a choice. Join the Cŵn Annwn or be given back to the sea."

"Wow, that's an interesting choice, very original and not at all overdone." She rolls her eyes.

It strikes me that she's not at all afraid of me. I blink. I don't know what to do with that. Even the people in Threshold, the ones it is our entire purpose to protect, are wary of us. It's a careful balance of respect, and I do my best to ensure I never abuse my power, but this witch doesn't know that. She doesn't know anything about me. "It's the only choice you have," I snap.

"Cute." She turns and looks around once more before facing me again. "But I'm abstaining from making any choices. The lizard man tried to stab me in the heart before he knew I was awake, so forgive me if I don't want to join your little murder club."

"But you'll steal from us." I hold out a hand. "Give it back."

"Oh, this little thing?" She holds up the flask as if she's never seen it before. "It's mine. Old family heirloom."

"Why, you—" I bring myself up before I reach for her. "What's your name?" I demand.

"Evelyn." She flips the flask up and catches it deftly. "There's one all-encompassing rule of the universe, dear Captain. I'm surprised you don't know it."

Even as I know I'll regret asking, I sigh. "What's the rule?"

"Finders keepers." She grins. "This is mine. I won't give it back, no matter how much you snap and snarl at me. Really, you're taking the hound thing too literally. It's embarrassing."

That's about enough of that. She's obviously going to be difficult, and while that shouldn't be a death sentence, I can't let her undermine me in front of my crew. Not when Miles has spent months chipping away at the crew's opinion of me. Letting this witch talk circles around me will just give him more ammunition.

Like all ships of the Cŵn Annwn, we elect our captains by a vote. My authority exists only as long as my crew has faith in me, and their faith is already precarious at best.

If I lose the captaincy, Miles will take the vote. The first thing he'll do is stab that spear right through her heart.

I draw my power to me, as easy as breathing, and wrap her up in it. Evelyn squeaks, but I gag her before she can keep running her mouth, sealing her jaw shut. Her eyes go wide and then narrow, promising retribution.

I grip her waist and try very hard not to notice how enticingly soft she is. I lift her easily off the deck and toss her over my shoulder. Several of the crewman laugh when she makes an indignant noise, but Miles watches with narrowed eyes.

Let him watch. I haven't given him anything to work with. I hope.

Evelyn's not taking this seriously, but people often don't

when they mistakenly go through a portal and end up some-where they're not supposed to be. Not until it's too late. The laws are the laws. I can't bend them without risking myself and my crew.

Not even for a cute, mouthy little witch.

CHAPTER 4

Evelyn

THE AUDACITY OF THIS MOTHERFUCKER!

I fight against the invisible hold around me as the captain walks across the deck. Telekinetics are rare, and it's good that they are because they're a gigantic pain in the ass. If I could get to my spells on my chest, I should be able to break his hold, but he's got my arms pinned to my sides.

He's also got me over his shoulder like a sack of grain, and I will absolutely not be even a little affected by the fact that he doesn't seem to register my weight at all. Why should he? He's the size of a house. He's got to be at least six-five, with shoulders that block out the sky and skin tanned by spending so much time in the sun. Even upside down, I can tell that his crimson cloak fans out dramatically when he walks, like some kind of lone wolf character in a movie.

He might be handsome, too, in an earthy kind of way.

I haven't noticed, though.

There's no getting out of his hold for now, so I turn my

attention to the ship and crew. At first glance, it looked like a pirate ship from a movie, but it's not quite the same. The whole space is saturated with magic, and it's apparent in the way some of the bits and pieces are moving without any crew doing the moving. The big crimson sail overhead unfurls and the ship jerks a little as we catch the wind.

The other thing that's different is that everyone appears recently bathed. In fact, the ship smells . . . kind of nice. Like pine and lemon with the faintest whiff of mint. It smells a bit like the protection spell Bunny put into her cleaning spells. Makes me think of Sundays being hauled out of bed and put to work. I always bitched, but now nostalgia hits me so hard that I have to blink rapidly against the burning in my eyes.

Bunny isn't here, and I'm in danger.

I close my eyes and try to focus. The captain is moving rather smoothly, almost like he doesn't want to jostle my stomach on his shoulder, but that must be a coincidence. The guy just gave me the option of joining his merry band of murderers . . . or drowning. After that trip through the portal, I am *not* going out by drowning. No, thank you.

I'm in Threshold.

I still haven't processed *that.* I might have poked the captain about the Cŵn Annwn being myth—everyone knows both they and the Wild Hunt actually existed and still ride in the dark of certain nights—but I honestly thought Threshold wasn't real.

Once upon a time, the realms used to be much closer to one another. People and creatures could jump them easily, which is where a lot of stories of myths and monsters come from. No one knows what happened to make crossing all but impossible, only that it was a very long time ago. So many generations have passed that people have stopped wondering.

But . . . Threshold? A realm that's still connected to every other realm in existence? The possibilities make my palms itch.

The captain shoves open a door and the light dims as we leave the deck. I honestly don't know what I expected. Nothing about this ship matches expectations for . . . pirates? I'm not sure if this crew even qualifies as pirates as I recognize them.

Cool air brushes my bare skin and wet clothes and makes me shiver. The captain sets me on my feet and I waste no time looking around. There's a large desk near a trio of massive windows that look out over the water and the wake of the ship's passing. Polished wood floors. A door on either side of the room.

It's bigger than I expected, and I pause to take in the space again. I'm no architect but I'm *certain* the walls go well past where the end of the ship should be. Is this a pocket realm? But then how is it looking out at the water we've just sailed through?

My attention goes to the desk. It's not made of any wood I recognize and the surface shimmers a little. Magic? I try to take a step forward but I'm still bound with the captain's power.

I glare at him. Gods, but he's even more attractive now than he was when I first opened my eyes. Dark hair that's just long enough to be termed roguish. A nice square jaw that probably shatters the fists of anyone who tries to punch him. A well-muscled body that is obviously used to hard work, clothed in fitted pants, a loose black shirt with a V that gives a tantalizing glimpse of a broad chest sprinkled with hair, and a duster I want to steal right off his back. His eyes are almost as dark as Lizzie's . . . No, best not to think about Lizzie or how furious she looked when I saw her last. How *murderous*.

If I can get through a different portal, I really will be beyond her grasp.

I tuck the thought away. It's a potential plan for the future, but first I have to navigate this mess I've found myself in.

The captain surveys me with a critical eye, his expression all forbidding lines that do *not* give me a thrill. "If I remove your gag, will you behave?"

Absolutely not. I try to look sincere as I nod. He doesn't seem convinced, but the power wedging my jaw shut eases. I open and close my mouth a few times. It doesn't actually hurt—he was remarkably gentle, with superior control—but I'll take any drop of guilt I can dredge up. It's an excellent lever to get people to do what you want.

Unfortunately, there's none to be seen on his face. If anything, he looks more irritated. "I didn't hurt you, so stop playing that game."

"Maybe I have a glass jaw."

"You don't."

He's right. I abandon that line of manipulation and move on to the next. "I didn't mean to end up here. There was a glitch in the portal I was using. I have a family that needs me. Children. Four of them. If I don't get back, they'll starve."

He might as well be carved from granite. "What are their names?"

I blink. "What?"

"Your starving children. Their names." He snaps his fingers. "Quickly."

"Dean, Sam, John, and . . . Cas."

The captain doesn't seem convinced. "Even if that were true, which I highly doubt, it makes no difference. We have our laws for a reason."

"Your laws. Not mine."

"You're in Threshold, Evelyn. They're your laws now."

The way he says my name is so severe, I don't know what to do with my body's reaction to it. I simultaneously want to flee the room and climb him like a grumpy tree. Which is just further proof that my hormones cannot be trusted.

First Lizzie, who was totally willing to let me die and will undoubtedly try to hunt me down and kill me for betraying her.

Now this captain, who gave me the option to join his crew but obviously has no problem killing me if I decline.

The best way to win a fight with a telekinetic is to never start one. The second best way is to knock them silly in a dirty attack and then run like hell. Neither is an option right now. I'm on a ship in the middle of an ocean. I have nowhere to run to, even if my arms were free.

There's an angle here. I just need to find it. "What's your name, Captain?"

He clenches his jaw like he might not answer, but finally he says, "Bowen."

"Nice strong name for a nice strong lad."

He doesn't smile. "You have a choice, Evelyn. Make it."

So we're back to that. I shift, trying to press against his telekinetic hold on me. The fucker is strong, I'll give him that. I *think* I could break the magic around me given the right spell, but the longer he holds me, the more I wonder if that's even true.

Most people have tells, even if you've only just met them. Their faces or bodies give them away, provide leverage to get what I want. Having a conversation with him is like beating my head against a stone wall. I don't think I can talk my way out of this one.

True fear licks up my spine, putting an edge of desperation into my tone. "Drop me at a portal. Any portal. Or throw me back into the sea and I'll find my own portal."

"We're days away from the nearest island. You won't make it without a ship."

If that's true, then he's probably right. I could theoretically propel myself through the water for a decent amount of time, but my energy reserves aren't unlimited, and I can't hold a spell for days on end. Especially one that would require so much power.

But neither of the other options are good. "Well then, I'm not choosing."

He flicks a glance over my shoulder to the door we just came through. "Not choosing is still a choice. *Any* choice that isn't joining the Cŵn Annwn is a choice for death."

I go cold in a way that has nothing to do with the pleasant chill of the room or my wet clothes. "What's to stop me from joining your little fan club and then betraying you the first chance I get?"

"There are vows."

Vows were made to be broken. Bunny's voice whispers through me. Maybe I can work with this? I shrug, feigning nonchalance. "Oh, well, in that case—"

"Whatever you're thinking, discard it," he cuts in. "In the event that someone breaks their vows and deserts, a hunt is called and the entire fleet participates. The longest a deserter has lived is three days."

Three days. That's . . . not a long time. "So you put a magical tracker on them when they take the vow. That's hardly sporting."

Bowen stares at me for a long moment. "This is not a game.

I'm sure you're very formidable, but you are no match for us. Take the vow and take it seriously. Mourn your old life if you must, but let it go." Shadows lurk in his eyes, but he blinks and they're gone. "You don't want the fate that awaits you if you try to run. Trust me."

He sounds so sincere, it makes me fight down a shiver of dread. I'm good at evasion, but this group is the *Cŵn Annwn*. The Wild Hunt exists in multiple folklore traditions, but the general consensus is that they're unstoppable. When they ride, smart people hide. Getting swept up in the hunt might mean you end up miles—and sometimes years—away from where you started . . . or it might mean you end up as *prey*.

The prey never escape.

These Cŵn Annwn either got their name from the myth or the myth got the name from them. Neither option is ideal for my odds of evading them indefinitely. *Three days*. I bite down on questions about that person. The way Bowen spoke of them, I bet he was part of that hunt. Were they just a normal person? Were they magical? Surely I have some kind of advantage over them.

I clear my throat. "Why the choice? Seems like guiding people back to their home realms would be just as good an option as anything. Having your crews staffed with reluctant people can't be good for business."

Again, a flicker, but I can't divine the emotion behind it. It seems too much to ask for that he agrees with me. Bowen finally shrugs. "I don't make the laws, Evelyn. I enforce them. Now, you've stalled long enough. If you don't choose, I'll choose for you."

I almost ask what choice he'd make for me, but I don't think

I want to know. He might have stopped his crewman from attacking me again, but he's obviously one hundred percent done with my shit, so it's just as likely that he'd toss me overboard to fend for myself if he didn't kill me outright.

Great.

Awesome.

I close my eyes and try to think. There's a way out of this. I just have to find out what it is. What I need is a loophole. No organization or person is free from things that they'd rather keep quiet. If the Cŵn Annwn has existed as long as it seems, I bet they have a boatload of secrets stashed somewhere. One has to be nasty enough to convince them to set me free from their group. *Without* a magical tracker attached to me.

Good thing I excel at stealing secrets.

Or, fuck, worst case, I can find a portal, jump through it, and start running.

Either way, under no circumstances will I spend the rest of my life trapped here, vow or no vow. I lift my chin and stare down Bowen. "Fine. Have it your way. I'll make a choice. I'll join the Cŵn Annwn." For now.

CHAPTER 5

Bowen

Y OU'LL JOIN." I STARE AT THE WITCH, WAITING FOR THE
other shoe to drop. She agreed too readily. I don't know
her well, but I've spent years dealing with an unruly crew,
half of which became Cŵn Annwn with the same enthusiasm
as the woman before me . . . which is to say none at all. "Just like
that."

"I'm sorry, were you looking to tie me down and torture
me until I saw reason?" She lifts her brows. Her hair has already started to dry, and it's lighter than I'd first thought, not
brown but blond. It makes her green eyes look even greener, or
maybe that's the way the color is coming back into her pretty
face.

"I don't make a habit of torturing people. It's messy and they
tell you only what you want to hear. It's not a good way to get
information."

Her brows inch higher. "You're not joking, are you? How
horrifying."

I find myself flushing, and resent that she provoked even such a small reaction. "Torture is not a joking matter."

"I don't think you'd know a joking matter if it slapped you in the face." She wiggles, pushing against my magic binding her. "Now that I'm one of your crew, you should let me go. You're violating a whole lot of maritime law right now."

"I'm doing no such thing." She's right on one thing, though. I should let her go. Her chest is heaving in a very distracting way, pressing against the sheer fabric of her top. It's more challenging than it should be to keep my gaze on her face. "The only maritime law in Threshold is what the Council of the Cŵn Annwn make it. You're not in your realm anymore. Adjust."

"Adjust," she repeats slowly. I can practically see her twisty mind working overtime, looking for an angle to leverage and give her the advantage. "Wait, you said 'Council.' You have a ruling body?"

She's going to be a pain in the ass. I can already see her searching for an angle to exploit. For the briefest moment, I'm tempted to follow Miles's lead and toss her overboard to be someone else's problem. I discard the thought immediately. That is not how we do things on this ship. "Pray you'll never have cause to meet them. They are not as nice as I am." There's no avoiding Lyari entirely, not when captains are required to stop in periodically and show our face to the Council, but I very intentionally set my routes to avoid the Southwest so they have no excuse to call me to task more than strictly necessary.

"Nice," she says faintly. "Right."

She's still not taking this seriously, but there's little I can do about that. "Once you give your vow, I'll release you and get you set up in your new bunk."

"A bunk. Of course." She wrinkles her nose. It's a cute nose, and I hate that I notice that cuteness. "Oh well, let's get this over with. What's the vow?"

"I pledge myself to the Cŵn Annwn. To hunt when the moon is full and howl for the death of monsters. I will bathe in their blood and protect the weak."

"Charming."

"It's tradition." I hold up my hand. "It requires a bit of blood before you speak it." I see her sly look only because I'm watching her so closely. And I'm watching her so closely only because she's a threat, not because I like the way the low light plays in her bright green eyes. Unnaturally green, almost. Uncanny.

"Of course it does. Can't have shady characters going back on their word." She grins. Trouble. This woman is *trouble*. I have a whole ship full of the same kind of people, so I should be used to it by now, but there's something about Evelyn that makes my skin prickle. Bringing her onto the crew is a mistake I'll end up being the one to pay the price for, but there's no other choice. The laws are laws for a reason. It's not for me—or anyone else—to ignore them because they're inconvenient.

I nod at her chest. More specifically, at the tattoos there. "I've never seen a witch cast spells like that."

"Baby, I think we both know you've never met a witch like me." Her grin widens and her uncanny gaze drops to my hips.

It takes every bit of self-control I have not to react to the sheer insinuation in her tone. She doesn't mean it. She's attempting to provoke a response. If I give her the benefit of the doubt, I could admit that she's probably terrified out of her mind and attempting to get through this situation on pure bravado.

I'd be a fool to give her the benefit of the doubt. She might be scared, but that's not the dominant emotion. I doubt this woman has ever walked into a situation and not immediately looked for ways to turn it to her advantage—and steal some shit along the way.

The vow will hold her. It's held everyone else, and I see no reason for her to be the exception, even if she thinks she can wiggle her way out of it. I focus on my magic binding her and free one of her arms. I swear I see her considering an attack before she smiles sweetly as if she's not a threat at all. "I'll need something to cut myself with in order to make this vow."

Again, my instincts demand I keep anything resembling a weapon out of this woman's hands. Unfortunately, as a witch, she *is* a weapon. Especially with those spells inked onto her chest. Most witches I've encountered over the years are able to prep only a small number, limited by whatever spell material they carry on their person. With the spells tattooed onto Evelyn, there is no need to prepare. The only limit is her capacity for magic.

I reluctantly move closer and pull a dagger from the sheath on my belt. I don't pass it over to her. Instead, I catch her wrist and flip her hand palm up. Her skin is startlingly soft. I have no business noticing that. I press the tip of the dagger to the fleshy part of her palm.

Evelyn stares at the tiny dot of blood. "That's it?"

"The amount of blood matters little. You, of all people, should know that. Even a drop is linked to your life force. Now, the vow."

She frowns a little, the expression so fleeting it's gone almost as soon as I register it. "Do you have many witches on your crew?"

"In a moment, they'll number at one." I gave her palm a pointed glance. "You're wasting both of our time. Either make the vow or I toss you back in the ocean."

"Someone should really petition this Cŵn Annwn Council of yours to let them know that their rules suck."

I don't bother to respond to that ridiculous statement. The Council doesn't make the rules. The originals did before they disappeared into the waves of history. No Cŵn Annwn has seen *them* in longer than anyone can remember, and some of our people live thousands of years. None among my crew has that kind of life span, but there's an old hunter who is quartermaster to the *Harpy*. Once, when we happened to make port at the same time, we shared a drink. The stories he told, passed down from his grandfather who lived just as long as him, were enough to make me grateful that the originals don't bother with us any longer.

It's best not to do anything to draw their attention or cause them to stir from wherever they reside now. I'm not sure any of us would survive it if they did. "The vow, witch."

She huffs out a breath but relents after a moment of pained silence. "I pledge myself to the Cŵn Annwn. To hunt when the moon is full and howl for the death of monsters. I will bathe in their blood and protect the weak."

Winning this fight should feel more momentous than it does. Instead, all I feel is exhausted. This is only the first battle of many with this woman, and I'm already fighting on several fronts aboard the *Hag*. One wrong move will be enough to tip the careful balance I've fought so hard for . . . the same balance Miles is constantly striving to undermine.

"It's done." As much as I would like to keep this woman

restrained until I can assure her good behavior, it's no longer an option. I reluctantly withdraw my magic and set her carefully on the floor.

Evelyn brushes at her clothing in a way that is obviously designed to distract. "I've never been a pirate before. Where are we headed, Captain? Off to steal some rich merchant's booty?"

"I thank you never to use the word 'booty' in my presence again." I motion for her to precede me. "We're hunting a sea monster. It's been terrorizing one of our local villages, so it's our job to remove the threat."

"Wow. So you actually do things beyond kidnap helpless civilians? How noble."

"Yes, *we* actually do more than that." I hold the door open for her and follow her back into the sunlight. It's impossible to avoid noticing how it caresses her light hair almost lovingly. As if her energy draws the sunbeams more than anyone else on the deck.

"Kit!"

"Up here, Captain." Kit descends one of the ropes so quickly that I wince in sympathy. Ne lands on the deck with a boom that sounds like a cannon going off, and strides toward us. Kit is a tall person with warm dark brown skin and the kind of shoulders that could hold up a mast in a hurricane. Ne is also one of the few crew members who Miles can't sway. I trust nem to get Evelyn settled in without causing an incident.

Kit eyes Evelyn. "Not a mermaid, after all."

"She's a new member of our crew. See her outfitted and give her a bunk." I barely resist the urge to tell nem to keep a close eye on her. It's unnecessary. Kit can take care of this without letting Evelyn's cunning words sway nem to some kind of foolish action. If Miles hasn't managed to do that after months of campaigning, Evelyn won't in a few short hours.

"Sure thing, Captain."

"You." I give Evelyn a long look. "Don't give nem any trouble."

"Wouldn't dream of it."

Kit makes an obvious attempt to hide nir smile. "This way, miss."

"No need to stand on formality. Call me Evelyn." She smiles up at nem, every inch a charming beauty.

It's only as they walk away that I realize I'm missing something. I touch my empty sheath and where my dagger was just a few moments ago. Irritation flares. How the fuck did she pickpocket me again? I wasn't even close to her this time. It shouldn't have been possible. She didn't do magic. I'm certain of that, at least.

I'm going to have to keep an eye on her. A close one. That thought should fill me with dread, but for the first time in years, a slow curl of anticipation goes through me. This woman is nothing like the rest of my crew, or the other people I've encountered in Threshold. It feels like the winds have shifted, but I don't know yet if it means a blessed trip—or if there's a hurricane bearing down on us.

I turn for the helm and nearly run into Miles. He doesn't look any happier than he did earlier. His irritation is there in the way his skin has shifted to a dull orange and his tongue flicks out at regular intervals. He looks over to where Kit leads Evelyn down to the crew quarters. "This is a mistake. The rest of the crew thinks so, too."

"They would after you've been dripping poison into their

ears about her." I can't quite keep my anger from my voice. "You had no right to try to kill her before we gave her the choice."

Miles turns his inky eyes on me. "There's a reason most witches don't survive in Threshold for long. Kill her now, kill her later, but she won't last and you damn well know it."

As with any group of varied peoples, the Cŵn Annwn has factions. I don't like thinking about it. We're supposed to be a unified group. It *should* be cut-and-dried—the laws exist, we follow them, end of story. Unfortunately, not everyone feels that way, and they don't treat all trespassers equally.

They don't treat the locals equally, either.

I brush that thought off. This is different. Some of our people consider witches to be monsters. Which means they don't give witches the choice I just gave Evelyn. They kill them on sight.

I hold Miles's gaze steadily. "She took the vow. She's part of the crew. A strike against her is a strike against me and the rest of the Cŵn Annwn. I trust you'll keep that in mind."

"No need to threaten me." He holds up his hands, but he's got a glint in his eye I don't like. She's part of the crew as long as I'm captain, but should that change, her protections disappear the moment he takes the position. The Council might rule the Cŵn Annwn, but each individual ship is governed by its captain, and some play faster and looser with the rules than others.

"It's not a threat. It's a reminder. Call for a vote if you want, but until you do, I am captain of this ship, and you *will* obey me."

"Yes, you're captain . . . for now."

There's nothing else to say to that. I move past him to where Dia stands at the helm. She's a wizened old crone, but she's half fae, so gods alone know how old she actually is. For all that her medium-brown face is lined with wrinkles and her hair is white peppered with black instead of the other way around, she's spry on her feet and has the sharpest mind I've ever encountered. "Captain."

"Dia. How are we looking?" We haven't been moving as quickly as I'd like; the winds seeming to work against us from the moment we got our orders about this particular sea monster. We don't have many details beyond the fact that it's killed several people in the village on Sarvi. But most of our orders come in like that—there are deaths and we're sent to investigate and remove whatever monster is responsible.

Dia's brown eyes glaze over into milky white. Her magic is one of the strangest—and most useful—I've ever encountered. She's a weather mage who, by some twist of family lineage, rather than being able to control the weather, has precognition linked specifically with weather patterns. We're almost never caught unawares in a storm because she's on board.

She finally shakes her head and her eyes clear. "We have a problem. That little squall we intended to use to speed our way along has developed into a ship killer. We can skirt the edges of it, but it will take us significantly off course and add nearly a week to the journey." She taps one wizened finger against the helm. I let her think. I know this part of Threshold as well as she does, but I've long since learned that the best way to manage the strong personalities in my crew is to let them have their say. Especially when I'm in agreement. "If we cut to the west, we can make port in Yaltia just as it hits. Rough ride, but nothing we can't handle. Storm should be through in the next day. That way we only lose two days instead of seven."

It's no competition. I glance at Miles. For once, he doesn't seem inclined to argue for the sake of asserting his own dominance. He shrugs. "Sounds like a plan."

I hate that it feels like he's giving *me* permission instead of the other way around. "You know what to do."

He nods and starts barking orders, and the crew shifts like a well-oiled machine to meet the new demands.

There's the added bonus of Yaltia being close enough to the attacks that they might have more updated news about what kind of situation we're headed into with this particular monster. My crew is experienced and good at what they do, but every bit of information we can gather ahead of time is worth its weight in gold.

It will also give me an opportunity to see if the witch intends to keep her vow . . . or attempts to escape at the first opportunity.

CHAPTER 6

Evelyn

AFTER THE POCKET DIMENSION TRICK THAT IS THE CAP-
tain's quarters, I shouldn't be surprised when Kit leads me
through a door at the bottom of the staircase and into a space
that is blatantly too big to be contained within the walls of the
ship. I look at the polished floors and the hallway studded with
easily a dozen doors. "Neat trick."

"It is, isn't it?" Kit smiles. Ne isn't like Miles or the captain.
There's something relaxing about nir presence that feels a bit
like ne is exuding Xanax from nir pores.

I press my thumb to the glyph tattoo just below my left collarbone, but the sensation doesn't change. So, not a spell. Perhaps it's a feature of nir ancestry. I don't think ne is human, or
at least not a flavor of human I've encountered before. "Are you
from my realm?"

"I doubt it." Ne heads down the hallway, nir long strides eating up the distance and forcing me to hurry to keep up. "Unless

you're from a realm where all but the tallest peaks have fallen into a toxic sea and most of the population lives on airships."

"Nope." I knew there were countless realms out there, a patchwork quilt of existence that boggles the mind, but I never had to think about it before. The most realm-hopping anyone does these days is when they make deals with bargainer demons. And then they hop only to *one* realm, instead of ending up in Threshold.

Holy fuck, I'm in Threshold.

Eventually, that is going to sink in fully, but for now I'm still in survival mode. I don't bother to ask Kit about the parameters of the vow. No reason to show my hand ahead of time. "If the ship sinks and I'm in here, do I sink, too?"

"Yes." Ne points to the door at the end of the hallway. "Through there is the mess hall and med bay. Your room will be here." Ne moves to a door identical to the others. It leads into a relatively nice room that would be at home in any college campus across the US. "Bathroom is shared with your roommate, Lucky."

I blink. "Each of these rooms has its own bathroom?" I went through a *heavy* pirate phase back in my teen years, and the whole life seemed rather glamorous until Bunny sat me down and talked about scurvy and poop decks and the reality of how damned stinky everyone was over those long voyages. It effectively killed any true desire to be a proper historical pirate.

This is something else entirely.

Kit bursts out laughing. "Trust me, it's better for everyone this way. Before the captain sprang for the extra-large magical expansion, there were more fights over showers than there were over meals or shifts. Beyond that, with as varied as the crew is, everyone's needs are a little different."

I can see how that would be true, but it doesn't explain why Bowen—er, the captain—would care. "He's paying for it with what?"

Kit's open expression shutters. "Best you talk to him about it if you want more information." Ne hesitates. "Everyone needs a bit of a time to adjust when they're first brought on. That will buy you some grace, but not if you're trying to make trouble. I suggest you don't abuse it."

I give nem a wide-eyed look. "I wouldn't dream of it." I know how to work a long con, though I don't normally have the patience for that sort of thing. I also can't take for granted that anyone would lend me a willing ear on this ship. It's entirely possible—probable, even—that they are all as murderous as Miles or as horrifically boring and law-abiding as Bowen.

I haven't seen anyone as attractive, though.

No.

No, absolutely not.

I might have terrible taste in partners, but even I have to have limits. A grumpy, uptight pirate paladin would have Bunny emerging from whatever plane of existence she's landed on in her afterlife to slap the shit out of me. Not that Bowen would consider himself a paladin, but if it walks like a duck and quacks like a duck, it's a fucking paladin.

Never fall for a paladin, little bird. Their first love will always be their god, and you'll come a distant second. If that god demands your bleeding heart on an altar, they will weep and wallow in guilt, but they'll hack the organ right out of your chest without hesitation.

"It's not so bad." Kit's voice interrupts my dark thoughts. Ne watches me with sympathy in nir dark eyes. "No one on this ship sought out this life, but we've all made the best of it. I know it doesn't feel like it right now, but the captain is a good man and we do good work. Important work."

"Killing monsters."

Ne nods. "Just so."

I shouldn't do anything to piss off these people more than I already have, but restraint is not one of my virtues. "Funny thing, that. We have monster killers in my realm, too. Who gets to decide who's a monster and who's not?" I won't pretend like there aren't monsters who hunt among the human population, but plenty of those monsters aren't paranormal in the least. The hunters in my realm don't go after *them*, though. Too often, those hunters use "monster" to label anyone who doesn't adhere to their criteria of what makes a person human.

Plenty of those groups had witches on their list not too long ago.

Some of them still do.

Kit stares at me for a long moment and shakes nir head. "You're going to be a giant pain in the ass, aren't you?"

"Undoubtedly." I fight for a smile, a real one. "I do appreciate the welcome, though. I'm not one to handle being outmaneuvered gracefully, but I'll do my best to settle in." *At least until I find a way out of this mess.* I don't know what my plan is yet, though. Run? Try to find out more about this Council that seems to make even the captain uneasy and somehow blackmail them into sending me home? What I need is more information, and the only way to get that is to bide my time here on the ship.

Going back to my realm means contending with Lizzie and the fact I stole something she will most definitely want back. I'm not foolish enough to think that the fact that we've shared a bed will soften her toward me. I know how she deals with betrayal—blood and violence. She really sounded like she meant it when she threatened to kill me.

"Dinner is in shifts. You can take first, which is in about an hour." Kit points at the chest at the foot of the bed. "Spare clothes are in there. We'll outfit you properly when we make port next, but you should find something to tide you over until then. Report to the kitchen after you eat. You don't seem like you're experienced with sailing, so that's a safe place to start working until Miles finds a permanent place for you." Ne turns without another word and leaves the room.

I count to ten slowly twice before I allow my knees to buckle and slump to the edge of bed. What a mess. Too much, too fast. My hands are shaking despite my best efforts. Stress and fear have a way of coming out no matter how good my control. I take a breath and let my body have its reaction. No crying—I'm nowhere low enough to shed actual tears over my circumstances—but my chest goes tight and my skin hot as tremors rack my limbs.

Fifteen minutes feels like an eternity, but it isn't nearly long enough for someone to come looking for me. Exhaustion weighs me down and I flop back onto the mattress. *Okay, Evelyn. Think. There's a way out of this, but you don't need a solution right now. If they need to make port to gear you up, then that will be your first chance to run. In the meantime . . . behave.*

Easier said than done.

I force myself into motion. A quick search through the chest comes up with a sad assortment of clothing. I finally find a pair of pants that fits well enough and a loose white shirt that would do any pirate on the cover of a romance novel proud. There are no bras to be found, so I grimace and set aside my damp one. Shoes are also a problem, and I'm exceedingly glad I was wearing my boots when I went through the portal.

The bathroom is rustic, but it's got running water and an honest-to-gods toilet. I frown at it for several beats before I decide I don't care about the semantics of disposal. For all I know, the human waste feeds the magic keeping this pocket dimension going.

I take a quick shower, braid my hair back from my face, and dress in my new clothes. I can't help humming "It's a Pirate's Life for Me" under my breath. This whole situation is just too ridiculous. Or at least that's the bit I have to focus on to prevent myself from having a full-on breakdown when faced with the reality of my circumstances.

The door opens and a person with gray-blue skin, short dark gray hair, and eyes with no white walks in. They're built curvy, a few sizes smaller than me, and have a face that I would term innocent . . . if not for those eyes. Or the delicately pointed ears peeking out from their mop of hair. Another half fae, though if their other half is human, I'll eat my boot.

"Lucky, I presume?"

"Yes." Their voice is soft but strangely rough. "The captain wants you in his quarters."

My brows wing up. "Forward of him."

Their lips quirk in something that's almost a smile. It flashes teeth that are . . . very, very sharp. The more I look at them, the more they remind me of a shark in human skin. "He always dines with new crew members on their first night aboard. It allows him to give them a full rundown of expectations so there are no . . . misunderstandings."

Oh. Of course. That makes perfect sense to avoid unnecessary complications and friction. And Bowen strikes me as too much of a control freak to leave that up to his quartermaster or another of the crew. As little as I like the idea of more time spent alone with him, I'd rather deal with him than his quartermaster any day. "Sounds great."

"You know the way?"

I bite back a snarky reply. I'm supposed to be endearing these people to me and that's impossible to do if I keep snapping at them. More than that, Lucky gives me the impression that they would be too happy to take a bite out of me if I annoy them. "I do. Thanks."

There are more crew members about as I move through the hall and back to the door that leads to the rest of the ship. People of every shape and color and a few with distinctly nonhuman features. The only place I've seen a crowd even close to as diverse as this is the Shadow Market that occurs during Samhain, and even then I can identify most of the types of paranormals who attend. The same can't be said of this crew.

I step out the door and nearly run into the quartermaster. His scaled skin is a deep red that makes me take a step back before I catch myself. I'm certain it was green earlier. Mostly certain.

He flicks his tongue at me. "Tomorrow, you're on first shift in the kitchen. Skirt your duties and you'll be punished."

"Oooh, promise?" *Damn it, why did I say that?*

He narrows his eyes. "It's dangerous at sea. Troublemakers have a habit of suffering accidents. Keep that in mind, witch."

I don't have time to come up with a snappy reply before he shoulders past me and disappears belowdecks. Apparently he won't be joining my fan club anytime soon. Shocking. I head for the captain's quarters, and it's only as I'm opening the door and stepping instead that my nerves threaten to get the best of me.

Or maybe it's the sight of the captain that brings me up short. He's changed in the time since I saw him last. He's still wearing that damned crimson cloak, but beneath it, he has on fitted black pants tucked into knee-high boots and a white shirt that looks to be an exact match to mine.

In fact, his eyes narrow at the sight. "Did you steal my shirt?"

For once, I'm innocent of any thievery, but I'm not about to let that get in the way of my reputation. "Finders keepers, remember?"

He opens his mouth as if he's about to demand the shirt back but seems to catch himself before the words escape. Probably because it would be an abuse of power to demand a member of his crew strip. *Paladins, am I right?*

He shakes his head. "Sit down and let's get this over with."

CHAPTER 7

Bowen

MY ENTIRE CREW KNOWS MY CUSTOM OF SHARING A meal with new members the first night they are aboard. It'd be strange if I skipped that ritual with the witch. People might get the wrong idea, and that would only give Miles more ammunition against me. I saw the way my people watched me on the deck earlier. There's doubt where there wasn't any a mere month ago.

The worst part is that I don't know how to combat it. I am a good captain. I've been trained by the best to be honorable and fair. We do our duty and answer the orders sent by the Council to kill monsters to protect Threshold, and the crews are rewarded generously as a result. I've ensured that this ship is as comfortable as possible and no one is going without.

I might not be the most charming or effusive captain, but I take care of my people. I never thought there'd come a day when that wouldn't be enough, but no matter what I do, Miles continues to chip away at the goodwill my crew holds for me.

Evelyn's arrival may just be the final thing to sway the majority of them to vote for him. It certainly will be if I start acting against type.

It still might have been better than standing in a room alone with Evelyn, who is wearing what I'm nearly certain is one of my shirts. On her, the V in the front looks downright indecent. The pants aren't much better, clinging to her round thighs just as lovingly as her denim did earlier. I realize I'm staring at her body and I jerk my gaze back to her face, but it's no better than last time. It's not that she's beautiful, though she is. The danger is in the glint in her uncanny green eyes that invites anyone present to be in on the joke.

Considering I'm pretty sure that I am the joke in this scenario, I'm not a fan.

Best to get this over with. I motion to the small table tucked up against one wall. "Shall we?"

"By all means." She turns and walks to the table, which is a mistake of its own, because it gives me a view of her full backside. I'm going to need this woman to wear different pants that don't cling to her body so closely. She is the very definition of a distraction. Maybe I can ask Kit to find her something. Ne is built both taller and with enough muscle that surely Evelyn would swim in nir clothes . . .

I don't know what's wrong with me. I've been around beautiful people before, and I've never lost my cool quite so quickly or effectively. The fact that she's one of my crew members only complicates things further. No matter what else is true, there is a deep power imbalance between me and the rest of my crew. The sole exception is perhaps Miles, but I barely tolerate the man and I'm certainly not going to jump into bed with him. I take my pleasure in port towns with partners who expect nothing but the pleasure I'm happy to give. It's an equitable give-and-take where we all leave satisfied. Such a thing is impossible if I'm living in that person's proximity day in and day out.

"What's got that frown on your face, Captain?" From the playful tone in her throaty voice, she has some idea. "Cat got your tongue?"

"I would like my dagger back."

Evelyn smiles even wider. "What dagger?"

"The one you lifted off me earlier today. If you want to get along here, stealing from your crewmates isn't the way to go about it." I move to the small tray that was left a few minutes before she arrived and carry it to the table. "You seem to think this is a game. It's anything but."

"And *you* seem to think I'm nothing more than a treacherous thief. Be careful there, Captain. Keep that up and you're going to hurt my feelings." Every time she says "Captain," it feels like she reaches across the table and strokes one of those pink-tipped nails down my chest. She's doing it on purpose. She has to be.

Except . . . what if she's not? What if I'm misreading things entirely?

I haven't had much interaction with witches over the years, and none like her. But even I know that in most realms witches are the descendants of a human who had children with a paranormal person. Humans are not inherently magical on their own, but they are a great conductor for magical energy in their progeny. It's entirely possible one of Evelyn's ancestors had a child with some flavor of paranormal person that draws people in naturally. A succubus, or a siren . . . except it's unlikely to be the latter, when they're all but extinct in every realm.

Thank the gods for that. I've seen the damage one can do when their song is unleashed. My skin heats at the memory. Best they not be left to wander about, spreading their . . . *chaos* . . . wherever they go.

Either way, if Evelyn is exuding this attraction naturally without intention, then I'm a bastard and a half for even engaging with it. I uncover the food and push her plate toward her. "Tell me about yourself."

"Here's a pro tip for free." She peers at the food as if trying to divine what it is. It seems simple enough to me, if heavy on the fish, but maybe they don't have the same varieties where she's from. Evelyn looks up at me through her eyelashes. "When you're mining for information, it helps to coax it out instead of demand. With that tone, I'm liable to think this is an interrogation instead of a conversation."

She's right, but I can't help it. I'm uncomfortable and offbalance—and I'm hardly the most charming person at the best of times. "Answer the question, Evelyn."

"If you insist." She picks up a fork and pokes experimentally at the fish before shrugging and taking a bite. Her green eyes go wide. "Oh. This is really good."

"We have several brownies in the kitchen. They take great pride in turning out fare that is far too good for those of us in the crew. We've learned not to question it—or to wander into the kitchen without invitation."

"Brownies? How does one of them end up in Threshold, let alone several?"

Something uncomfortable squirms through me. "A family unit was forced through a portal by the owner of their house. We fished them out of the sea much the same as we did with you."

Evelyn goes still. For once, there's no amusement on her pretty face. She frowns. "You don't see a problem with that at all? I suppose I'm to blame for jumping through a portal without getting all the information about its destination first. I'll own that. But surely even you can see the lack of justice where they're concerned? It wasn't their choice, foolish or otherwise, that brought them here."

The squirming inside me grows in strength. I swallow and do my best not to let the sensation present as an outward fidget. I took no pleasure in their vows, but I would have taken even less in their deaths. "The law is the law. Like I told you earlier, intent matters less than the fact they ended up here."

"Fascinating. You're like a windup toy. Question the laws and that's your only response."

"In a world that touches on every realm in existence, surely you can understand how important it is to have rules. Without the Cŵn Annwn, it would be anarchy. Monsters would slip from realm to realm, hunting those who are ill-equipped to deal with them and killing indiscriminately." I give up on trying to be still and drag a hand through my hair. "Things are the way they are for a reason."

"Why are the Cŵn Annwn the ones who get to make the rules?"

I'm temporary distracted by her popping an olive into her mouth and chewing slowly. I shake my head roughly, trying to focus. "What do you mean?"

"I would think the question is self-explanatory. There was a time in my realm when the myths about the Cŵn Annwn didn't exist, which would suggest there was a time when they *didn't*. Or at least when they kept to whatever realm spawned them. Who set them up as the protectors of Threshold? This system benefits someone. I'd like to know who."

"It benefits the people of Threshold," I say through gritted teeth. "Even with us doing our jobs to the best of our ability, there are people we can't save. Without the laws in place, even more would die in horrific ways. Our origins matter less than what we accomplish in the present time."

"Yikes." She makes a show of shuddering. "Maybe that's true. Maybe it's not. Either way, it's not very pirate-y, anti-authority, anti-capitalist of you to be sailing around, scooping up refugees, and giving them a bullshit bargain where there's only one option because the other outcome is *death*. Come on."

She takes a few more bites while I sputter.

"Listen, I'm not from around here, but at least ask some questions, man. You're in a cage just like the rest of us. Don't you want to know the boundaries?"

"Did you not hear me when I said we save lives?"

"I heard you." She sips her wine and makes an appreciative noise that I'm too frustrated to, well, appreciate. "I still don't think it outweighs the lives you've ruined by forcibly recruiting them to your cause."

I have been one of the Cŵn Annwn for twenty years. Ever since I woke up, thirteen years old, soaked and half dead on the deck of a ship. This ship, in fact. I never did regain my memories of my life before that point, but Ezra, the former captain of the *Crimson Hag*, brought me under his wing like I was his own son.

He took as little joy in following the laws of the Cŵn Annwn as I do, but he never faltered.

I won't falter now.

"I told you what would happen if you broke your vows. That same fate awaits anyone who does. The Council may keep a loose grip on most of our captains at this time, but that's only because they are still fulfilling the role set out for them in Threshold. If a captain went against that? If *I* went against that? Not only would they make an example of me, but they would do the same with my entire crew. It's not just a single life that hangs in the balance of these decisions, Evelyn. I have to think of my people."

"Sure." She shrugs. "Like I said, I understand you not breaking these laws if the consequences are so dire. But I'm curious by nature, and I don't think it's a bad thing to question why things are the way they are. It's the first thing my grandmother taught me."

I'm pathetically grateful for the chance to shift this conversation into safer territory. Though, truth be told, I want to know more about Evelyn and what kind of life she must've lived to turn her into the person she is today . . . and to cause her path to cross mine. "Your grandmother raised you?"

"I was orphaned at six. Bunny picked me up and I never looked back. She taught me everything I know." She stares at her plate, but it's blatantly obvious she's looking into the past.

I recognize the grief that flickers over her face. I feel the same when I think of Ezra, gone now three years. The ship's just not the same without him. Even years later, there are times when I'm faced with a difficult decision and I find myself looking to where he used to stand behind the helm. I always feel foolish when I do it. He gave me every bit of advice he could when he was alive. He trained me to be able to make these decisions on my own, once he was gone.

It doesn't mean I don't miss him, though.

"How did you end up here?"

I expect another laugh, or maybe a playful comment, but Evelyn freezes. Is that true fear on her face? She carefully sets down her fork. "We're still on the move, right? We're nowhere near where I came in?"

"We're leagues from there now." I lean forward. "Why?"

"I damaged the portal, but Lizzie is too damn smart to have only one route available. There's got to be another one in the house, if not more. How do portals even work in Threshold, anyway? I should have asked that the moment I woke up." Her words tumble over each other in her apparent panic. "It was really foolish of me to steal from her, but it seemed like a good idea at the time, and she didn't have to be such a bitch about kicking me out of her house when I didn't even want to be there to begin with. She practically kidnapped me. Which I wouldn't have been opposed to, except for the whole 'her family showing up and killing me for fun if they stumbled on me' thing. Really, I was justified in stealing from her."

I blink. "Lizzie is a . . . friend? Girlfriend?"

"Lizzie doesn't like labels. And neither do I," Evelyn says primly. Or at least she tries. She's gone pale, her movements becoming jerky. She's still talking too fast, even for her. "But I suppose if you were going to put a label on it, 'lover' is as good as any. That's not the point. The point is that there's a decent chance she'll follow me to Threshold on sheer principle, since she threatened my life and all. If she does, we're all in danger.

She's a bloodline vampire, and the power she wields is . . ." Evelyn shudders. "Trust me that I don't know a single person who could survive a fight with her. I certainly couldn't."

I don't know what it says about this Lizzie that Evelyn went through a portal, ended up in the space between realms, and was attacked while still barely conscious, and yet none of that caused the same amount of fear she's exhibiting right now. It makes me want to reach across the table and take her hand. To comfort her. To promise I will stand between her and whatever danger this Lizzie presents.

The impulse is so strong I almost talk myself out of it on instinct. But I'm the captain, aren't I? It's my responsibility to see to the well-being of my crew, and that includes their emotional well-being. That logic feels flimsy as fuck, but I move before I can think too hard about it.

I reach across the table and take her hand. Little tremors work through her fingers. It makes my chest feel funny. "You have nothing to worry about. Threshold is vast, and despite all we've talked about with people wandering here by accident, it truly doesn't happen as often as you'd expect. Portal travel is usually confined to whatever realm the portals themselves exist in. Even in Threshold, our portals to the network of realms are limited to the islands. One portal for one island, and while they're stationary here, they aren't in their home realms. It's all but impossible to come here on purpose. It defies probability to believe she could follow you, powerful vampire or no."

"If you believe that then you don't know Lizzie."

I squeeze her hand. "Even if you're right and she somehow manages to defy the odds to track you down, you're part of the Cŵn Annwn and the *Crimson Hag*'s crew now. This whole crew, including myself, will stand between you and any threat that arises."

Evelyn stares at our joined hands for several beats. When she lifts her gaze to mine, she doesn't look particularly reassured. "While I appreciate the attempt at comfort, if Lizzie comes here, we're all fucked."

CHAPTER 8

Evelyn

I DON'T KNOW WHAT I WAS DOING CASUALLY EXPLORING the ship earlier. I should've been thinking about Lizzie. I should've been thinking about the fact that there's no way she had only a single portal in her house, no matter how difficult Bowen claims it is to get to Threshold. She has another way here; I'm sure of it.

I look around Bowen's cabin again, this time with an eye for a map. No matter how magical a realm, no matter how often things move within its boundaries, there's always a map that can guide the way. Or at least there normally is. I don't see anything of the sort. "How do you navigate?"

He gives me a long look. "If you're thinking of escaping, I will remind you yet again that it's an impossible task. Even if you could find your way to one of the islands that contain the portals out to the various realms, a full half of them are actively hostile to humans. Even down to the air, Evelyn. I realize you didn't choose this life, but surely it's better than dying."

Of course it's better than dying. But being free is significantly better than being actively conscripted into what is starting to feel like a cult. "Look, I won't pretend I'm not considering escaping, but that's not why I'm asking."

"Lizzie." The derisive way he says her name irks me. He's dismissing a threat he really shouldn't.

"Yes, Lizzie. This is serious, Bowen."

He studies me for a long moment, and I hate that I can't quite cover up my fear. At least it's useful in this moment. His dark eyes go soft and he sighs. "Very well. Come here." He pushes to his feet.

The sheer *size* of him is so damned distracting. No one should be that big. It's rude, honestly. I almost smile before I remember why we're having this conversation, and then my fear comes rushing back. It doesn't matter what he says, but all information is worth having, so I rise and follow him over to the desk I clocked when I was in here earlier.

It was dark while we ate, but when Bowen waves his hand over it, the surface flares to life. It must be keyed to him. Bright colors swirl, finally settling into what appears to be a map. It's mostly blue with islands scattered throughout, some in black and some in purple.

I point to one of the purple ones. "Why is this different?"

"Not all the islands are stationary. Some migrate in regular patterns. Some blip in and out of existence on their own schedule. Tracking them isn't a perfect science, but we do the best we can. Right now, a full half aren't present because of various factors of time and season and their own internal schedule."

I study it further, grateful to have something to focus on that isn't what I'm running from—*who* I'm running from. I try to count them, but am instantly overwhelmed. "There are so many." And each represents a realm just as large and diverse as the one I grew up in. The thought staggers me. I knew the universe was big enough to be unknowable, but the proof in front of me makes my head spin. "Wow."

"You see," Bowen says gently. "This is why I'm not concerned about a threat a single vampire poses. It's no easy task to navigate Threshold, even if she were to somehow make it here."

I'm not totally reassured, but maybe he has a point. "If you say so."

"This is also why the Cŵn Annwn are necessary. This map represents the people who live in Threshold, yes, but it also represents lives beyond number. Allowing predators to use Threshold to slip in and out of other realms is out of the question."

I don't want to agree with him at all, even on this, but there are reasons we have some pretty horrific legends about monsters in my realm. And I'm not talking about the so-called monsters that are vampires or shifters or, yes, witches. I'm talking about the ones that destroy cities to get their preferred prey of choice. There's a reason so many legends about dragons exist, and that quite a few of them have rumors of virgin sacrifices attached.

Not even the hunters in my realm would be able to take down a dragon.

Even so, it's hard to blame a dragon for ensuring that it feeds itself when it's been stranded in a strange realm. What is it supposed to do? Die? That's ridiculous. Surely there's an answer that doesn't involve killing it. I don't have one readily available, though, and I doubt Bowen will appreciate me questioning his beloved Cŵn Annwn further. He's feeling sympathetic toward me now, and I'll admit to being wowed by the map, so might as well try to foster some goodwill, right?

"So what's your story?" Even as I ask the question, I tell myself I'm only doing it to get more information to leverage in my aim for freedom. It's not because I'm actually curious. This pirate might be sexy in a kind of rugged way, but he's rigid and unbending while I'm as fickle as the wind.

He's also standing between me and my freedom, which makes him the enemy.

Again, he pauses so long I think he might not answer. Again, he surprises me by doing it anyway. "I was pulled out of the sea when I was thirteen. Right here, in fact." He points to a spot on the map in the middle of the blue. "I have no memory of my life before then, and no idea how long I was actually in the water. I was in pretty bad shape when they found me. I've been on the *Crimson Hag* ever since."

I stare at the spot. I don't have any concept of actual scale, but it seems like it's a very long way from any of the nearby islands. If the ship hadn't happened to be in the area when he came through, he would have died. The thought makes my chest hurt. He was just a kid. "Seems like it happens a lot."

"Like I said, not as much as you seem to think. But when people fall through portals that are glitching or otherwise interfered with, it randomizes their exit, which means they don't always end up on dry land."

"How many people die just because they drop into the water without a ship around?"

He hesitates. "There's no way of having a proper number, but it can't be that many."

I don't know if he's saying that to make me feel better or make himself feel better. It doesn't seem to work on either front. No wonder he's such a stick-in-the-mud. He has nothing to compare his current reality to, and even if he did, he's been conditioned to see things a certain way since he was little more than a child. I'm sure all the realms are harsh in their own way—mine is no exception—but Threshold is particularly so. A flash of sympathy goes through me before I aggressively wrestle it down.

It doesn't matter what this man has gone through. It doesn't matter that I feel a strange sort of kinship. Neither of us has anyone. No, that's not true. I might have lost the last of my family when Bunny died, but I have friends. A community.

And an enraged vampire ex who no doubt wants to rip every drop of blood from my body.

I shudder before I can catch myself. Bowen looks like he wants to reach out, but stops himself before he can do more than shift his hand an inch. "You have nothing to fear here. You're one of us now. I said we'll protect you and I meant it."

It's startling how badly part of me wants to believe him. To just . . . give in. Whether I have friends at home or not, I can admit I've been adrift for most of my adult life. Maybe some people turn eighteen and suddenly know what their purpose is, but mine has been elusive. The thought of joining someone else's, especially when they promise to protect you and treat you like family, is more attractive than I want to admit.

It's also a trap.

I want no part of a group that requires unquestioning obedience. I sure as fuck am not down with this vague mission statement about killing "monsters." And I'll never be okay with them forcing innocent people into their ranks under threat of death.

I aim for a charming smile, but I feel strained around the edges. "Like I said before, you don't know Lizzie if you think there's nothing to fear." Easier to focus on the threat she represents than the longing inside me that I spend far too much time ignoring. It's inconvenient that it decided to pop up its ugly head right now.

His brows draw together. Really, he's almost adorable in his frustration. "What do I have to say for you to believe me? I will defend you with my life. I will kill any threat against one of my crew. You're safe. I promise."

I don't know what to say to that. It's both a horrific outcome and strangely comforting, all at the same time. Because the truth is that I don't want Lizzie dead. Even if it means I will be safe. I care about her, vengeful vampire or no. Bunny always said I was too sentimental, and I can't even pretend she's wrong.

But that doesn't mean that I'm suicidal . . . or a fool.

I clasp my hands and lower my head, letting my shoulders drop a little. The very picture of dejection and fear. I bet good money Bowen can't read emotions or the energy around a person the way some paranormal folks can. Which is a relief, because while I can lie to myself enough to create a false emotion, it's exhausting. Easier to lie with my body and words. "You don't understand. But I do appreciate the fact that you're willing to protect me. I know I've hardly been the easiest crew member to deal with."

Bowen gives another of those sighs that sound like he's

carrying around the entire world on his broad shoulders. "No one is eager to join the Cŵn Annwn, Evelyn. You're not the first one who's had to go through an adjustment period. You won't be the last. Just try to go easy on yourself . . . and on us."

Not fucking likely.

I give him a trembling smile. "I'll do my best."

He's still watching me as if I'm a snake that crawled into his bed, but there's a softening around the edges of his harsh mouth that conveys I'm making progress. Battling someone tooth and nail is exhausting, and he would rather believe I'm a coward than continue to fight. Truly, I don't know how he's managed to stay captain of such an unruly bunch of pirates for so long if he's this gullible. That said, I am not a fool. I can't afford to assume I have him by the nose.

I glance at the map again. It's less useful than I had hoped. The islands aren't labeled, and even if they were, it would take me hours to read them all to determine which one contains the portal home. I'll have to find another way.

"Why don't you go to bed, Evelyn?" Did his voice just get deeper? I could swear it did. He seems closer, too, though I swear he didn't move an inch.

Even though I know better, I can't help lifting my head and looking up into his dark eyes. Serious. Gods, he's so incredibly serious. It should be aggravating in the extreme, but with him looking like he's about to drop to one knee before me and offer me his sword . . . I'm only human. My stomach flutters and heat courses through me. I don't mean to lick my lips, but I'm all too glad I did when his gaze drops to my mouth and his attention sharpens on me.

The moment draws out, weighty and filled with the possibility of bad decisions. This man was literally threatening my life earlier today. It's not like he was happy about it, though.

That thought is enough to snap me out of my lustful haze. What the fuck am I doing? He's the enemy, even if he seems to get sexier by the minute. I know my standards are in the ground, but they have to exist in some capacity, and wanting to press myself against his hard body and see if I can drive this paladin pirate out of his mind is a clear violation of them.

I take a quick step back. Bowen tenses like he might close the new distance between us, but he shakes his head slowly. "Ah. What was I saying?"

"You were sending me to bed." Damn it, my voice has gone low and throaty, as if I'm inviting *him* to my bed.

"Right." He takes a careful step back from me, and then another, finally going so far as to round the desk and sink into the chair behind it. "We're making port in the very near future. We'll get you equipped with everything you need there. I know this is an adjustment, but you're an adaptable woman, and I have no doubt you'll make the best of it."

I pull in a breath and try to get my head on straight. "Adaptable is my middle name," I say faintly.

It's not until I exit his cabin and feel the fresh sea air on my face that I realize what he said. We're making port. That means a town. That means I'll have a chance to escape. I thought it might take weeks before an opportunity arose, but apparently some god somewhere is looking at me with a kind eye. Finally.

The possibility of getting out of Threshold is almost enough to bury the fact that I very much wanted Bowen to kiss me back there. And if he had, I would have been incredibly tempted to put that desk to good use. It's more than a little depressing to realize how deep my recklessness goes, but at least something good has come out of it.

Port. Escape. That's all I need to focus on.

Even as I consider this turn of luck, the wind picks up until my hair whips around me, nearly harsh enough to draw blood. I shiver. I know better than to tempt fate, even if Bunny firmly believed that fate was hardly fickle enough to be altered by silly thoughts of a single person. Bunny knew a lot, and she went through some serious shit in her life, but I've always believed that fate is exactly as fickle and malicious as any other entity.

I have a feeling I'm going to be proven right yet again. The thick storm clouds gathering in the sky certainly seem to think so. I've lived through plenty of storms, but I've never experienced what appears to be a hurricane while standing on the deck of a boat. It feels like being a thimble in a bathtub. Even with magic, can we survive the violence currently riding the waves and air?

"It's not a good idea to be out here, at least until you find your sea legs properly."

I turn to find a short old crone standing a few feet away. She has medium-brown skin creased with the laugh lines of a life well lived, and the hair that's mostly pulled back into a tight bun is nearly white. Even though the deck shifts sickeningly beneath my feet, I bow to her a little. If there's one rule I live by, it's to respect my elders. "I was just on my way to my room. It wasn't this bad when I started dinner."

She shrugs. "It doesn't take much to get Llyr's panties in a bunch. The weather when we're at sea is changeable and sudden. You'll get used to it."

It takes several seconds for her words to penetrate. Llyr, as in the Welsh god of the sea. I give her a long look, but it's impossible to tell if she's merely making a metaphorical reference, or if she means that the literal god of the sea gets his panties in a bunch. With the elders I've interacted with over the course of my life, it really could go either way. When you've lived long enough, not even literal gods are impressive.

"I'm sure I will." I might have a relatively antagonistic relationship already with several members of the crew, but this woman has a soothing vibe that I find myself reluctant to leave behind. Or maybe there's something about the stranger that reminds me of my grandmother.

She pulls out what appears to be a hand-rolled cigarette. "I'm the navigator. Have been for decades. I was brought on under the last captain, Ezra." She produces a flame from somewhere and lights the end of her cigarette. It's only when she exhales a cloud of smoke that I realize it's not tobacco she's smoking.

I grin. "Care to share, Grandmother?"

She lets loose the cackle that would do any witch proud. "Girl, I like you, but I'm no one's grandmother. You can call me Dia." She passes over the joint and watches with interest as I take a long inhale. "It will get easier. I know that sounds like a trite statement, but it's the truth. I wasn't happy when Ezra gave me the choice, either. I tried to kill him a dozen times before it sank in that there was no escape." She accepts the joint back. A few puffs and she blows an honest-to-gods smoke ring. "The Cŵn Annwn are not to be crossed. It took me a while to figure *that* out, but I'm a slow learner. Doesn't mean you have to be. This ship is a family, if sometimes a dysfunctional one. You could be happy here if you give it enough time."

She's being genuine, so I don't tell her that I have no intention of sticking around long enough to be embraced by this so-called family. It's nothing personal.

I accept the joint back and take one more long drag, letting it burn all the way down my throat. "The old captain didn't have a problem with you trying to kill him?" I can't imagine getting the drop on Bowen. His damned telekinetic power gives him an instant advantage. My spells are faster than those of most witches, but he doesn't need more than a thought to attack or defend.

She lets loose another of those amazing cackles. "To him, it was practically foreplay." She grins, her eyes nearly disappearing in the deep wrinkles of her face. "It turns out, it was practically foreplay for me, too. Ezra and I had a lot of fun in our day."

There's not much else to say to that. I stand next to her and smoke for a few more minutes, watching the sky grow darker and more violent. It's getting challenging to keep my feet. Especially with the weed in my system, making my head fuzzy. "You sure we're not going to sink?"

"Nah. This is barely a fizzle. It will be fun." She presses a hand to the center of my back and guides me to the door leading down to the cabins. "Get some sleep, girl. There will be plenty of work for you in the morning."

CHAPTER 9

Bowen

AFTER THE DINNER WITH EVELYN, IT'S A RELIEF TO FO-
cus on work. No new correspondence has come in via the
message system enchanted into my desk, so our plan to take
refuge in Yaltia during the storm will work just fine. With that
plan solidified, I head out onto the deck.

We've only caught the edges of the storm Dia saw, but it's a
nasty one. I take the helm as the crew follows my shouted orders. I don't love storms for the danger they present, but I can't
deny that there's a peace in moments like these. I'm here, pitting
myself against nature herself. There is no past, no future.
There's only this moment of trying to stay alive.

As always, it's over far too soon.

Miles appears at my side, his scales glistening in the rain. His
tongue flicks out. "The island has been sighted. We're almost
there."

Sarah is up in the crow's nest as usual, relaying what she
sees to Miles by way of her magic, using the wind to transfer her

words as if she were standing right next to him. There was a time when she spoke to me directly, but she's firmly among Miles's supporters, and now prefers to relay her directions via the quartermaster. A small rebellion, but a marked trend in how some of the crew treat me.

There's no time to worry about it now, though.

We easily avoid the rocks surrounding the island, even with the storm driving us at unsafe speeds. The relative shelter of the bay allows us to slow our pace enough to dock safely. I shove my wet hair out of my face and drag in a harsh breath. "We should be good, but check for damages and make sure everything's lashed down. This one's going to be a bitch, and I don't want us to see any damage that might delay us. Let the crew know I expect them to be on their best behavior while in town."

Miles gives me an unreadable look. "We're Cŵn Annwn. We keep them safe. They should be greeting us like gods."

It's an old argument. I find that the people who join the Cŵn Annwn fall into three categories. The first is like Evelyn, who resent their new lot in life and have no desire to learn the history of the Cŵn Annwn. The second is like Miles, the people who see the status that being part of the Cŵn Annwn brings and think that respect is owed to them simply for being part of the crew. The third . . . well, people who shoulder the responsibility and carry out thankless task after thankless task, each more dangerous than the last, all while keeping an eye on the responsibility we've inherited? We're a lot rarer.

"You tell them, Miles. Or I will." And we both know how *that* will go. The crew may trust me to keep them alive and to guide them, but they don't like me. I'm too rigid when it comes to the laws. At least that's what I've been told. Miles has used that to his advantage again and again, but I don't know how to be any other way. We are *not* gods to be worshiped. We act in service to the people who live in Threshold and beyond. But that belief isn't very popular these days among the Cŵn Annwn, both among my crew and beyond.

His tail twitches restlessly. "I'll tell them, Captain."

I watch him walk away. Again, I wonder if today will be the day that he challenges me for the captainship. It's only a matter of time. Ezra always told me that the best kind of partnership between a captain and a quartermaster is a slightly contentious one. The quartermaster looks after the crew's interest, while the captain is the one who keeps their eye on the prize and guides both crew and ship. It's natural that there would be conflict from time to time, but things with Miles are constantly fraught. I'm becoming increasingly certain that if he challenges me for the vote, I'll lose. And then I don't know what I'll do.

I don't know who I am if I'm not captain of the *Crimson Hag*. "So that's our port."

I don't jump out of my skin, but it's a near thing. I didn't hear Evelyn approach. Now she's standing at my side as if she's been there all along. She's changed back into the clothes she was wearing when we pulled her out of the sea, but she must've done something to magic them, because the rain doesn't seem to touch the fabric. Or her hair, for that matter.

I step back and look at her properly. There's a fine bubble around her that the rain slides off. "Neat trick."

"Work smarter, not harder." She's still eyeing the small, sleepy town with far too much interest. She's going to run. It's nothing more than I expected, but I can't help the frustration that blooms in response to the realization.

I don't have time to be chasing down a wayward witch who breaks vows as easily as she makes them. "Do I have to lock you in my cabin for the duration of our stay here?"

Her brows wing up. "There you go again, flirting with me."

I hate myself a little bit for blushing in response. Hopefully she can't see it in the low light and stormy weather. "I'm not flirting with you." I might have been thinking about kissing her after dinner in my cabin, but I wasn't *flirting*.

"Are you sure? Because threatening to lock me up in your cabin sounds particularly flirty." She shifts closer until she's nearly pressed against me. "If you had me in your cabin all to yourself, what would you do with me?"

Everything.

I barely manage to keep the instinctive, unforgivable answer inside. She's trying to provoke me, to make me uncomfortable enough that I won't pay attention to what she's up to. I may be interested in her, but I know better than to let it color my interactions with her. At least I hope I do. I've never felt so completely foolish around a potential paramour.

What am I thinking? Potential paramour? This woman is a godsdamned menace. She is fair of face and lush of body, but she's already proven to be a ball of chaotic energy. Besides, I'm the captain. No matter that I would never abuse my power, there *is* a power imbalance between me and the rest of my crew. I have to keep my interest locked down.

I belatedly realize that I'm staring at her in awkward silence. Usually I'm not so damn awkward; she seems to bring out this side of me in particular. It's irritating. "Go back to your cabin, Evelyn. You can go ashore with the rest of them at first light." It won't be first light. Everyone will sleep in, courtesy of a long night and the fact that most shops won't open until well past dawn.

She gives me a long look and smiles sweetly. It's a liar's smile. This woman doesn't like me, and she doesn't want to be here. It's mildly insulting that she thinks I would believe her to be docile after only a few hours. "Yes, Captain." She salutes in a charmingly irreverent way and turns with a click of her heels.

I can't help watching her big ass in those tight pants as she walks away. I have no doubt that the extra swing in her step is because she knows I'm watching. The little witch. It's only when she disappears back belowdecks that I think to check whether she lifted something else off me.

Sure enough, I'm missing the ring from my thumb on my right hand. How did she manage that? She never got close enough to touch me properly. It's wildly unfair that she's slipping things from my body and I don't get the benefit of feeling her touch.

I shake my head. Hopefully the storm passes quickly and we're able to get back on the water soon. Being at port, and so close to the portals each respective island offers, makes my skin itch.

Or maybe it's the fact that I highly suspect Evelyn will be sneaking away the moment she thinks my back is turned. With all the spells at her disposal, it's entirely possible that she'd be successful. Unless . . .

A slow smile, feeling foreign on my lips, settles over me. The little witch has gotten one over on me several times since she came aboard. Perhaps it's time I turn the tables on her properly. It's not something I would normally engage in, but there is very little about the situation that's normal.

She's going to run, and she thinks I have no idea. If I happen to get ahead of her, to lie in wait . . . Is she actually breaking her vow and fleeing if she's running *to* me?

Something strange and fizzy takes root in my stomach. I'm not sure what to think of the sensation. It almost feels like excitement, but that can't possibly be it. I catch sight of Dia over by the mast, the bright orange spot near her lips making her easy to pick out. "Dia."

She doesn't rush, but then I don't expect her to. I'm also not a captain who expects people to drop everything and sprint to me the moment I call. My navigator strolls over to me and holds out a joint. "Care to join me?"

"You know I never touch the stuff."

She shrugs. "You should try it sometime. Might loosen up that sphincter a bit."

I never know what to say when she makes comments like that. They're highly inappropriate, but this woman has been on the ship for longer than I've been alive. If Ezra was something of a grandfather figure, I suppose that makes Dia a grandmother figure. It doesn't mean that she gets special treatment, exactly; more that she chooses which orders she feels like obeying, and no one can force her to do otherwise. *I'm* certainly not going to. "You'll be up for a bit yet?"

She inhales deeply, and exhales a perfect circle and then another inside it. I'm not sure how she's managing that in the rain, but Dia is plenty magical at times. "That depends. Why are you asking me to watch over the helm?"

There's no point in lying. She'll know if I do, and then she'll just ignore my request. I blink rainwater from my eyes. "The witch is going to try to escape. I mean to stop her."

"You could just let her go." She flicks ash away. "If she's so determined to meet her bloody fate, you could just allow it. No one escapes the Cŵn Annwn. You know it, and I know it."

That's the problem. I can't stand the thought of Evelyn's green eyes going faded and blank in death. I've seen enough life snuffed out from this world. I'm sure if I explained as much, Miles would say that I'm soft and unforgivable and further erode the crew's faith in me. I'm not the kind of stern shit a captain of the Cŵn Annwn should be made of. Maybe it's even true. There are more than a few captains, like Hedd of the *Audacity*, who have no problem hanging crew members who question too many orders.

But if Evelyn flees and a hunt is called, it won't matter that I'm not a captain like *that*. I won't have a choice about joining in.

"I would rather catch her now, while there's a chance to save her, than catch her with a blade in my hand."

Dia considers that. I can't read the thoughts on her wrinkled face. I don't bother to try. She's never had a problem telling me exactly what she thinks, and I highly doubt this will be the exception to the rule. "Go on, then. If you leave now, you can get ahead of her." She takes another drag. "She'll know better than to try to seek shelter in the village, so she'll head into the trees around the perimeter. If I were a betting woman, I would say she'd head east. It's easier going that way, and it will take her farther from the sea."

Farther from me.

"Thanks." I move back so she can take my spot. "The crew knows the protocol. I'll be back to relieve you as soon as I've dealt with the situation."

She cackles. "Take your time, Captain. These old bones were

made for the sea. I have no interest in land." A sly light comes into her dark eyes. "Maybe give that girl a good ride. That might be enough to convince her to stay."

My face flames, and there's no way *she* doesn't see it. "That's not why I'm doing this."

"I know." She grins. "But no reason you can't have a little fun along with doing your duty."

She's still cackling behind me as I flip up my cloak hood and move to the railing. A deep breath and I wrap my power around myself and lift off the deck. I cross the water in seconds and descend to lightly land at the outskirts of the village. It's still early enough that dawn is barely a hint in the sky on the horizon. No one will be out and about for a while yet.

I consider the various routes through and out of town before deciding that I agree with Dia; the witch will go east. Now it's only a matter of finding a good spot to wait until she makes her attempt.

Each of the islands have evolved to match the portals they contain. This one is no different. The trees are monstrous, thick and curling things that are blue and green and purple. I hate being on this island, to the point where I avoid it whenever I can. I've never quite been able to put my finger on why, though. There are other islands that are even more unsettling. Islands where trees grow upside down. Islands where there's no organic life to be seen, just rocks and dirt and death. Even islands where gravity seems to shift based on the time of day.

None of them make me feel like this one does.

The small hairs at the back of my neck stand on end as I turn in a slow circle, squinting against the rain falling in sheets around me despite the interwoven branches overhead. I'm close enough to the village to see the ladders and the lift that lead up to the walkways strung between trees. Even on a clear day, the buildings themselves are almost indistinguishable from the trees they're built into and around. Today, with the rain obscuring my vision, they might as well not exist at all.

I'm surprised the residents left the ladders down, but I don't know why. There are predators in these woods, but they don't venture close to the village. They certainly don't have hands to climb ladders.

No, the sensation bothering me isn't one of being hunted. I'm all too familiar with that. Instead, this almost feels like . . . memory.

I shake my head and do my best to ignore the feeling. I'll deal with the witch and then make my way back to the ship. We're well stocked, so there's no need to go up into the village to negotiate or trade. My crew knows the rules, and they know the consequences of disobeying them. All in all, it should be an uneventful stop.

If not for the witch.

I turn and head east, deeper into the trees. The sensation plaguing me only gets stronger with each step I take. I've never been out this way before, but judging by the well-trodden path I follow, others have. I continue down it, grateful for the rain making it hard to see.

I don't know what's wrong with me. This place isn't familiar. I've been to the village before, but I've never walked this path, never spent time in these woods. There's no reason for me to be feeling like I could name every one of the array of blue flowers climbing a nearby tree trunk. They're pretty. That's all I need to know.

That's all I *do* know.

"This is far enough." I use my magic to rise to land on a well-hidden branch. It's easily thicker around than I am, and it's one of the smaller branches. I don't even need to use my powers to balance as I crouch and survey the path below. Yes, this is a good spot. Now all that's left to do is wait.

CHAPTER 10

Evelyn

ONE OF THE FIRST SPELLS I LEARNED ON MY OWN WAS the ability to quiet my steps and any noise of my passing. Combine that with the invisibility Bunny taught me, and I was *very good* at sneaking out as a teenager. These days, it makes me one hell of a thief.

Not that I capitalize on that . . . too often.

I wait in my cabin until the sounds of the crew moving about fade. And then I wait a little longer. My roommate appears to be dead to the world. That might even be literally, because I'm nearly certain they're not breathing. It's the sort of thing I got used to with Lizzie, but it still makes little shivers work their way down my spine. Living creatures are supposed to breathe.

I cast the spells and slip out of bed, careful to take my bag with me. Out in the hallway, there isn't another soul in sight. As I climb the stairs and step out onto the deck, the rain engulfs me. It would've been nice to keep my dry spell going, but I can hold only so many spells active at a time. Right now, stealth is the name of the game.

I catch sight of Dia lounging next to the helm and have the most ridiculous urge to tell her goodbye. There's no point. I don't know her and she doesn't know me. One conversation does not a friend make. I'm probably feeling sentimental because I miss Bunny, and while Dia is hardly a carbon copy of my grandmother, I think the two of them would've gotten along like a house on fire.

Grief rises in a wave so strong, it makes my knees buckle. I have to close my eyes and press my hands to my chest to still their shaking. As much as I hate this time of year, there's a part of me that relishes it. Will I start forgetting her when the grief fades? The thought makes me sick to my stomach. Already there are bits and pieces that have disappeared into the depths of the past. The human mind was not meant to hold information indefinitely, and without her here to reinforce those pathways, I've forgotten the exact timbre of her laugh. Was it really just like mine, or has my mind tricked me into thinking that?

Now is not the time or place to focus on that.

I swallow down the tears threatening and head to the side of the ship. There's no gangplank in place, which is nothing more than I expected. I swing myself over the railing. At least there are plenty of nooks and crannies to use to climb down to the water. I could probably jump, because the sounds of the wind and rain would cover up the splash, but it's not worth the risk.

It's a miserable, if short, swim to shore. By the time I stagger up the beach, I am quietly cursing Bowen's name. If he had just let me go, none of this would be necessary. Yes, technically I may have drowned in the sea if he'd tossed me back overboard, but I'm not in the mood to be grateful.

I shove my wet hair from my face and survey what I can see of the island. It takes me far too long to understand that the reason I can't see the village is because I'm looking in the wrong place. It's not on the ground at all; it's in the trees themselves.

At this point, I have to assume that everyone in Threshold is an enemy. I'm sure there are people here who don't fuck with the Cŵn Annwn. There have to be. The problem is that I don't know who they are, and I can't risk being turned back over to Bowen and his crew. I highly doubt they'll be sympathetic to my attempted escape. Entering the village is out of the question.

No, the better option is to stick to the shoreline . . .

Except even as I think that, I see the vicious-looking cliffs on the other side of the beach. Maybe I could scale them in good weather, but if I try to do it right now it's a death wish. "Okay, inland it is."

I skirt the edge of the town slowly, curiosity a live thing inside me. I think every kid goes through a stage where they're sure a tree house is the greatest invention mankind has ever made. I even had one when I was young, a little room that was built with more twigs than anything else, but it was *mine*. A place where I could hide when the world became too much. I kept little treasures there, pretty rocks and flowers I found in the trees that bordered Bunny's house.

This village is . . . not like that at all.

It's difficult to see in the rain, but these are very clearly buildings created with *living* in mind, rather than a childlike escape. Some of them seem to be carved into the giant trunks of the trees themselves, while others are built in great spirals through the branches.

I pick out little hints of the people who must live here. Flowerpots line one of the walkways, their blooms spilling over the railing in a brightly colored stream. Someone forgot their laundry hanging on a line and a dress flaps wetly in the storm. Down here on the ground there's a painting that was obviously done by children, judging by the vibrant colors and the awkwardness of the figures. I stop in front of it and study the lines that are slowly beginning to run as the rain washes them away. Humanoid figures that appear to be dancing. A rainbow. Flowers. Kid shit.

I wish I had more time to explore. I would love to see what kind of things shops here might sell, or to spend a night at an inn so high above the ground, with only the sway of the branches in the wind as company. To meet the kind of people who live here and in the realm this island connects to.

Fanciful, foolish thoughts. The village isn't more magical than any other. It just happens to exist high off the ground. Dawn is already making its presence known. I have to *move* if I want to get out of here before someone notices I'm missing.

If I can find this island's portal out of Threshold, then I am one step closer to being home. Traveling between the realms might be all but impossible, but that doesn't mean it's flat-out impossible. There are bargainer demons who are able to do it, and I bet my best spell that there are other types of paranormal who can as well. I just have to find them.

But first, I have to get out of this godforsaken realm.

I hitch my bag higher on my shoulder and start for the trees. I like being outside, but that doesn't mean I like being *active* outside. Up until this point, the thought of going for a hike has ranked right up there with bamboo shoots under my fingernails, but surely it won't be that bad traveling through an island connected to a strange realm. Yes, I can hear something skittering in the underbrush. Sure, those spiderwebs look like they're made by something about the size of a small pony. And I guess maybe I should be worried about that pair of yellow eyes glowing in the distance, too.

"Damn it." I grab my bag with white knuckles. "I am the baddest witch around. If anyone fucks with me, I'll blow a crater in this damn forest."

Unsurprisingly, my attempt at bravado does little to actually make me less scared. I faced down murderous pirates and a cranky Lizzie. I fought in the tournament that's held at the Shadow Market every Samhain. I'm a fucking witch. Creepy forests should be perfectly within my wheelhouse.

Except that's a shitty stereotype with no basis in reality.

After a brief debate with myself, I drop my stealth and invisibility spells. Both work well against humans, but if what I'm facing in this forest is more animalistic in nature, then scent will betray me faster than anything else. Better to have something defensive prepared.

I take a couple steps into the trees and fight back a shiver. The air was hardly balmy without the sun warming the sky, but within the trees, it's downright frigid. "I get it, okay. Creepy forest. Spooky chills." I wave my fingers. This is *fine*. There's no one else around. If I have to talk myself through this fear in order to keep going, then it's a small enough price to pay. It's not like anyone is witnessing this weakness.

The eyes in the distance have disappeared, and I'm not sure

if that's a blessing or a curse. The creature they belong to may have decided I am more troublesome than I'm worth . . . or it may be stalking me right now.

Cheerful thoughts. *Happy* thoughts.

I pull out the dagger I lifted from Bowen and press its tip to my thumb. Not all magic needs a blood component, but it's a nifty shortcut in a pinch. My tattoos do most of the heavy lifting. Each one is inked with a specific combination of components unique to that particular spell, and I have to reink them after I've used up that particular spell. Some of them are single-use only. Some I can tap a few times before I need to recharge them. Either way, the tattoos are one of the best decisions I've ever made.

Putting in extra effort for no damn reason doesn't make you a saint. Efficiency isn't a bad thing, as long as you don't forget your roots.

If I get stuck in Threshold any longer, I'll be forced back to those roots. Somehow, I don't think they have tattoo guns lying around. I want to get out here before I have to find out.

I am most definitely stalling.

I press my thumb to the glyph that triggers a medium-strength defensive spell I can hold for a prolonged period of time. It won't save me from getting bruised up, but it should stop a killing blow.

Now there's nothing left but to get moving. I curse under my breath and pick the direction where the trees seem not quite so impossible to navigate. "I can do this. I have to do this." I take three large steps . . .

And run face-first into an invisible wall.

I bounce back and land on my ass, my nose smarting fiercely. "What the actual fuck?"

Something grabs me by my ankle and lifts me into the air. I fire off a spell on instinct, but there's nothing to make contact with. It just flies off into the trees with a faint sizzle. When I bend and grasp at my ankle for the rope that must have snared me, my fingers find nothing to unwind. Only air. I'm not being held in a trap of any earthly making. It's magic. And I know only one aggravating motherfucker who can move things with his mind.

I twist and flail, my hair making it nearly impossible to see. "Where are you, you asshole?"

"That's a bold statement coming from a vow breaker." His voice sounds near me, but not too near.

I don't know whether to be incensed or relieved that Bowen is the one responsible for my current predicament. On one hand, it means he anticipated my escape and was out here laying a trap for me. On the other hand, it's not some new enemy to contend with. For better or worse, Bowen is somewhat of a known factor. At least in theory.

"Let me go."

"So you can run again?" He scoffs out of sight. "I don't think so. You and I are going to have a frank conversation."

Not this again. Surely he can't be so intentionally dense that he thinks he'll convince me to see things his way. Yes, I've been a bit of a liar. But all that is out in the open now. There's not much I can say to make him believe I won't run again, and rightfully so. "How about, instead of doing that, you go find a dead horse to beat?"

He's silent for several moments too long. "I am assuming that is some kind of metaphor, because the alternative seems out of character for you."

For fuck's sake. How am I supposed to talk to this man? I realize I'm in another realm with different cultural touch points, but it still feels like talking to someone's great-grandfather who's barely come to terms with the moving pictures on his television. I drag in a deep breath and strive for patience. "Bowen, put me down."

Instead of listening, his magic turns me to face him and gathers my hair away from my face. That, more than anything else he's done since I've met him, terrifies me. I've met telekinetics from time to time, enough to know that the big explosions of power are actually the easy moves. It's the small, delicate tasks that require the most control.

Bowen doesn't hurt me. He doesn't snag even a single strand of hair. *Holy shit.*

"I understand you aren't the kind of person whose nature it is to take threats seriously." He moves out of the darkness between two trees and crouches in front of me, a few feet away. Gods, but he's a handsome fucker. I didn't think he was going to win any beauty pageants when I first saw him, but it seems like he only gets more attractive every time I look at him. His broad shoulders block out what little light there is; they even seem to block out the rain still cascading down around us. He snaps his fingers in front of my face, forcing me to focus on him. "Take me seriously now, Evelyn. You say you know the reputation of the Cŵn Annwn. What do we do?"

I'm still too freaked out by his display of control to come up with a smart-ass comment. "You hunt," I say through numb lips.

"Yes, we hunt." He leans forward, his dark eyes devastatingly serious. "If you run, you will force us to hunt you. You will force *me* to hunt you."

"I am—"

He keeps going as if I hadn't tried to speak. "Leaving Threshold won't be enough to save you. While the Cŵn Annwn don't normally hunt in the other realms themselves, there are times when it's necessary to do so. A rogue member of our group is one of them. This isn't something you can outrun, Evelyn. Hunting is what we do. When we find you—and we will—there will be no trial, no opportunity to use your witty words to defend yourself. We will rip you limb from limb and paint the ground bloody. Do you understand me?"

I can't catch my breath. I want to blame the buzzing in my head from being upside down, but fear is its true source. Because he's not blustering. He's not yelling or making ostentatious threats. He's merely stating a future as if it's a given.

If I run, they will kill me.

Tomorrow, I will tell myself that I wasn't about to piss my pants in terror. Tomorrow, I will start thinking of a future where I can work around this inevitability. Tomorrow . . .

Right now, all thoughts have fled from my brain. "Why are you doing this to me?"

"I am trying to *protect* you."

Bowen doesn't want to hurt me. I think I knew that, but it's never been clearer than it is in this moment. By all rights, my sneaking off the ship should count as breaking my vow. I certainly intended for it to. And yet he's not ripping my limbs from my body and painting the forest with my blood.

Yes, he's holding me captive. But he sounds so fucking exhausted that I have the strangest urge to give him a hug. I don't know what the hell that's about.

"I need you to tell me that you understand me, Evelyn."

Just like that, whatever fight I have left drains away. At least for now. I nod, and even as scared as I am, I still note the fact that he adjusts his magical hold on my hair to ensure it doesn't pull. Who *is* this man? To be so careful with me, and yet deliver one of the most horrific threats I've ever experienced. Because he's not bluffing. He threatens the same way Lizzie does: A statement of fact. An explanation of consequences.

I don't know if I'm going to get out of this one.

"I understand," I finally managed.

Bowen's magic moves around me as he turns me right side up and sets me on my feet. My blood immediately rushes from my head and I stumble. When he catches me, it's not with his magic this time.

It's with his hands. They're very nice hands. Wide and rough in a way I can feel through my thin shirt. Strong, too.

It must be tangling my senses and confusing my instincts. That's the only explanation, and not even a good one at that. Because instead of stepping away and putting some necessary distance between us, I lean in closer.

Worse still, I grab the front of his shirt and yank him toward me.

And then I kiss Bowen.

CHAPTER 11

Bowen

I WISH I COULD SAY IT HAPPENED TOO FAST FOR ME TO avoid. It's a lie. The truth is that I let Evelyn pull me down and take my mouth. I didn't even hesitate. I wanted to kiss her more than I wanted to do the right thing.

So much for honor.

She tastes like freedom. Like the air against my face and the sea beneath the rolling deck of my ship. I'm no poet, but the first stroke of her tongue against mine makes me want to be.

I don't make a conscious decision to move, but she lets out a tiny little whimper and then my hands are in her hair and stroking down her back, urging her to press more tightly against me. She's so fucking soft, it drives me wild. I cup her full hips and make a sound that's damn near a growl.

I need to stop.

A mere minute ago, I was threatening her in the most violent way possible. I have no business grabbing two fistfuls of her ass and lifting her so she can wrap her legs around my waist. I sure as fuck shouldn't turn and take several staggering steps so I can press her against the nearest tree.

I do it anyway.

All the while, she kisses me as if she might never get another chance, as if she wants to imprint every sensation on her very soul. I feel exactly the same way. I want more. I want everything. And yet I would be satisfied merely kissing this woman for the rest of my days.

Her tongue is just as quick as her words. She teases me, advancing and retreating in turn, almost seeming to taunt me. What am I saying? Of course she's taunting me. Her hands are in my hair, tugging until she has my mouth exactly at the angle she prefers. There's no hesitation. If there was, maybe I could stop myself from thrusting against her.

She makes that intoxicating whimpering sound again. It's the most beautiful thing I've ever heard. I thrust against her a second time. I'd like nothing more than to rip the pants from her body so that I can have complete access to her, but I have enough of myself still present to not give in to that animalistic urge.

She digs her heels into the small of my back, urging me closer even as she rolls her body against the hard length of my cock. I want to tell her to stop. I want to tell her never to stop. I don't have the breath to do either.

Her movements become more desperate. Instinct has me matching them even as I fight against the pleasure shooting down my spine and gathering in my balls. I have already made a fool of myself for this woman too many times in our short acquaintance. I won't do it again. Not here. Not like this.

Evelyn tears her mouth from mine and her whole body goes tense. I have to move fast to cup the back of her head to prevent her from smashing it on the tree behind her. "Oh fuck, Bowen." She shudders, clasping me to her.

Did she just . . .

Her fingers clench rhythmically in my hair and the tension eases out of her body. Surely not. Surely I'm misreading things. "Did you just—"

"Not another word."

That all but confirms it. She orgasmed. "But I didn't even—"

Evelyn covers my mouth with her hand. "Not. Another. Word." Her skin is warm against my lips. I almost kiss her palm, but think better of it at the last moment. "Let me down."

I don't want to. It's not only the desire surging through my body in time with my racing heart. I like how soft she is, how good her legs feel clamped around my waist. "We should talk about this," I speak against her palm. I don't know what I'm saying. I just need to prolong the moment until I have to step away and reality will come rushing into the new space between us.

"Suffice to say we are *never* going to talk about this." She shivers and her thighs tighten around me. "This is complicated and the last thing either of us need is complicated. This is a terrible idea, and I am at my allotment of terrible ideas for an entire lifetime. Let me down, Bowen."

I let her down. My cock is a painful length against the front of my breeches, but just as I feared, reality splashes me in the face with what I've just done.

Evelyn is a traitor. I might have stopped her this time, but she'll try to escape again. I already felt sick at the thought of hurting her before I knew what she tasted like. I can't afford to hesitate if it comes to that. If I do . . . that will make me a traitor just like her.

It would mean that all the terrible things I've done since Ezra pulled me out of the water were for nothing. That they meant nothing.

That, more than anything else, snaps me out of the haze of desire. I'd accuse her of casting a spell on me, but lust doesn't need magic to spark to life. I wanted her from the moment I saw her. I never would have made the first move, but when she kissed me? Yeah, that wasn't magic propelling me forward.

It was need.

I carefully set her on her feet and step back. Even in the darkness, I can see the flush in her cheeks and the way her lips are plumped from kissing. It makes me want to kiss her again. It makes me want to howl at the fucking moon at how unfair this whole situation is.

"You can't run again, Evelyn." I hardly sound like myself, my voice low and ragged. "Don't make me kill you. Please."

She looks away and then finally faces me fully. "I can't make that promise."

Even saying that is breaking her vows. Or it would be enough to qualify for some captains. *Miles would argue for it.* "Evelyn."

"Don't say my name like that."

"Like what?"

"Like I'm infuriating you and you want to kiss me again."

That startles a ragged laugh out of me. "You *are* infuriating, and I *do* want to kiss you again."

"Bowen! Don't be charming. It's upsetting and confusing."

She's the charming one, especially now that she's flustered. It makes my chest feel strange to know that I'm the one who flustered her. This woman is dangerous in a way I'm not prepared to deal with. I've had lovers over the years, but none have come close to what Evelyn has accomplished in two short days.

She makes me . . . *crave*.

"Come back to the ship."

"I don't have much choice, do I?" She casts a look filled with longing toward the darkness of the trees. "I don't think I was made for the sea. I miss the earth beneath my feet."

That strange feeling in my chest twinges hard enough that I press my hand there as if it were a physical sensation. I don't like her sad. I *have* to make her sad to keep her alive. "Come on."

A low sound stops me cold. It's not quite a growl, more of a hiss of pure menace. Evelyn turns to peer into the darkness, but I grab her arm. "Don't move."

"What is—"

"*Silence*, woman." I stare over her shoulder at the two glowing eyes that seem to hover in midair just over her shoulder. If I hadn't been so distracted by her, the beast never would have gotten so close. "When I tell you to run, run back to the village like your life depends on it. Because it does."

A fine tremor works its way through her body, but I don't have time to worry about her fear right now. I'll have to time this carefully. The creature will pounce and there will be one moment to get out of the way. These animals have the ability to partially shift planes of existence, which allows them to dodge attacks both physical and magical.

How do I know that?

We've stopped at Yaltia a handful of times over the years, but I've never once ventured out of the village itself. I took one look at the houses in the trees and any curiosity I felt shriveled up. Up until this moment, I would have sworn I have no idea what resides in this forest.

The eyes shift, sinking a few spare inches. The beast is about to pounce. I shove Evelyn toward the village. "Run!" I draw my magic forth even as I pull my largest knife from my boot. Not bringing my sword was a foolish thing to do, but I hadn't expected to do more than gather up a wayward witch. Fighting for my life wasn't on the agenda.

I get my first clear look at the creature as it stalks out of the darkness, a giant black cat with a startling patch of white on its chest. Its shoulders are massive, likely coming up to my chest if it stood still long enough, and its claws are easily as long as my hands. The glowing eyes hold an intelligence that is hardly animal. There's menace there, hate even.

The beast launches itself at me. I throw up a shield, and it blinks out of existence. There one moment and gone the next. It reappears on the other side of my shield, far too close. The damn thing teleported. I knew it could do it, but seeing it verified is something else entirely.

Holding a shield around my body is all but impossible in a fight, and it won't do any good against an enemy like this. Instead, I go on the offense. I strike with a concentrated blast of magic aimed directly at its head.

The damned thing dodges, leaping straight up so my magic passes harmlessly below it. "Fuck." It obviously has experience fighting magical humans. I'm in trouble. If I can't strike and I can't defend . . . this might be it for me.

I barely have time to process that thought and the conflicting emotions it brings when a ball of violently purple fire smashes into the cat's side. It howls in agony as the fire wraps around it, freakishly fast. The beast blinks out of existence, but when it reappears, the fire is still spreading through its fur.

With a cry that makes my skin prickle, the cat turns and flees deeper into the trees. Instantly, the fire goes out. It doesn't stop running, though. I watch it disappear before I turn to where Evelyn crouches.

Her fingertips are filthy from carving the rough circle she occupies, and she's breathing just as hard as I am. She looks up at me, her green eyes glowing nearly as brightly as the cat's had. "I didn't want to hurt it."

I blink. "What?"

"I couldn't let it kill you." She weaves a little and plants her hand on the ground. Her hair falls forward to hide her face from me. "And it's too close to the village. A child could have wandered this deep into the woods. It's not like we walked far to get here. It's only a matter of time before it kills someone." Her voice is clogged as if she's fighting back tears.

I move closer on pure instinct. "You saved me."

"It's not right to kill animals just because they're dangerous. By that logic, both you and I should be killed, too."

Gods above and below, my thieving witch has a bleeding heart.

I don't stop to think. I scoop her into my arms. "You didn't kill it, and it's smart enough to move on to an easier territory to hunt. You saved my life and probably the lives of at least one villager." I press a kiss to her temple on pure instinct. "And the villagers *would* have killed it after it took one of their own. You did a good thing, little witch."

She gives a sad little laugh. "I know what you must think. It's a silly thing to be sad about. But we humans fuck up too much shit, you know? It's not the wild's fault that we're so determined to show up where we're not wanted."

I hug her even tighter to me. "Are you going to ask me to track down the beast and heal it?"

"What?" This time, her laugh sounds a little bit closer to the woman I'm coming to know. "Of course not. There might be others, and while I'm sad at the thought of hurting it, I don't want to die. Or for you to die." She tilts her head back and looks at me. Her brows draw together. "You really would do it, wouldn't you?"

I don't want to. The thought of venturing deeper into the trees makes my skin threaten to crawl right off my body. I don't know that it would return to this place once it's healed, but it's possible. The beast being so close to the village is a recipe for disaster. If the villagers weren't able handle it themselves, the Cŵn Annwn would be summoned back to this place to deal with the problem. And they . . . *we* . . . wouldn't stop until it's dead.

"It would be a bad idea to track it down and heal it," I say finally.

"Oh, Bowen." She rests her head on my shoulder. It feels rather nice. "I'm going to let you carry me because that was a bit of a reckless move on my part, to pull that spell with so little prep, but don't think it's because I like you."

I smile against her hair. "Of course not."

"I don't like you."

"Mm-hmm."

She sighs. "Right. I don't even sound convincing to myself. Whatever. Take me back to the ship, Captain. I'll be a good little sailor, at least for a while."

CHAPTER 12

Evelyn

BOWEN DOESN'T SAY ANOTHER WORD AS HE CARRIES ME around the perimeter of the village and back to the ship. Probably because he's very much a man not overly in touch with his emotions and I'm doing my best not to weep over a murderous cat monster.

Bunny always said I was too soft when it came to furry friends.

Then again, she suffered from the same affliction. She constantly fed strays and nursed sick creatures back from the brink of death, and she never met a swan she didn't want to talk shit to as if it were human.

She wouldn't have faulted me for defending myself . . . except I *wasn't* defending myself. I was defending Bowen. I could have run like he ordered me to. Truth be told, I had started to. It was only when I looked back and realized the cat could teleport to avoid his magic that I realized exactly how much trouble he was in.

The fool didn't even have his sword, and it was absolutely my fault. He came out here to bring me back, to save me from myself. The fact that he didn't bring a weapon with him speaks volumes . . . and it was going to get him killed fighting that beast.

If he died, Miles would take over the *Crimson Hag*, and that outcome is unacceptable. That's the only reason I saved him. Yep. It doesn't matter that I didn't have that thought until just now. Totally checks out.

Bowen stops and I lift my head to see that we're near the docks. Not close enough to be seen by the ship, but there's no way he can carry me back without someone noticing. I clear my throat. "I'm good. You can put me down."

"Evelyn." His arms tighten around me, ever so briefly. "Thank you."

My traitorous heart gives a little thump. Too much has happened in too short a time. From my thwarted escape attempt, to my ill-advised kiss, to the humiliation of coming from a little dry humping, to the attack by the giant cat.

"What was that thing?" I've never seen anything like it. We have big predators back home, and some of them are even paranormal in nature, but that was on another level entirely.

"Cat-sìth." He frowns and shakes his head. "I have no idea how I know that. I've never seen one before."

He sets me on my feet and I can't help searching his expression. It's bothered in a completely different way than I'm used to. *I'm* not the cause of that frown. "Just because you haven't seen one doesn't mean you don't know what it is. I've never petted a lion but I can identify one on sight."

His lips curve a little but his eyes are still distant. "I don't . . .

I'm nearly certain I've never heard that term before." He shakes his head again. "It's no matter. Ezra gave me a lot of lessons when I was an unruly teenager. It's entirely possible it's rattling around in my head from that time."

I don't know him well enough to press, even though I can tell he doesn't actually believe that. "Maybe it's your home realm and that's why you know."

Bowen's expression shuts down. I didn't realize how much he's relaxed and opened up until it's gone. "That's not it. I have no past before the Cŵn Annwn. Stop trying to create a problem where there is none."

It's on the tip of my tongue to point out that no one pops into existence at thirteen, no matter what flavor of paranormal they are, and Bowen is clearly from the same source as humans. The Cŵn Annwn didn't birth him.

But I'm tired.

The spell took a lot out of me. Every being with magic has a limited well inside them. It refills regularly, unless something wild happens, but you have to be careful not to drain it completely. I've never gotten close. I'm not close now, but I've used more than is comfortable. I need some food and a solid night of rest to recover.

Strategically, saving Bowen was a bad move; I could've used his distraction to escape and even now be putting miles between me and whoever comes hunting. But the thought never crossed my mind. I reacted on instinct, and at this point I think it's well established my instincts are shit.

All this to say that I don't have the time or energy to fight with him. It's hard enough to stand here without weaving on my feet. "If you say so."

He frowns at me. "Do you need a healer?"

"I'm fine." With my luck, he'd use that opportunity to stick a tracking spell on me, and then I'd have to dismantle that before I could attempt to escape again.

And I *will* be attempting to escape again. Just . . . not right now.

"Evelyn." He waits for me to look back at him before he continues. "As soon as the weather clears, we'll be heading out. It's important that you don't do anything to delay that. People have been killed by the monster we're hunting. We're still not sure the exact type it is, but we *are* sure of that. It's our job to ensure no one else dies."

Just like we did with the cat-sìth.

The thought makes me sick to my stomach. "You know, I'm a liar and a cheat and a thief, but I've never murdered anything—or anyone—before. I'm not looking forward to changing that."

"It's not murder if it's a monster." He's doing that thing again, the one where he opens up his mouth and someone else's words come out.

I hold his gaze. "How do you know that? You just said you don't know the shape of it, only that it's killed people."

He sighs. "Sometimes our orders don't have all the necessary details. It's just how it works. We are trained to adapt to whatever monster we might face. The Council trusts us to be able to handle it even if we don't know the full parameters of what we're walking into."

"There you go again. Throwing around that word as if it actually means something. I suppose breaking your vow makes you a monster, then? Since you kill people who run."

Bowen pauses, and sighs. "I understand what you're saying, but it's different. There's no choice."

"That's the thing about life. It's nothing but bad choices." I'm soaked to the bone, exhausted, and more than a little heartbroken. I turn and start toward the ship. This whole thing was a mistake. Not just because Bowen caught me . . . and then gave me a particularly stellar orgasm.

Nothing but bad choices, indeed.

If I had escaped Lizzie's house without jumping realms, there's every chance that her family would have killed me. And not in a quick, painless way. Lizzie didn't become who she is in a vacuum. She was formed that way by birth and a very long life of conditioning. I imagine her parents are even worse. The thought makes me shiver.

A warm weight settles over my shoulders. Bowen's cloak. Even as I tell myself not to, I pull it closer and inhale deeply. His cedar scent settles something inside me just as much as the residual warmth inside the cloak does. I don't know what to think about it, so I don't think about it at all.

I trudge back to the ship. In the predawn darkness, it's still and silent. There's also no gangplank. *Damn it.* The thought barely crosses my mind when Bowen's magic wraps around me and lifts me into the air. His grip wobbles a little before he steadies me. I glance down to find his expression strained. He used a lot of magic tonight, too. Even though he's got to be just as exhausted as I am, he's still going above and beyond to ensure I have an easier time getting aboard. It's unnecessary and frivolous and . . . damn it, it warms my heart.

The rise up the side of the ship is slow going, nearly as slow as if I'd climbed it myself. It gives me too much time to think. With the delicate way he's holding me, even in his exhaustion, there's a part of my brain that can't stop analyzing the possibilities. I was too scared out of my mind earlier to register exactly how sexy it is that he has this level of power. Of control.

I'm not scared right now.

Who needs bondage ropes when your partner can hold you down with their mind? Can lift you and move you and *touch* you without lifting a single finger?

No. Not going there.

Except I've already gone there, haven't I? The lid is off that Pringles can and now I know exactly how good he tastes, how he holds me as if I'm the most precious thing in the world, how he *growls* when he's about to lose it. A woman could get addicted to being touched like that, to affecting her partner that deeply with only a kiss and an embrace.

I have no illusions about how I look. I'm fat and sexy and I've had no shortage of partners over the years. But it's always been a game, a push and pull for fun or dominance or, in Lizzie's case, a perverse desire to unravel her epic control. I was never successful; even in the throes of orgasm, she was as cold as ice. It made me want her more.

Bowen isn't like that. There's no game here. He's so devastatingly serious. I don't know how to deal with it. I *shouldn't* deal with it. No matter the attraction I feel for him, I'm leaving.

Yes, the Cŵn Annwn are scary, but so is Lizzie. I was already planning on spending the rest of my life dodging her. Tomato, tomahto.

Bowen sets me gently on the deck and physically climbs up

instead of using his magic for himself. As I suspected, he looks like he's weaving on his feet when he hauls himself aboard a few moments later. He shakes his head when I go to shrug off his cloak. "Keep it for now."

It's impossible not to notice how the rain plasters his white shirt to his broad chest. The fabric is practically transparent, clearly displaying every curve of muscle and scar. There are a *lot* of scars. It makes my heart pang strangely, but my heart has always been a fickle creature. Of course it would feel empathy for this man who is just as much monster as the cat-sìth.

"Thanks." Without another word, I turn away and head belowdecks. Lucky is nowhere in evidence when I duck into our room. It's just as well. I'm not in the mood to deal with their strange attitude.

I peel off my drenched clothes yet again and glare at them. That's two botched escape attempts—one from Lizzie's mansion and one from the *Crimson Hag*. Maybe the clothes are cursed. Next time I run, I'll wear something else.

Granted, nothing fits quite right from the clothing I've been given, but that's a battle for another day. There is magic that can bolster sewing and stitching, but I never bothered learning it because I'm downright garbage at both. As Bunny always said, *Stick to what you're good at.*

My inhale sticks in my throat. Gods, what am I doing? This was my best opportunity to escape and I barely made it a few hundred yards. Bowen saw me coming a mile away. I never stood a chance.

How in the gods' name am I going to get free? I've wiggled out of some sticky situations over the years, but this is by far the stickiest. There has to be a way . . .

I flop onto my bed and, with only the most fleeting feeling of guilt, pull Bowen's cloak around me. I have no business finding comfort in the reminder of my captor, and yet here I am.

Sleep takes me between one breath and the next, exhaustion sucking me down into the depths.

CHAPTER 13

Bowen

THE STORM PASSES RIGHT ON SCHEDULE. WE SPEND A full twenty-four hours docked, just long enough for interested crew members to avail themselves to the hospitality of Yaltia. The bar owner will be happy with their income from all the drinking, and I sent Kit to secure proper clothing for Evelyn.

Not that the witch makes another appearance in that time. I tell myself it's a blessing that she's not underfoot and causing trouble while we get ready to set sail. It doesn't stop me from having to forcibly turn away from the door belowdecks over and over again as the storm decreases to a sprinkle of rain and a playful breeze, and then dies away completely a few hours later.

She doesn't need me to check on her. She's *fine*. There's nowhere more protected from outside attack than the *Crimson Hag*, and my crew knows better than to do more than good-natured ribbing with each other. The same can't be said for other Cŵn Annwn ships, but . . .

I can control only this ship and this crew. I can't worry about the others. If I try to battle every injustice in this world, I'll end up in the sea, feeding the mermaids. Ezra taught me that it's vital to pick your battles, and protect those you can because it's impossible to protect everyone in an unfair world. Some times that lesson chafes more than others.

"I got what you asked for, Captain."

I nod at Kit. Ne has a bag in nir hands, and it looks significantly fuller than I expected. I raise my brows. "Did you buy out the whole place?"

Ne grins. "Not at all. Yaltia gets plenty of traffic through, so they keep a good stock of things for our people to trade with."

In a realm of constantly moving islands—and portals— stationary trading locations are worth their weight in gold. There are four permanent islands of some size in Threshold— Sarvi, Drash, Lyari, and Three Sisters. The latter is technically three islands, as their name would suggest, but they're in such close proximity with each other that they gained a single name for all three.

Yaltia sits at a perfect intersection amid the routes between the permanent islands, which means a significant amount of traffic. Its position makes Yaltia an invaluable stop for supplies on some of the longer voyages.

I almost take the bag from Kit, but common sense gets ahold of me at the last moment. I have a ship to run and a crew to manage. As much as I want to lay eyes on Evelyn and see for myself that she's recovered from the burst of magic that saved us, there are other things that require my focus.

Like the sea monster menacing Sarvi. According to the updated report that appeared on my desk last night, it's killed several more people. Teenagers who were swimming on a beach that should have been safe. There's no escaping the guilt that haunts me. We couldn't have sailed through that storm, and yet our delay feels like a failure. People died because of it. *Kids* died because of it.

Additionally, the deaths seem to suggest it's settling into a hunting territory, rather than attempting to go back to whatever realm it came from. Not that fleeing would save it. Once a monster garners enough attention, it requires the Cŵn Annwn to go hunting outside of Threshold. Even if it never crossed into our territory. I'm sure my little witch will have something to say about *that* on the rare occasion it comes up.

"Take it to her, please."

Kit raises nir eyebrows. "You sure you don't want to hand deliver it yourself?"

I almost choke. Only years of Kit's ribbing have given me the practice not to react. "I hardly think that's necessary."

"Necessary isn't any fun, Captain." Ne grins. "We all see how you look at her. How she looks at you. A gift from the handsome captain wouldn't go amiss."

I will not blush. I will *not*. "I am the captain of this ship and fraternizing with any of my crew would be highly inappropriate." It's a good thing Kit is human. Ne is without a lick of magic, so ne can't see the memory of Evelyn's mouth imprinted against mine from a mere twenty-four hours ago.

"You know that's not actually a law, right?" Ne shakes nir head. "Live a little, Captain. We might be named for the Cŵn Annwn, but none of us are immortal. Life's too short to pass up what little joy it has to offer." Ne turns and walks away before I can come up to a response to *that*, which is just as well.

The next few hours are a flurry of motion as we cast off and head north around the perimeter of the island. Then there's only the open sea from horizon to horizon. Out here, I feel like I can finally breathe.

It's an illusion.

Threshold is peppered with islands, both permanent and traveling. We're never more than a few days from one of them. Not all are inhabited, or even contain fresh water, but they serve as a reminder that we're never really free.

I pause. *Where did that thought come from?* If I didn't know better, I'd track down my witch and accuse her of planting it right in my head. It's a false accusation. She might be partially responsible for the strange thought, but it's not magic at its source. It's her incessant questions. *Why* do we do things the way we do? It's her grief over the harm she caused a vicious beast intent on our deaths.

I never expected that from her.

She hasn't done much that I've expected since we fished her out of the sea.

"Good winds."

I watch Miles walk up, my mood souring. "We'll make good time to Sarvi despite the delay." I haven't seen much of my quartermaster in the time we were trapped in Yaltia's bay by the storm. He went ashore with a good portion of the crew. No doubt he used that time well to continue to gain favor among them.

The vote is coming. I can sense it the same way Dia can sense weather patterns. I do my best to operate above reproach, but I'm only human, and the code of honor that Ezra instilled in me doesn't sit well with some people. It will take only one moment, one bad choice, and Miles will have his victory.

The thought should fire me up, but I'm so fucking tired. I want to blame it on being worried about Evelyn sneaking out again, or on the hundred other little details and concerns that go with running a ship and keep me up at night.

I'm starting to wonder if this exhaustion isn't years in the making. Evelyn's presence on board didn't cause it. She only revealed what was already there, simmering below the surface.

Miles stops next to me and turns easily to face the same way. I nod to Sarah and she gives us a little boost with her magic, filling the sails and sending us skimming across the waves away from Yaltia. I tell myself I don't breathe easier with each league between us, but it's a lie.

Seconds tick by, and then minutes. This is the longest Miles has spent in my presence in weeks. I glance at him. "You need something?"

He shrugs. "Just making sure the plan for Sarvia hasn't changed."

I don't like the casual way he asks that, as if there are layers beneath the seemingly simple words. Miles speaks plainly most of the time, which makes the times he *doesn't* all the trickier. "Why would something change?" I finally ask.

His tail flicks, the smallest movement but telling nonetheless. "The woman is in your head."

"She's not in my head." I speak too quickly, too harshly. He's not saying anything I haven't thought myself, but hearing it from Miles sets my teeth on edge.

"Are you sure?" His voice is bland. "Nothing worth reporting has happened since she came aboard?"

Something like guilt blossoms on the back of my tongue. There's no way he could be talking about the cat-sìth. It wasn't an official hunt, and the only witness to what happened was Evelyn. *She* didn't tell anyone; of that, I'm sure. Miles is trying to trap me into admitting I've done something wrong. I make an effort to loosen my grip on the helm. "You obviously have something you're chewing on. Spit it out."

"Lucky woke up to find their bunkmate missing. No one saw the witch for several hours that first night on Yaltia . . . not until Sarah witnessed *you* coming back aboard with her. If she broke her vow—"

"She didn't." I can't let him pursue that train of thought. I might be willing to give Evelyn the space to come to terms with her new life, but Miles won't. He's more than proven that since we pulled her out of the sea. "She wanted to see the island, so I took her on a quick tour."

"In the middle of the night, while we were trapped by a vicious storm." His disbelief might as well be a physical thing between us.

If I let him chase down this argument, he's going to catch me out. There's no good reason for Evelyn—or me—to have gone ashore when we did. Not unless we were up to no good.

Or she was, and I was hauling her back before anyone could notice she'd slipped out.

Better to change the subject entirely. "While we were in the woods, we happened across a creature I've never seen before. It could shift planes. Have you ever heard of a giant cat that can do that?"

Miles flicks out his tongue, tasting the air. As if testing for a *lie.* "Is it something we need to take care of?"

"No. We handled it." Let him read what he will from that vague statement. He'll assume we killed it. We didn't, but with it being so injured, it's sure to leave the village behind and move on to easier—less dangerous—prey. It's not a sure thing, but . . .

The line of thought makes me uneasy. It feels like mental acrobatics, and that's not something I usually indulge in.

"But no, to answer your question, I've never come across such a beast." He narrows his beady dark eyes. "Why do you ask?"

Because apparently I've heard of this creature. I know its name and far too much information about it. Information I have no right to. Not that I'm going to admit as much to him. He's already feeling me out for weakness to exploit. There's no reason to hand him one for free. "If it's something that's more common than I realized, it would be useful to train the crew in how to deal with it."

"No reason for *you* to worry about it. You won't be captain for much longer." He turns and walks away without another word.

I watch him go, dread weighing my shoulders down. If we've moved to overt threats, then he thinks he's all but assured the vote. I'll have to deal with that soon . . . but not yet. First, we have people to save.

I turn my attention back to the horizon. I'll deal with Miles after we handle the sea monster. Even without knowing the full details about what we're about to hunt, it's likely to be some kind of serpent. From the most recent report, the teenagers were killed on the beach itself, which means the creature came out of the water, at least partially. That, combined with the fact that it's attacking in the shallows, removes a number of options.

Sea serpents are common enough in Threshold, but all of our native ones stick to the depths, except during breeding season. Even then, they historically stay clear of the islands with people. The ones who haven't end up dead. Which created something of a natural evolution, I suppose.

It's the transplants we have problems with. While the islands are the only places where portals exist, over the generations, some of the islands have descended beneath the waves. Our records are clear enough when it comes to the ones we've lost for one reason or another, but just because the island is inhabitable to nonaquatic people doesn't mean their respective portals stop functioning. When monstrosities from the sea arrive, those are the portals they use.

If I feel pity for them, I remind myself that I have more responsibility to the citizens of Threshold than I do to some creature who's lost its way. There's no good method of returning it to the realm where it came from, and even if there were, that's not what the Cŵn Annwn do. We hunt. We kill. End of story. It weighs on me, but I owe *everything* to them.

These thoughts do me no good. There's no problem to solve here, for all that Evelyn would have me believe there is. She's working an angle, and I have to remember that.

And I do . . . right up until I see Kit stride back onto deck. I motion nem over, even though I have no good reason to do so. Ne knows it, too. Kit grins and ambles over. "What's up, Captain?"

I'm in danger of making a fool of myself, and I can't seem to stop. "Did she get the clothing okay?"

If anything, Kit's grin widens. "Of course. She oohed and aahed over all the pretties. I made sure to tell her to give her thanks to you, not anyone else." Before I can come up with a response to that, ne gives me a finger wave and heads toward the stern.

I didn't give her clothes so that she'd have a reason to seek me out or thank me. And yet I'm looking forward to being in her presence again all the same. I can't get the memory of her in my arms out of my head. Her absence over the last twenty-four hours should've been enough to banish the worst of it, but it's not the case. If anything, I crave her more.

This is a problem.

I'll just add it to the list.

CHAPTER 14

Evelyn

I CAN'T HIDE FOREVER. WHEN MILES FIRST ASSIGNED ME TO the kitchen, I resented it, but it's honestly been a nice reprieve from . . . everything. I have some experience with brownies, so I don't step on their toes the way some of the rest of the crew does. In return, I don't have to do the hard labor that comes from working on deck or worry about dealing with the quartermaster, who obviously hates me. I tell myself that it's worth the exchange.

But I can't help missing Bowen.

It's ridiculous to miss the man who's my captor, who's aggravating in the extreme because of his unwillingness to bend. But after three days, I find myself back on deck, pulled there by the excitement of the crew as we near our destination. I stay out of the way as best I can, and make a careful path to the railing.

Overhead, the skies are clear of clouds and painted a blue that's almost unreal. It reminds me of summer days back home, and longing hits me so hard, I actually flinch. It's so strange that

I can be in this magical place and yet the sky looks so familiar. Brilliant and blue and absolutely endless. I try to appreciate the fact that I'm in Threshold, but it's hard to be positive these days when I feel so conflicted.

Our destination lies in front of us, an island that is significantly larger than the last one. It curves out to the east—or at least I think it's the east—and then back around out of sight. There doesn't seem to be any place to access from this direction; the whole coast is high cliffs that remind me of the pictures I've seen of Ireland. Except these ones aren't white. They are a magnificent green shot through with blue and gold and silver, so bright they take my breath away. The metallics catch the light as we sail northwest.

"You want to be belowdecks for what comes next."

I jolt and turn to find my roommate, Lucky, standing next to me. I didn't even hear them approach. For the first time in our acquaintance, a small smile curves the edges of their lipless mouth. It's hardly any expression at all, but on them it's practically a shout of joy.

"What do you mean?"

"Here there be monsters." They let out a harsh laugh. "It's no place for people like you." They press one hand to the railing and hoist themselves over.

It happens so fast, I'm left standing there with my mouth open as they plummet to the water and sink beneath the surface. I spin, ready to shout that there's a person overboard, but Kit hurries up, nir face in hard lines. "You shouldn't be out here, Evelyn."

"So everyone keeps saying." I lean over the railing, but Lucky is nowhere to be seen. "They just—"

"I know." Kit takes my arm and turns me away from the railing. "They're our scout. Lucky's half mermaid, which means they don't ping magical systems the same way a probe would—or run the risk of drowning. They're fine. But you won't be. We don't know quite what we're up against, and the captain would have my head if something happens to you."

There's no time to digest that, not with nem hustling me back toward the staircase that leads belowdecks. "But—"

"Next time." Ne picks up nir pace. "You need to—"

I never find out what ne was about to say. There's a giant roar that raises the hair at the back of my neck, and the entire ship lists violently to the side. Kit catches me in nir burly arms, but we still both slam against the opposite railing. It's only nir strength that keeps us aboard.

I look around frantically, but the rest of the crew seems to be doing okay. Some of them are even laughing, the fools. At least until Lucky flings themself onto the deck, dripping seawater everywhere. Their black eyes are wide and panicked. "Dragon!"

Just like that, the entire vibe changes.

"Gunners, to your stations!" Bowen's roar snaps everyone into motion.

Kit curses under nir breath and thrusts me away from the stairway. "There's no time to get belowdecks now. Hurry. There's space at the helm behind the captain. He'll keep you safe."

For once, I'm not interested in arguing. I've been in plenty of fights over the years, and I know how to take care of myself, but this is a different animal entirely. Fighting by yourself is one thing. This crew is a well-oiled machine, and even as fear is a live creature inside me, they move as if directed by a single mind. I know that's not magic at play, which means it's Bowen's leadership.

Apparently I'm not moving fast enough, because his magic wraps around me and hauls me to a small space at his back. I don't know what it says about me that I find its gentle grip comforting instead of aggravating, but now isn't the time or place to examine the sensation.

It also isn't the time to notice how magnificent he looks, his strong hands guiding the helm and the wind blowing his dark hair back from his strong face. He's wearing another crimson coat, and as much as I hate what that color represents, I can't deny that it looks stunning on him.

"Stay behind me. I'll keep you safe." He doesn't look at me.

There's no time to reply. The ship veers in the other direction, tipping so violently that I slam against Bowen's back. Again, his magic grip surrounds me, carefully keeping me in place.

But I only have eyes for the creature rising out of the waves next to the boat. It's the most magnificent, terrifying thing I've ever seen. Massive and serpentine, but with a face that is both reptilian and strangely catlike. It's a deep blue color, with a lighter underbelly, similar to a great white shark. The better to blend in while it hunts.

Its roar has me covering my ears with my hands and fighting not to crouch as if that would make a difference in this fight. Movement at the other side of the ship makes me pivot, and a great white noise fills my thoughts as my brain tries to comprehend the sheer size of the thing. Because that's its tail, whipping violently about, hundreds of yards from its head.

It strikes at the mast, but it doesn't make contact before

hitting an invisible wall. I know that wall. I walked into it the other night. It's a shield Bowen has constructed with his magic. Sure enough, I feel the tremor that works through him in response to the contact. That took its toll. He's stronger than I can comprehend, but not even he can keep this ship safe indefinitely against that kind of strength.

"Get the spears!"

In response to Bowen's command, Miles and Kit appear, along with several crew members I know by sight, if not by name. Each holds a long spear in their hands and has a determined look on their face. No fear there. I barely understand it.

I recognize the spears, though. They're the same type of spear that Miles tried to impale me with on my first day. I might hate the fucker, but I can't deny he wields the weapon like he was born to it. He uses his entire body behind the strike, sending the spear hurtling through the air with more strength than I could have anticipated.

It impales the dragon, lodging between its scales. We might as well have stuck a toothpick into a giant. Or at least that's what I think until it explodes.

The dragon howls in fury and pain, and strikes at the ship a second time. Again, Bowen deflects it.

"I can . . ." But what can I do? I have several long range spells, like the fire that I used against the cat-sìth. But they require prep, which would be impossible to do with the shipping moving sickeningly beneath my feet. If I try, I'll end up in the water.

That's the last place I want to be.

"Stay where you are."

In another situation, I would disobey just to do it, but I don't really want to die, so I do what Bowen says. Crew members launch a second, third, and fourth spear—javelin?—at the dragon, earning another round of explosions and a third attack.

This time, Bowen grunts a little when he deflects it.

The next one might get through.

Oh fuck. I don't know what to do. Bunny had a lot of rules, but only one when it came to dragons. *Do not, under any circumstances, fuck with a dragon's hoard. Most of them are old bastards who can't stir themselves to eat a pesky witch, but they'll burn the entire world to the ground to protect and reclaim what's theirs.* But surely that doesn't apply here? From what Bowen's said, his orders came only a few days before they found me, which means it's likely this dragon hasn't been in Threshold the entire time.

Think, Evelyn. You have a brain for a reason. If most dragons don't attack unprovoked, then . . .

Another swipe of its tail shakes the shield around the ship so hard that the deck shifts beneath my feet, derailing my thoughts. "How many more hits can you take?"

I don't expect Bowen to answer, but he turns his head slightly and mutters, "A couple. I'd have a better chance if I went on the offensive, but I can't afford to leave the ship defenseless."

I can't help there, either. I know a handful of shielding spells, but a good shield doesn't let anything in—or out. I might be able to keep us safe, but then we wouldn't be able to attack. Beyond that, my strength is no more bottomless than Bowen's is. If the dragon keeps attacking, it *will* get through. End of story.

I hate this.

I don't want this fight, but I also don't want to die.

Even as I debate with myself, Kit and a trio of crew members rush to the side of the ship to replace Miles and the other three who just attacked. I can't see that they're actually doing any damage, and every time they land a strike, the dragon attacks in kind.

In fact, it didn't strike our ship until we threw fucking spears at it. Which doesn't mean it wasn't going to attack, but we definitely went on the offensive first. Of course we did—the dragon has been eating people, and even if I don't love the Cŵn Annwn, I can admit that that's probably not a good thing. Probably.

No, damn it. I'm doing it again. Looking for an angle where there is none. We're fighting for our lives here. There is no angle.

There's always an angle, little bird. If you haven't found it, it's because you're not looking hard enough.

Dragons *protect*. That's what I was thinking before the last strike threw me off. So what is this dragon protecting?

I don't mean to move away from Bowen's back, but I find myself drifting closer to the railing nearest the dragon. It hasn't attacked again. It's twisting and roaring and causing a huge fuss, but it hasn't struck the ship again.

It feels almost . . . defensive. *Protecting.*

Instinct guides me, and I spin toward the center of the ship where Lucky stands. They have a sword in their hand and a grin on their face, showcasing their sharply pointed teeth.

I grab their arm. "What else did you see down there?"

They shake me off, their black gaze pinned to the dragon. "Get off me."

"It's protecting something, isn't it?" I grab their arm again and shake them. "Tell me!"

Lucky snaps their teeth at me, which startles me enough to release them. "We'll deal with the baby after we deal with the mother. Don't get impulsive."

A baby.

A *mother*.

Even in my realm, we know better than to antagonize a wild creature defending its young. I don't know if this dragon has really killed people, but wouldn't it make more sense to send it home? Or to do literally anything than to murder it for the sin of existing in its natural state?

This is wrong.

No one pays any attention to me as I charge up the railing to the upper deck. With the dragon curled around the center of the ship, that's where everyone has congregated. I pause just long enough to note that there are plenty of crew members who don't seem overly eager about this whole process. That hasn't stopped them from grabbing weapons. Something to worry about later.

Bunny taught me never to go anywhere without chalk on my person, and so I have a stick tucked into my pocket. No one bothers me as I sketch out a messy circle and write the glyphs from memory. This won't hold forever, but hopefully it will hold long enough.

I pull my stolen dagger out and cut shallow lines on my forearms. I'll need my hands if it comes to a fight. A quick drag of my fingertips through the blood and I press them to the wooden deck and speak the words to trigger the spell.

Not a moment too soon, either.

Miles launches a spear that will take the dragon in its throat. My shield locks into place a breath before it can leave the perimeter of my spell. The spear explodes in midair.

Every eye on the ship snaps to me.

CHAPTER 15

Bowen

I'M GOING TO KILL THE LITTLE WITCH. I'M NOT GOING TO have a choice. I don't know if she has a death wish or she thinks she's calling a bluff that doesn't exist, but she's forcing my hand.

As I charge to her location on the upper decks, I keep my barrier around the ship in place. Just in case this is a trap. I try to step over the lines of her circle, but a secondary shield bounces me back. "What the fuck are you doing?"

"It's a mother. She's defending her baby." Her green eyes practically glow with emotions. "*This* is wrong."

Something like horror twists in my stomach, but I muscle it down with the ease of long practice. Being one of the Cŵn Annwn means making hard decisions. It always has. The greater good is the only thing that matters. "Mother or not, it's killed people on this island."

"Who told you that?"

I jerk back. "You can't seriously be questioning the honor of my people? Of the Council?"

Evelyn doesn't drop my gaze. For once, there's no amusement or subterfuge on her face. Only fury. "She only attacks after we attack. Her first appearance happened after Lucky went into the water. Look!" She flings her hand out to where the dragon hovers partially out of the water.

It's still writhing in pain, but . . . she's right. It hasn't attacked. More than that, now that I have a moment to pause, I can admit it hasn't used any of its more devastating attacks. It doesn't matter what realm they come from, dragons are magical down to their very blood and bones. The creature has more catastrophic strikes. It hasn't used them.

I don't want to see the pain in those giant golden eyes. I don't want to feel sympathy curling in my chest. It fucking hurts. It makes me doubt, which is even worse.

No. I'm not going to start doubting now. I've read the initial order and the updated report. This dragon has killed people. Teenagers. There can be no mercy. "This is what we do, Evelyn."

She glares up at me, completely fearless even as her magic flickers around us, her strength obviously coming to its end point. "Why?"

Why. Why. Why. All she asks is *why*. "Drop the shield, Evelyn."

"No." Her voice shakes as badly as her body does. She has her hands planted to the deck and the glyphs glow sporadically as her magic attempts to keep them charged.

True fear makes my voice harsh. "You're draining yourself too fast. Drop the fucking shield right now."

"No," she gasps. Evelyn jerks her head to the side. "Look."

Even as I tell myself not to, I obey the command in her voice.

The dragon has quieted, the wounds inflicted by Miles and Kit knitting themselves back together, aided by the creature's natural healing magic. It surges downward, creating a wave that sends us farther out to sea.

Then it dives below the surface. A few moments later, it breaches the water before diving again. This time it's not alone. A smaller dragon winds around the mother, and then they're gone, heading away from the island.

At my feet, Evelyn collapses and the shield drops.

It doesn't even occur to me to chase the dragon. I bend down and scoop my witch into my arms in a single motion and then start for the stairs. Miles meets me at the top. He's so furious that his movements are sharp and more reptilian than humanoid. Even his claws are longer.

The only thing that gives lie to his fury is the triumph in his dark eyes. "What the fuck was that, Captain?" He flings a hand toward where the dragon has disappeared. "We have to go after it and finish the job. Or have you fallen so far, so quickly that you will renounce your vows?"

I'm not entirely certain that Evelyn is breathing. This is the moment. The breaking point. If I don't say or do something right now, I run the risk of losing everything. I open my mouth, but . . . I glance down at the woman in my arms. Too pale. Even as I watch, her green eyes flutter shut and she goes limp. "Fuck."

I shoulder past Miles and charge down the stairs, roaring for our healer, Aadi. The crew mills around, looking uncertain, but Aadi alights next to me almost instantly.

"Take her to your cabin. I'll look after her while you deal with this."

I don't know how I'm supposed to deal with anything when

I'm so fucking worried about my little witch. She aggravates me unlike anyone else, but the thought of her not recovering makes me sick to my stomach. I kick open the door to my cabin, Aadi close on my heels. "I need her to be okay."

"And *I* need you to give me some space to work." She waves an azure-and-silver wing at me. "Give me ten minutes to stabilize her and then you can come back."

I don't want to leave for even that long, but I can hear Miles and the crew arguing just outside the door. I have to *think*. I have to deal with this. If they vote me out now, they'll kill Evelyn. Fuck, they might kill me, too, but that's less of a concern.

I drag in a deep breath and square my shoulders. I will never be the most charismatic captain, but damn them, I *will* have obedience. At least for now. I stalk out onto the deck. The whole crew isn't here, but enough of them are for it to be a concern. "Set course for the island. I want to talk to the person who made the report to the Council."

Miles shoves to the front of the crew. "We're wasting time. That woman is a traitor, and if you're not willing to do your duty, then give her to the sea and let nature take its course. We need to finish what we started with the dragon."

Some of the crew rumble in agreement. I take the time to meet each of their gazes individually. One by one they fall silent. When I speak, everyone listens. "I will find out who among the villagers gave the report and ask them the questions I have after this encounter. At that point, I will make the decision about what to do with the witch. Should we need to hunt down the dragon, we will hunt down the dragon. It headed to the west, and it will take days before it reaches another island. If it even does. Hunting is what we do, and I will not rush this." I motion at Dia. "Take us around the island to the village."

"Careful, Captain." Miles doesn't raise his voice, but the threat is clear nonetheless. "If you keep defying orders of the Cŵn Annwn, you might be in danger of being branded a traitor alongside that witch."

I stare at him until he drops his eyes. It takes longer than it normally does. At this rate I wouldn't be surprised if Miles skipped the vote and tried to slip a knife between my ribs. "Everyone to their stations. I will go into the village after the witch awakes. Everyone else will stay behind." It's a risk, but Dia will keep them in line. At least long enough for me to return.

Taking Evelyn is also a risk, but I need her to understand once and for all that we are not monsters. She's so determined to think the worst of me—of us—and maybe if she hears how many people the dragon killed, she'll stop fighting me.

Maybe then she'll stop trying to escape.

The opinion of one woman should not be enough for me to alter the entire course of our ship, but right now I don't give a fuck. I turn on my heel and walk straight back into my cabin.

Evelyn, the damned troublemaker, is awake. She blinks up at me while Aadi coaxes healing magic in the air above her body. "What happened?"

It's Aadi who answers. "It's not safe for you to drain your magic to such low levels. Thankfully, your body gave out before your magic did. Otherwise, we might not be having this conversation."

It's been only a couple days since she saved my life against the cat-sìth. Surely she's recovered enough that this magical incident stands on its own. I can't help the guilt that viciously courses through me. She's the one who fucked up and yet *I'm* the one who's feeling bad about it. I don't know how she does this without saying a single word, but she manages to again and again.

"Get her up and walking. We're making a stop." I should leave it at that, but I hate how fear crests in her green eyes. I should be happy—if she's afraid enough, maybe she'll start making smarter decisions—but I never want this witch, this woman, to fear *me*. "We're going to talk to the villagers about the dragon attacks."

"I'm ready to go." Evelyn sits up, disrupting the beautiful ribbons of magic Aadi is weaving.

The bird woman huffs. "You're as terrible a patient as the rest of them." She pins me with a look. "She's going to be dizzy for a bit. Don't let her fall and hurt herself further."

It's on the tip of my tongue to offer to carry Evelyn, but that's not a reasonable offer to make. The impulse isn't reasonable, either. Everything about this woman has me twisted up in knots. The worst part is that I don't know if I want to untwist myself . . . or urge her to bind me tighter to her.

I know what her answer would be. After all, her main priority is getting away from me. Or at least, away from the Cŵn Annwn. But it might as well be the same thing because I *am* the Cŵn Annwn.

I walk to the door and hold it open, watching her closely as she stumbles toward me. "Don't fall."

"And deprive you of a chance to catch me?" She moves past me, each step becoming steadier. "Hold your breath, Captain."

The crew has cleared out, but I feel their attention on me as we sail into the bay where the village resides. Very few of them are happy with this turn of events, but they can join the club because I'm not happy, either. I have never questioned my purpose. I'm trying very hard not to question it now.

Except isn't that exactly what I'm doing? The order came directly from the Council. I've read it on my desk half a dozen times since Evelyn came aboard. It might be a little sparser on the details than some orders are, but it's clear enough. And the follow-up confirmed that the dragon killed more than a single person, though even one death would be enough to condemn it.

I've never done a separate investigation of an order on my own. I've never even considered that I would need to. I shake my head hard. No, damn it. I'm not a traitor. I'm only doing this for Evelyn, to ensure that she accepts the reality of her situation and stops doing things that will force me to hurt her.

I desperately want her to stay safe, even from us. Especially from us.

Neither of us speak as I use my magic to lift us down to the dock. The village isn't visible from our current location, so I motion for Evelyn to precede me down the dirt road that leads into the trees. It's only then that I see the strange look on her face. "What's wrong?" I turn to follow her gaze, trying to find the danger that must've put the stricken look on her face. "What do you see?"

"I recognize these trees," she says softly. "They're just like the ones that grow around my late grandmother's house."

A strange feeling comes over me. It's not outside the realm of possibility that several realms have the same kind of trees. Some of them are damn near identical to one another. There's no reason to think we happened to land on the one island out of hundreds that actually leads back to Evelyn's home realm. The odds are astronomical. Beyond astronomical.

"That's not why we're here."

"If I gave you the slip, I might not end up home, but I have a feeling this realm wouldn't be that unfamiliar." She's still speaking softly, almost as if she's musing aloud.

Again, that strange fear takes hold of me. "It doesn't matter if the realm is familiar or not. If you run, you will be hunted."

"I'm already being hunted. That's nothing new." She starts up the path, leaving me to follow. By the time we reach the trees, one would never know that she had been injured a mere hour ago.

Reluctant admiration mixes in with my fear for her. She's so damned fierce, and she might get knocked down regularly, but she bounces right back up. Yes, her honor seems strangely questionable . . . but I'm not even certain I believe that anymore. Someone without honor doesn't weep for the life of a vicious monster. She did what she had to do to protect me and herself from the cat-sìth, but it brought her no joy. I understand that all too well.

We reach the village in short order, and it's only because I'm watching Evelyn so closely that I see her miss a step, that I see the recognition in her green eyes as she surveys the buildings and the people moving about their day.

This island's portal really does lead back to her realm.

She's going to make a run for it again.

CHAPTER 16

Evelyn

THE BUILDINGS AND PEOPLE IN THIS TOWN COULD BE pulled straight out of a history book. At least if that history book drew from multiple different cultures spread across the world. There are the distinct roof lines of pagodas, and their inverse in rumah gadang with spiked gables. I even catch sight of several turf houses on the perimeter. The chaotic mix somehow comes together to create a cohesive whole.

The people are equally varied. There is every skin tone and body type imaginable. It must be market day, because there's a bit of a crowd gathered in the open space between buildings. Stalls with brightly colored awnings offer fruits and vegetables I recognize—apples and pomegranates and squash. People haggle over prices in a way that's so familiar, it actually hurts.

Human. They are all undeniably human.

Just to be sure, I pull my drained reserves of magic and cast it out in a faint circle. Sure enough, they're human, albeit of a magical variety. The people closest to us give me a sharp look as I scan them, but they quickly look away when they see Bowen at my back. Their fear is so transparent that it actually gives me pause.

I look around again, and sure enough, people have melted away from us until we're standing in a large circle. They haven't actually fled, but I see a parent grab their child's arm before the kid can run into the empty space. They sweep up the child and hurry away, their expression stricken. "Bowen—"

He wraps a careful hand around my wrist. "Don't scan them. It's rude."

"It's not *me* they're reacting to," I say softly. They watch him with a wariness one would give a hungry wolf that wandered into their midst. I study his expression, wondering if he sees it, too. The Bowen I've come to know would be incredibly bothered by this reaction, and sure enough, there's a new tension in his shoulders. But he still doesn't seem to be fully registering exactly how wary these people are. "Is this how every village reacts when you come into it?"

"Evelyn." His voice is deeper than normal. Despite myself, I inch closer to him. This man exerts a pull of gravity all his own. "Stop trying to distract me from the fact that you're looking for an exit."

For once, I hadn't been. I don't imagine the portal will have a giant sign announcing its presence overhead. It certainly won't be in the village center where anyone could tumble into it.

I bet it will be like portals in our world, hidden in fairy rings, in forked trees over water, and in mirrors. Well, maybe not the last. The portals have existed since before the technology to make mirrors was created. So they have to be natural.

But that's neither here nor there. At least right now. He brought me here for a reason, and I want the answers he's offering. I want *him* to have the answers he's seeking. It's possible that my instincts are wrong about how off this situation is . . . but I don't think so. "We came here for a reason, right? Let's get to questioning."

For a moment, it looks like he wants to argue with me, but he finally curses under his breath and starts down the main street, towing me behind him. I could break his hold easily. I choose not to for reasons I'm not about to examine.

With every step, I catch scents that are both familiar and not. A person with pale skin and freckles is roasting meat and carving it bit by bit to serve in wraps of some sort. Another, with dark brown skin and the kind of wrinkles that speak to a life well-lived, is frying vegetables and tossing them into a bowl with broth and noodles. A third with light brown skin and a bald head is shaving ice into cups for a group of small children.

We move past the food to the stalls that have people hawking everything from jewelry to textiles to bundles of herbs. The last makes me pause for a moment, but there's no stopping Bowen's forward momentum.

Every single person flinches when they see us. When they see *him*. It happens exactly the same, over and over again. The first glance of curiosity. The second to note his size. Then they see the crimson cloak and their expressions shut down. Some of them actually look terrified. Surely Bowen realizes this is not the reaction of people grateful for the Cŵn Annwn's interference.

The street ends at a large stone building that's familiar from the trip I made to Europe after graduation. The memory is a smear of alcohol, sex, and grief, but even in the midst of that, I remember the churches. This isn't the largest I've seen—its size is on par with the rest of the buildings along the main street—but it's certainly got all the details. Right down to the gargoyles perched on the corners, looking down disapprovingly.

"What gods do they worship here?"

"A large variety. Just like every other island." Bowen pushes through the doors as if he's been here before. Inside it's even more beautiful than the outside. The multicolored glass paints the floor in abstract art that shifts with the clouds overhead. The benches are not the most ornate I've seen, and the pulpit is plain wood, but there's a vibe in here that speaks of history. Of power. I don't fuck with organized religion, but as Bunny used to say, it's foolish not to know all the varied kinds of beliefs and magics.

Especially since some of them would like to see us six feet in the ground.

I don't get a chance to soak up the atmosphere, though. Bowen isn't hurting me. He's certainly not dragging me along behind him. But his pace discourages lingering, and if I stop, I'm not entirely certain he'd notice for a few steps.

A man steps out from the door near the back of the building. He's short and slight, his skin a cool dark brown. I expect him to call for help. It's what I would do if an angry-looking Bowen was bearing down on me.

This stranger does the same sequence of glancing, realization, and fear that everyone else has so far. The only difference is that his fear melts away instantly, replaces by derision. "A visitor. How lovely."

Bowen stops roughly ten feet away. He doesn't drop my

hand, though. When he speaks, his tone is perfectly even and respectful. As if he doesn't care that he's obviously not welcome here. "We were called here to remove a dragon that had been plaguing your shores. I would like to talk to the person who reported it. We've had a bit of issue dealing with the beast, and any information you can impart would be incredibly valuable."

The man shakes his head sharply. "You came for nothing, then. No one in town reported anything to that Council of yours."

Bowen's hand spasms around my wrist, and it surprises me enough that I make a small noise. He releases me instantly, but he doesn't take his gaze from the man. "That's impossible. I saw the report myself. I was told that several of your young people had been killed."

"That part's true enough." The man looks away, some of his fury dissipating into sadness. "Several of our young people took it upon themselves to encroach on the dragon's territory despite our warnings. We knew she was breeding, and temperamental as a result. One does not get between a mother and her young."

I could cut the tension in the room with a knife. I don't know if this man is the leader of the town, a priest, or something else altogether, but he obviously dislikes Bowen as much as the rest of them. I step forward, drawing his attention. "I'm Evelyn."

For a moment, I think he'll just demand we get out, but he finally relents. "I'm Elijah."

"Bowen." Bowen looks at me. There's no victory in his eyes, just sympathy as if delivering bad news. He thinks he's right and that it will change my mind, but he takes no pleasure in it. "The dragon killed several people, just like the report said."

"I can confidently say that none of my people made this

report you speak of. I don't know how your Council came by this information, but it wasn't through official means." Elijah crosses his arms over his chest. "It's not often that dragons come to our shores to nest, but it happens every generation or so. It's a gift to be alive when it happens. There's a spot on the cliffs that allows a view of the beach from a safe distance. The people on this island have been gathering there for as long as the dragons have been coming. Or did you think that our village's population is enough to generate the crowd outside?"

Now that he mentions it, there *were* a lot of people for a town small enough to be termed a village. "So it's an event."

Bowen tenses. "People *died*."

"Yes." Elijah sighs. "Every generation, some of our people are foolish and trespass where they shouldn't instead of sticking to the safety of the cliff view. I won't say they earned their fate, because death is a terrible consequence for foolishness, but I hardly think the creature should be punished for human error."

I watch Bowen closely. I won't pretend I know him well, but even I can see the conflict passing over his face. This isn't what he expected. Considering how he and the rest of the Cŵn Annwn talk, it isn't what I expected, either.

After all, we have monster hunters in my realm, too. Most humans would rather kill the monster in question than wonder if maybe the fault is held by all. It's true that there are monsters who specifically target humans, but this isn't the same. *This* is like provoking a mother bear after she's just had a cub. Tragic as the loss of life is, it's not that unexpected.

"But the report . . ."

Elijah cuts him off with a wave of his hand. "There was no report as far as I'm concerned. Leave the dragon alone. Within a month, she'll return to her home realm with her youngling. Our people will steer clear of the western beach until then, so there should be no further incident."

This time, it's me who reaches out and takes Bowen's hand.

Elijah pauses without turning back. "I understand what the Cŵn Annwn claim to be doing with their hunts, but most of the time all you're accomplishing is compounding a tragedy into something catastrophic. No one should be punished for protecting their child, regardless of whether humans consider them to be *monsters* or not. It's what any of us would do in her situation. Murdering her and leaving her child motherless is not the answer." He finally turns to look over his shoulder at us, his expression severe. "Or would you kill the child as well for the sin of being born?"

He's not saying anything I disagree with, but it's as if his words are stones thrown at Bowen. Every sentence makes the big man's shoulders drop further. I slip my hand into his and manage a smile, though it feels stilted. "Thank you for your time."

It's more than mildly alarming to be able to lead Bowen to one of the pews and guide him to sit down. It's on the tip of my tongue to make a joke to break the awful storm growing in his expression. I don't. "Are you okay?"

"He's wrong." He doesn't say it like he believes it, though. "He has to be wrong. We *protect* people. They're grateful for the protection."

How much to push? It's hard to say. But there might never be a moment where I can get through to him. I don't have to take a hammer to him; all I need is a scalpel. "How many villages or towns meet you with open arms? Or do they all greet you like this one, as if *you're* the monster hiding under their beds?"

"What?"

"Typically when there's a savior coming into town, people are excited to see them. It's a celebrated thing." I've seen it happen with the hunters back home. People fear the dark and they elevate those who are willing to take up their weapons and fight monsters beyond knowing.

That's the problem, though. I won't pretend there aren't monsters lurking in plenty of shadows, but a lot of people look at something Other and decide it's monstrous simply because they don't see themselves reflected back.

In my world, it's all too easy for the monster hunters to become more monstrous than the beings they hunt. Judging by the looks people gave us when we walked through the village, the same is true for Threshold.

"Some people don't understand," he mutters. "They think we're there to snatch their children to join our ranks. That's not how the laws work. We *protect*. We don't kidnap and murder, no matter what Elijah says."

It strikes me that I could fall in love with this fallen hero of a man. The way he clings to his laws as if everyone holds them as sacred makes me want to hug him. "Not every Cŵn Annwn is you, Bowen. You're not naive enough to believe none of them abuse their power. That's not even getting into the fact that apparently the Council fabricated the report that led to your order to kill this dragon. How many other reports have they fabricated that you just didn't catch?"

"I can't . . . This isn't . . ." He stares down at his hands. "This is fucked."

"Yep." I bump my shoulder against his. "The only question is what you're going to do about it." I don't expect a single conversation to knock his entire alignment out of order, but surely he can see that chasing down the dragon is wrong?

Bowen leans back against the pew with a sigh. "I would like to know who's making reports on behalf of people who aren't interested in being saved."

"Only because there wasn't anything to be saved from." I have to wonder how many generations of dragons had their young on that beach while the village kept their silence. I would wager there's been more than either of us could possibly guess. "Are you going to hunt her down?"

"No." He shakes his head and his voice firms up. "No. It's a waste of time and resources when she'll return to her home realm on her own. As long as she doesn't hurt or kill anyone else, it seems . . . cruel to kill her. Let alone the youngling." His expression is troubled. "No matter what else is true, he was right about that. It's wrong to deprive a child of its mother, when she was only trying to protect them. I don't like that she killed people, but . . ."

"It's more complicated than you realized," I fill in.

"Yeah. A lot more complicated."

That soft feeling in my chest grows. I knew there was much to be admired about this infuriating man, but the fact that he's adapting so quickly? It breaks my heart that I won't be around to see his final evolution.

If he even has one. The Cŵn Annwn don't seem the type to allow their people to question orders.

A frisson of fear shoots down my spine. No. Damn it, *no.* Bowen is not my problem. Even if he was, I'm not the one people go to when they need help or protection. I'm a good time and a fun escape, but I'm not a harbor against storms.

But . . . I don't want to see him hurt.

"I know the crew won't be happy to hear that, but maybe you can find a way to pitch it that sounds reasonable and won't cause a revolt."

He finally looks at me. One corner of his lips curve. "Worried about me?"

"Maybe." I huff. "Okay, fine, yes, I'm worried about you. You were about to sacrifice yourself against a cat-sìth to save my life. Your instincts are suspect."

His dark eyes see too much. Thankfully, he keeps his observations to himself and rises. "Let's go back to the *Hag*. Hopefully I come up with a brilliant argument in the meantime to convince them not to mutiny."

Again, that awful concern for him arises. I've seen how some of the crew talk about him. You hear a lot of things in the kitchen, and while I had no intention of staying in Threshold longer than strictly necessary, it was impossible not to notice that the crew is divided into three factions. Those who think Bowen walks on water. Those who believe Miles is more of a proper representation of what the Cŵn Annwn should be. And those who haven't made up their mind yet.

It still boggles the mind that these fearsome monster killers decide their captain by . . . vote. From the gossip I gathered, there are times when it might come down to a fight or a straight-up mutiny, but generally that's not how leadership passes. The captain who's voted out is dropped at the nearest port—as long as they still has some goodwill with the crew—and then they're left to find another Cŵn Annwn crew and join up, starting at the bottom of the heirarchy.

In the time since Bowen pulled me out of the water, he

seems to be losing people's support daily. "Will this decision be the one that finally tips the balance in Miles's favor?"

"It's possible. Probable, even." Bowen shrugs. He holds out a broad hand, and even though I definitely don't need help standing, I take it and allow him to tug me to my feet. He doesn't respond to my question until we step out of the building and into the faint sunlight. "There are a lot of individuals who are loyal to me, but the crew as a whole is a fickle beast and Miles is good at knowing exactly what angle to take to get them to listen to him." He shrugs again. "It doesn't matter. It's the right thing to do."

Again, that awful urge to protect him arises.

Watch out for yourself first, little bird. No one else will.

Bunny's rule rings hollow as we trudge back down the dirt path toward the dock. She's not *wrong*. I have no intention of staying with the Cŵn Annwn, and even if I did, I would balk at hurting Bowen, even indirectly. I can't imagine Miles would let me stay aboard if he became captain; it's far more likely that he would finish what he started the day I arrived and try to kill me. Out on the water with the entire crew at his back? I don't stand a chance.

Damned if I flee, damned if I stay.

I'm so wrapped up in my dark thoughts that I don't realize Bowen has stopped walking until I bounce off his back. "Hey!"

His power rises so fast, it feels like a hunting bird diving past me. I jump away, but he's not focused on me. His attention is on the docks, and farther out to the bay. The bay that is currently empty.

"Where the *fuck* is my ship?"

CHAPTER 17

Bowen

MILES TOOK IT."

"*What?*" I spin to find Dia leaning against a tree, her ever-present joint perched between two fingers.

She exhales a cloud of smoke. "He got them to take a vote. He won handily, but couldn't get them to agree to brand you a traitor. That will only hold until you do something foolish, though." She eyes me. "Or *more* foolish."

Her words hit me with the force of boulders. They took a vote. They took *my fucking ship.* I knew this was coming, but part of me never believed it would actually happen. I was voted in as captain after Ezra died during a particularly vicious storm; his declining health until that point and the fact he made a point to tell me he was proud of me before sending me below all add up to the fact he knew he wasn't long for this world, and he chose the way he left it. I've made my peace with that in the inter-vening years, but he served as captain for my entire life in Threshold—and a good decade before we ever met. I honestly thought I'd do the same, leading the crew of the *Hag* until the sea finally took me into its embrace.

"It's gone. Everything's gone." The world goes a bit hazy around me. "I've lost everything. They had no right."

"You know better. They had every right. A captain is only a captain as long as he has his crew behind him. They lost faith." She takes another long inhale.

Betrayal lays thick and cloying on the back of my tongue. I have to swallow hard several times to keep from gagging on it. I know I need to pivot, to plan on what I'm going to do next, but I can't think. I can't do anything but *feel*.

I've been this crew's captain for years. I've guided them through good times and bad, and I've always—*always*—put the laws of the Cŵn Annwn first. I have curbed their excesses and ensured they lived lives worthy of the name they bear. I have been fair and, if I'm unbending, it's all for the cause. And it still wasn't enough.

"What are you doing here?" I sound bitter and angry, but there's no helping it. I *am* bitter and angry. "Why haven't you sailed off to indulge in your every excess? That's what Miles promised them, isn't it? To let them take what they think they deserve instead of reminding them that we *serve*."

"I've had my years of excess already. At my age, it all sounds like too much work." Dia pushes off the tree and heads for the town. "Besides, that ship doesn't feel like home with Miles at the helm. I expect a few people will jump crews within the next turning of the moon. Hard to say."

My entire life is crumbling around me. I'm teetering on the edge of absolute ruin and there isn't a damn thing I can do to stop it. Ever since I came to Threshold, emerging from the sea and into my new life, my entire identity has been wrapped up in the *Crimson Hag*. Starting as a cabin boy. Learning how to sail, how to navigate, how to *lead*, from Ezra, until I worked my way up to be quartermaster. I served in that position for years before his death and the vote that made me captain. "What the fuck do I do now?"

She sighs. "You'll figure it out, boy. This time of year, it'll be a week or two before a ship comes through that can ferry us back to Lyari, so might as well take the time to do some soul searching. You'll be starting from the bottom on the next ship, just like you did on the *Hag*." Then she's gone, melting into the trees as if she was born to it instead of the waves.

A pit opens up inside me and threatens to suck me under. Start at the bottom. New ship. New crew. New captain. And who will take me on? Over the years, I've butted heads with more than a few captains, and I never bothered to keep my disapproval hidden, not when so many of them have fluid interpretations of what the laws mean. If I go back to Lyari, I might be able to find a position in the city, serving the Council . . .

But to spend all my time on dry land? To twist myself into knots playing at politics when there are people in need of saving? People I can actually help, instead of arguing circles just for the sake of power?

The thought of that being my future makes something inside me threaten to shrivel and die. "I just lost everything."

"I'm sorry."

I turn to Evelyn. It's so tempting to blame her for this, but if her presence brought my problems to a head, they started well before her arrival. I've made my own choices. I can't blame her for my actions. If I'd let the waves take her, maybe I would have stayed captain for another few months, a year even, but Miles was always going to make his move. Evelyn only expedited it. With every decision since meeting her, I've stood at a crossroads of law and heart. Every time, I've chosen heart.

I am in a mess of my own making. It doesn't improve my mood to acknowledge that. "Let's go. We'll have to rent a room for the time being." I pause, studying her guileless expression. "This doesn't change your situation, Evelyn. If you flee, they *will* hunt you."

"What's the difference between you being stranded here and me being stranded . . . elsewhere?"

I give her the look that question deserves. "You know damn well the difference. Getting voted out of captaincy isn't a crime. Reneging on your vows *is*. I am required to join up with the next crew we happen across, at least long enough to return to Lyari. If I choose not to stay with that crew, I'll have to stay in the capital until I find a crew—or a job for the Council. Those are the only options. Not settling down on one of the other islands. Certainly not jumping through a portal to another realm. You have the same choices."

"Seems like semantics to me." But she falls into step beside me. "But I would kill for a good night's sleep and a meal, so I'm not going to argue with you here. Maybe later. We'll see what the night brings us."

What it brings us is to the little inn nestled just off the road near the entrance of town. With darkness falling, the crowd down the main street has mostly dispersed, though there's music and loud laughter coming from two separate bars. I stop and stare at the warm light shining through the windows. The people there seem happy.

As if this once-in-a-generation event really is something to be celebrated, rather than feared. I can barely wrap my mind around me.

The inn is run by a person with pale skin, dark hair, and a truly impressive mustache. They start shaking their head the moment I tell them what we need. "I'm sorry, but there's only one room available. You might try your luck with another inn, but to be honest, I'm surprised we have any rooms left at all. I'm certain the other establishments don't."

Frustration threatens to drown me. This is one stumbling block too many. The pottery on the shelves rumbles as my power slips the tight leash I keep it on. Evelyn puts her hand on my arm, and despite everything, that allows me to get a handle on myself. She smiles at the innkeeper. "That will be fine. Could we get a bath and a meal?"

"Of course." They eye me nervously. As if *I'm* the monster they fear. "The room has an inset hot spring and we have an agreement with the bar next door to have them bring over meals for our current guests. It's all part of the price."

Evelyn squeezes my arm. "Perfect. My friend has had a hard day, but we're grateful for the service."

"O-of course." They slide a key across the counter and snatch their hand back as if they're worried I'll throttle them.

The worst part is that I'm not sure if it's because of my display of anger or the crimson coat I'm wearing. I wasn't displaying any power at all when we walked through the crowd earlier. Evelyn might not think I noticed how people skittered out of our path, but it was impossible to ignore. Their fear rankled. It *always* rankles.

Evelyn leads me back to a surprisingly large room, complete

with a decent-sized bed and the promised pool of steaming water. It's a nice space, but I'm not in the mood to appreciate it. She moves around the room, touching things and humming a little to herself. Even the sight of her isn't enough to chase away the horrible feeling rotting away inside me. My entire life, everything I've worked and fought for and believed in . . . It feels like it's teetering on the edge of a massive wave. One wrong move will suck me under and I might never surface again. "Don't steal anything."

She gives me a sharp look. "I don't steal from normal people just trying to keep their business afloat. That's evil."

"You steal from me."

"Yeah, I do." She comes to stand before me. "You're not a normal person, Bowen. You're the villain in so many people's stories. Us villains have to stick together."

"I don't want to be the villain," I say quietly. I don't know what to feel or think. All I can see is my ship sailing off to the horizon without me, taking the people who were as close to family as I'll ever get. Not Dia, but I'm not foolish enough to think Dia will stick around. She's always moved to her own beat, and that may take her away from me. Even if it doesn't, she's not immortal.

Eventually she'll sail on seas I can't reach.

Evelyn reaches up and tentatively cups my face. "Most people don't want to be the villain. That doesn't mean they don't stumble into it by accident. I know you try to do good, and this hurts right now, but maybe you should use it as an opportunity to look around and see how things truly are."

It's too much. I understand what she's saying, what the evidence of the last few days is starting to point to, but it's too big to grasp. And under it all is the horrible suspicion that Ezra knew exactly what everyone believed the Cŵn Annwn to be and intentionally carved off those bits in his teachings as he raised me. I can't think about it. I'm tumbling beneath the surface, and if I start swimming one direction, I'm just as likely to be moving away from the air I desperately need as toward it.

So I don't think about it.

Maybe that's the coward's way out, but I don't give a fuck. All my problems will still be there in the morning.

I glance at the bed. I've been so wrapped up in my misery that the implications are only now settling in. A single room at the inn. One bed. With Evelyn, who I haven't stopped thinking about since I tasted her.

I take an abrupt step back. Honor didn't keep me from touching her before, but she's essentially trapped here with me. I clear my throat. "You can take the bed. I'll sleep on the floor."

"Bowen." The reproach in her tone is nearly enough to make me smile. "You can't be serious."

"Actually—"

"If you're making that offer because you regret the kiss in the forest and want to establish some boundaries, that's one thing." She moves with me as I turn, not allowing me to hide my gaze from her. "But if you're trying to sleep on the floor out of some misguided paladin guilt, then I won't have it."

"I do *not* have paladin guilt."

"You've been lashing yourself so intensely since your crew sailed off that I'm surprised you're not bleeding out on the floor." She crosses her arms over her chest. Well, *under* her chest. Her breasts aren't particularly large, but they're very present, and they press becomingly against the thin fabric of her shirt and . . .

Gods, I'm staring at her chest again.

I almost take another step back, but that would be running from her, and I'm not capable of doing that. I don't *want* to do that. "You don't have another choice but to room with me."

"For all the—" She rolls her eyes. "You might drive me batty, but that doesn't mean I don't want to strip you down and have my filthy way with you. For fuck's sake, Bowen, you made me come without taking off any of my clothes. If I didn't want you, I wouldn't be here."

"I've wanted you from the moment you stole that flask off my hip. That kiss in the forest was barely an appetizer. I couldn't justify doing more while I was still your captain, but my ship is gone and we're just two souls lost at sea." I shrug out of my cloak and toss it over the chair situated next to the desk. "Never think I don't want you, Evelyn."

Her lips curve and her gaze heats. "You sea captains love your water metaphors."

"Evelyn." Over the course of a single day, everything has changed. I'd be a fool to throw caution to the wind and fall into bed with her. I don't care. Everything is spinning out of control, and she might be a force of chaos adding to it, but she's also the person I find myself turning to again and again.

I'm turning to her right now. "Kiss me."

"It's not a good idea." Despite her words, she takes a step toward me. "The closer we get, the more it will hurt when it goes poorly. If you sleep with me, you're not going to be able to hunt me."

She's not wrong and yet she's missing one very specific point. I hold out my hand. "I was never going to be able to hunt you." Even if denying that order makes me a traitor.

She takes my hand and allows me to tug her close, to wrap my arms around her. I'll never get over how perfectly she fits against me, her body soft and giving and, *fuck*, I want her so desperately, I can barely hold myself still as she considers me.

"I know you weren't." She kisses me.

It's even better than last time. Now I know the shape of her. I know the way she melts against me at the first stroke of her tongue. I know the feel of her body pressing into mine. I know . . .

It's not enough.

I wrap my arms more tightly around her, and it's as if I'm holding the world itself. That's a wild thought, one completely unearned. It doesn't change the fact that it feels true. Ever since Evelyn came into my life, she's had me questioning things that I never thought I would question. And now that the truth has smashed my world to bits, she is the only thing that feels sturdy.

That thought is enough to make me break the kiss. "I'm sinking fast. I don't want to drown you alongside me simply because I'm grasping for something that makes sense."

"Bowen." She tugs on my hair just short of sharply. "All of us are drowning. Every single one of us. Anyone who says otherwise is a goddamn liar." She steps back. As much as I mourn the loss of her touch, watching her pull her shirt over her head and then shimmy out of her boots and pants is more than worth it. I've thought Evelyn was beautiful from the moment I saw her, but nothing could've prepared me for the sight of her naked, and her blond hair tangled around her face.

It turns out she *does* blush everywhere.

"You better say something, or I'm in danger of throwing myself into the bathtub and never coming up for air." The blush stealing across her chest deepens, but she holds perfectly still, her eyes on my face even as I drink in the sight of her.

I am not a man who always has the right words, or even knows the right thing to do most the time. But I do right now. I cross to her and sink to my knees.

She lets out a nervous laugh. "What are you doing?"

"The only thing a man in my position can do when faced with a goddess. Worship her."

"*Bowen*. You can't say shit like that. If Aphrodite exists, you're going to bring her wrath down on me."

I catch her wide hips and tug her several inches closer. My mouth waters. I can't stop myself from leaning down and kissing her dimpled thighs. Perfect. Everything about her is perfect. I guide one leg over my shoulder and open her to me. Her pussy is perfect, pink and practically begging for my mouth. "Do you want me to stop?"

"If you stop right now, I might turn into an actual goddess and smite you."

That surprises a chuckle out of me. "Can't have that." I trail kisses up her thigh, partially because I can't stand the thought of being this close and not having my mouth on her, and partially because I'm afraid if I get a taste of her pussy right now, I'll fall on her like a starving man. It's been quite a while for me, and Evelyn is no casual bed partner. She's right about the fact that this can't last, and yet I find myself not wanting to do anything to scare her away.

All the while, I stare up at her gorgeous body. I love that she blushes so thoroughly. I want to see her skin go pink with desire instead of embarrassment. I want to be the one to paint the color across her features.

And then I kiss my way to her pussy, and I think of nothing at all. She tastes of the sea, which is a strange thing to think and yet it feels like coming home. I know better than to believe this woman is made for me. That's not how life works. That's sure as fuck not how *my* life works.

But I don't know how I'm going to let her go at the end of this.

CHAPTER 18

Evelyn

IN THE TIME SINCE MEETING BOWEN, I'VE ENTERTAINED more fantasies about him then I'll ever admit aloud. Especially after that kiss. The man made me orgasm while dry humping in our clothes as if we were a pair of teenagers necking in the woods. It was humiliating and sexier than it had right to be. Of course it made me wonder what it would be like to properly get him into bed.

Nowhere in those fantasies were him falling to his knees, declaring me a goddess, and then proceeding to worship me with his mouth.

And he *is* worshiping.

He kisses my pussy with the same thoroughness that he kissed my mouth, tongue, and lips, lavishing attention on every part of me. I love oral sex. I always have. But there are definitely some partners who treat going down on me like it's either a chore or a task to check off their list. Rare, but no less frustrating, are the people so certain of their skill that they're more focused on preening than they are on figuring out what I actually like.

Bowen doesn't fall into either of these categories. I would say that he's lost himself in the taste and feel of the experience, but when I look down, his dark eyes are searing into me. He is perfectly present. And yet somehow swept away at the same time.

I dig my fingers into his long hair and tilt my hips. He follows my urging with no hesitation, shifting up to my clit. "Soft vertical strokes, use the flat of your tongue," I murmur.

He growls against my flesh and obeys. I was already teetering on the edge just from kissing him, and with his tongue moving against my clit, my legs start to shake. I bite my bottom lip. Holy fuck, that feels good. "If you don't stop, I'm going to come and end up in a boneless pile on the floor. Maybe a concussion, too." I don't know why I say it. I should just be able to ride this out and accept the orgasm, but the thought of him seeing me like that . . .

I don't know what's wrong with me.

I expect him to stop, or slow down, or maybe even speed up out of sheer arrogance. I should know better. Bowen's power wraps around me, as gentle as a summer breeze. It loops under the leg I'm supporting myself on and around my waist, perfectly distributing its touch so nothing squeezes me too tightly as he lifts me. He rises to his feet easily. I shriek, but he ignores me. He walks us to the bed and lays me down with so much care that I almost orgasm on the spot. All the while, he never stops licking me.

It's almost embarrassing how good it is. Which is the strangest thing to feel. There's no shame or embarrassment in pleasure, but it's been all of two minutes and my thighs are shaking and little tremors are working through my body as pleasure coils tight in my lower stomach. How the fuck is he doing this? The only other person who's been able to make me come this fast is Lizzie and only because she can summon my literal blood to where she wills it.

He shifts against me and then two of his blunt fingers press to my entrance. He eases them inside me, obviously testing me. He's not a small man, and two fingers is enough to stretch me almost uncomfortably. I love it. Especially when he curls his fingers against my inner wall, zeroing on the spot that makes what few thoughts I have left short out.

Then I look down my body and realize he's not using his hands at all. His magic might be holding me spread out, but his palms are against my thighs.

Which means it's his magic inside me.

"Bowen—"

The devil of a man finds the perfect rhythm, mirroring his tongue with his magical touch inside me, or maybe the other way around. It feels like the moment when a tsunami sucks all the water out to sea and you're left standing there, knowing the wave is coming for you while also understanding that you'll never be able to outrun it. I don't want to outrun this wave. Even if it terrifies me.

"Don't stop!" The looming orgasm might actually kill me, but what a way to go.

Bowen's only response is to give another of those devastating growls that vibrates against my clit. That's what sends me over the edge, except it's not an edge at all; it's a free fall with no end in sight. This isn't a cute little orgasm that comes and goes between ragged exhales. This is world-ending. It swells and swells, bowing my back and turning my muscles to stone.

And still he doesn't stop.

Not until a scream rips from my lips, an involuntary reaction that I barely have time to process before my whole body bears down and I squirt all over him. Only then does he change his pace. Bowen doesn't withdraw his magic, though. He fucks me slowly with it, easing me down without depriving me. When he lifts his face to meet my shell-shocked gaze, the entire lower half of his face is soaked.

His attention tracks down my body as if noting every physical response to that orgasm. I'm shaking like a leaf, but the feeling of his magic inside of me is shifting from comfort to something darker and sexier.

I drag in a breath. "What are you *doing* to me?"

"Do you want me to stop?" He sounds just as devastated as I am.

I don't know if that's a comfort or not. One of us should be steering the ship, but instead we're two drowning sailors, clinging to a piece of driftwood and hoping for the best. I want to laugh, but I don't have the energy. "Refer back to my previous comment about smiting you if you stop."

"Can't have that," he murmurs. He looks down to where he's still fucking me with his magic, one slow stroke at a time. "If you can take more, I have more to give."

Yep. This man is definitely going to kill me. I will welcome every moment of it. He'll send me to the underworld with a smile on my face, and what more can a witch ask for? "Give me everything."

Bowen makes a noise that's almost a laugh, but it sounds like it's strangled halfway through. "I don't have any contraceptive spells on me. I haven't needed one in quite some time."

I know it's just horny hormones fucking with my head, but I have to clamp my lips together to prevent myself from confessing my undying love. Tomorrow, I can remember all the ways I find him infuriating. Right now, he's too good to be true.

When I'm sure I can speak without embarrassing myself, I clear my throat. "I have one in place. A witch can never be too careful, you know."

He strokes his big hand up my thigh over my hip to press against my stomach. I would call it a calming touch if he didn't have two fingers' worth of magic still buried in my pussy. "Give me a few more orgasms, Evelyn. I won't last once I get inside you. I need to feel you come again."

Oh no, he's not getting away with that. I muster my body into motion and lean up to grab his hand and pull him forward until he covers me. "Are you going to roll over and go to sleep after you come, Captain?"

His jaw drops. "Fuck no. I've wanted you too long to be satisfied with a single time. I want you again and again and again, until we're both too exhausted to fuck."

I was hoping he'd say that. I kiss him, tasting myself on his tongue. I clench my thighs together, which serves only to drive his magic deeper. "I want your cock. At this point it's not a want, it's a *need*. Please give it to me."

He props himself up so he can see my face. "You're a menace."

"Guilty as charged." I snake my hand between our bodies and wrap it around his thick length. And it *is* thick. He's a big motherfucker everywhere. I tug, and he allows me to guide him by his dick until he's settled between my thighs.

He's still fucking me with his magic. I shake. "Is it—"

The feeling inside me shifts. Later, I'll let my mind be blown by the fact that he's got magic inside me and it's bringing only pleasure and no pain or fear. The control required will give me a bit of a meltdown . . . later.

Right now, I can't stop whimpering as he uses his magic to part my pussy lips. Opening the way for his cock. And still he keeps up that delicious stroke against my G-spot.

Considering how we started this encounter, it's so fucking sexy how he holds himself perfectly still as I press his cock down until it notches on my entrance. I drag a single finger down its length and wrap my hand around his base as best I can. I use that hold to guide him closer, guide him *into* me, inch by devastating inch. He's wide enough that it's on the far side of uncomfortable, but I don't stop. Not when my body is already melting for him.

"Evelyn." His voice is a ragged gasp. "Evie, you're killing me." Before I can ask him if he wants me to slow down, he grinds out, "Don't you dare stop."

I don't stop. I'm not doing most of the work anyway. He's the one thrusting at my gentle command, filling me so fully that I'm certain I'll burst into flames. It takes forever and nowhere near long enough for me to envelop him to the hilt. Bowen, my fiercely honorable pirate, holds himself perfectly still over me, in me, as tremors rack his body.

His expression is almost agonized. "You really are a witch, woman."

I would laugh if I had air to breathe. He might think I put a spell on him, but the feeling is entirely mutual. I can't get enough of him. Even now, I'm fighting to stay still, to not wrap him up in me until I don't know where I begin and he ends. I'm so fucking greedy for him that I truly hope what he meant about going all night, because I don't know if even that kind of marathon will be enough to satiate me. "Bowen."

Just like that, his shakes still. "Say it again."

I reach up and he lowers himself enough that I can hook the back of his neck and tow him the rest of the way. When I say his name again, I do it against his lips. "Bowen."

He rumbles out a sound that's part moan and part growl. Then he takes my mouth and begins to move between my thighs. For all his comments about going too fast, I'm the one who begins to spiral at the slow slide of his length inside me. He made me come too hard earlier; I don't know if I ever came back down properly.

It's all frenzy.

I move on instinct, doing anything to get closer, to hold him to me tighter. He's obviously of the same mind, because he works his arms between me and the bed, pinning me to his body as he grinds into me. Each stroke is barely a stroke at all, as if he's trying to reach some secret part of me deep inside and he can't bear to retreat more than absolutely necessary to thrust again.

I'm moaning. Maybe I'm whimpering. Fuck, I might be speaking some arcane language known only to lovers.

It doesn't matter, because he understands me. He gives me exactly what I need. Bowen uses his arm beneath my hips to lift just enough to hit—"*Yes, there.*"

And then I'm coming again and, holy mother of gods, I think I'm squirting again as he grinds into that spot over and over, milking every bit of pleasure from my body. Too good. Everything about this is too good. How am I supposed to walk away now?

You know how, little bird. One foot in front of the other.

CHAPTER 19

Bowen

I NEVER HAVE BEEN A MAN WHO QUESTIONS HIS PURPOSE. When I woke up on the deck of the *Crimson Hag*, I might as well have been a newborn for all the history I brought with me. Ezra became something of a father to me, and the Cwn Annwn Council my gods. Never to be questioned, always to be followed with a devotion that was more than earned. Or so I thought.

Nowhere in that worldview is there room for *lies*.

I still don't understand why the villagers here didn't report the deaths. Once a beast takes a human life, theirs is forfeit. Except . . .

"What are you thinking about so fiercely over there?" Evelyn trails a single finger over my chest. She's draped half on top of me, her body loose and sleepy.

"I didn't realize you were awake." True to our word, we had sex for hours before passing out sometime in the dead of night. Judging by the angle of light coming through the windows, it's close to midmorning.

She snuggles closer until I put my arm around her. It's very, very cute. "That's not an answer."

I want nothing more than to roll her onto her back and lose myself in the pleasure of her company for a few more hours. Even if I do, these thoughts will still be waiting on the other side.

I sigh. "When humanoid people end up in Threshold, they're given the same choice we gave you. It doesn't matter how they got here or what kind of person they are. They can join or die."

Evelyn's finger stills. "Yes?"

"Those we deem monsters don't get a choice. Every time we're called in, it's after a death has occurred . . . or so I thought. What if we've been butchering them simply for the sin of wandering where they shouldn't?"

She props her chin on my chest, her green eyes serious. "Would it matter?"

The question stings. "Of course it would matter."

"But it doesn't matter for the human-adjacent trespassers. Why would it matter for those you decide are monsters?"

She's not doing anything but echoing my own thoughts, and I still have to fight the ingrained urge to argue. It was so easy to do when I thought my position was unassailable. When I thought I was *right*. "It matters."

"Your laws have never been fair, Bowen." She kisses my chest and gives me a sad smile. "I think I understand a little better where you're coming from. Your ship was your family. They're all you've ever known."

Her sympathy grates. It feels too much like pity. "Ezra, the last captain, was essentially a father to me. But I'm too aware of the power imbalance between me and the crew. I don't know if 'family' is the right term."

"For what it's worth, I'm glad you had him. It's awful to be lost and adrift in the world without someone to anchor you." Her expression goes contemplative. "But that doesn't mean he wasn't perpetuating a corrupt system. In theory, laws are supposed to keep the peace and be fair, but I've never found either to be true. They tend to benefit the powerful and everyone else is left to drown."

Again, I have to fight against the instinct to argue. "The Cŵn Annwn—the originals, the ancients—are gods. Or as close to gods as exists in reality."

"And gods are immune from corruption? From being selfish and power hungry and trampling those weaker than themselves?" She smirks. "You must not have many myths here. In *my* realm, plenty of the prey the legendary Cŵn Annwn hunt are undeserving of that fate. Seems like it's the same here."

I feather my fingers through her hair, mostly because I can. Because she's in bed with me and I'm allowed to touch her. Because this is only temporary and I want to soak up every detail I can in order to sustain myself for what comes next. "They'll hunt you."

"We're not talking about me right now."

No, we're not, but I'd rather shift our discussion than keep digging into the foundations beneath my feet. I don't know what to think of any of it. Or how to deal with the loss of my ship and crew. We didn't always see eye to eye, but I thought even if I lost their vote, I'd earned more than being left on a random beach as they sailed away without saying goodbye. It stings. No, this clawing feeling in my chest cannot be described by a word as mundane as "sting."

"Give a man some time to breathe." I cup her jaw. "I know

you're going looking for your portal home. I wish you wouldn't, but I won't stop you." I don't have it in me to fight her, not anymore, not when she's been right to question everything and I've been the fool being led around by my nose.

I'm still not prepared to admit that we haven't done *some* good, though. Not every creature we've killed has been innocent, and there are plenty of people on my crew—not *my* crew anymore, damn it—who had nowhere else to go. People who were like me, without a past to mourn. They welcomed the fresh start and they've been happy on the *Crimson Hag*.

Or at least I thought they had.

Evelyn climbs up to straddle me. Gods, she's a beautiful sight, her body soft and rounded and so fucking perfect I could worship *her* for the rest of my days. But I still see right through her. "While I'm not opposed to letting you distract me with sex, that won't change the ultimate outcome."

She drags her nails lightly down my chest. "What if you're wrong?" She rolls her hips, rubbing her pussy against my rapidly hardening cock. "You were wrong about some things. What if you're wrong about this, too? There are so many realms, Bowen. Even if they find me eventually, I'm very good at running. I can live out a long happy life in the meantime."

I hook an arm around her waist and roll us. Evelyn's laugh turns into a little moan as I settle between her thick thighs. I love that she doesn't hesitate to dig her hands into my hair and tug me down for a kiss. It's good. Too damned good. I want her forever, even though forever was never on the table for us.

That thought is enough to have me lifting my head. "I'll miss you, Evelyn."

She worries her bottom lip. "You could come with me, you

know. I realize that's a wild thing to say when you've known me for a week, but I like you a lot and I *don't* like the idea of you getting yourself branded a traitor and murdered just because you're trying to do the right thing."

I think I love her a little bit in that moment. For the offer, but also for caring about my future. This woman drives me up the walls, makes me question everything I've taken as fact, and . . . I care for her. A lot. I am enticed by her kindness and her passion and her insatiable curiosity. "I can't go with you, love. My place is here."

"I thought you might say that." Her smile trembles a little, but even as I search for the right words to banish her sadness, she gets control of herself and brightens. "Well, no reason we can't have one hell of a goodbye, then. When do you figure a ship will come through here next?"

"Hard to say. This island is right in the middle of several trade routes, so it likely won't be more than a day or two."

Her smile drops for a beat before she reclaims it. "That quickly? Well, guess we better make it count, then."

"Evelyn."

"Bowen." She mimics my serious tone. "Do you have something better to do for the next day or two? Somewhere pressing to be that isn't pacing the beach and brooding while you glare at the sea."

Considering I had been planning on doing exactly that, I can't help but flush. "Wanting a plan of action isn't a bad thing."

"No, it's not." She hooks a leg around my waist. "But in this case, your plan is simple enough. Hitch a ride on the next ship that comes through. Head back to report to your Council or whatever and then pick a crew to join." She nips my jaw. "Start as a cabin boy. Work your way up to captain again. Maybe toss a giant rock at Miles's head the next time you see him."

That surprises a laugh out of me. "Miles was within his rights to call for a vote. He had the crew's confidence."

"Doesn't mean what he did was right." She shifts restlessly against me. I have her pinned too effectively for her to angle my cock to her entrance, but I can feel how devastatingly wet she is. How *ready*. "Either way, I don't want to talk about him right now."

I don't want to talk about him, either. But there's one last thing to say before I can give in to her desire and spend the next day or two buried inside her. "Before I go, I'll help you find the portal."

She freezes. "You don't have to do that."

"Yes, I do."

"Bowen, I'm pretty sure helping someone break their vows is treason. If they find out—"

I brush her hair back from her face, stilling her words. "If you're leaving, then I'll ensure you exit safely before I move on. You can argue all you want, but it won't change anything."

"You're a stubborn ass."

"It's been said before." My voice deepens with desire. It's taking everything I have not to shift down a little until my cock notches at her entrance. I need her to agree first. "Promise me, Evelyn. Promise that you won't try to go without me. I give you my word that I'll see you safely through the portal home."

"Oh, for fuck's sake. You went and gave me your word, so now I'm going to look like a big asshole if I sneak out." She sounds put out, but amusement warms her green eyes. "If you're going to insist on seeing me through the portal, then I guess I'm going to have to insist on sucking your cock."

I blink. "What?"

Instead of answering, she shoves on my shoulders to get me to roll onto my back. Evelyn wiggles back until she's kneeling between my thighs. She strokes the twisted scar on my right thigh. "What happened here?"

"Kraken."

Her brows wing up. "No shit?"

"No shit." It had been an ugly fight that almost killed me and everyone onboard. It was only by working together that we managed to send it to the deep, and even then, I'm not entirely certain we killed it.

There were no more deaths attributed to the creature, at least.

She shifts her touch to my hips, dancing her fingertips over the sensitive skin of my lower stomach. For a moment, it looks like she might ask me another question, but instead she dips down and takes my cock into her mouth.

Last night was a frenzy, a need to get closer to her, to have nothing between us, to escape the horrible thoughts in my head and finally—*finally*—get my fill of this wicked little witch.

This is different.

With the warm morning light filtering through the narrow windows, there are no shadows to hide within. There's just this woman, her green eyes seeing too much, as she dismantles me with her clever lips and tongue and, yes, teeth. She doesn't go directly to suck me down. She . . . plays. Evelyn flicks her tongue against the underside of my cock and then presses open-mouth kisses along my length.

For my part, I am seconds away from losing it. I'm *always* seconds away from losing it with this woman. My body is strung tight with tension, and evil woman that she is, she laughs a little as she cups my balls and makes me jolt. "Relax."

"If I relax, this will be over too soon."

"Mmm." She works her way back to the head of my cock. "We have all day, Bowen. Come in my mouth, eat my pussy, then we'll relax in the bath for a bit, and when we're both recovered, you can bend me over the edge of the bed and fuck me from behind."

I grab fistfuls of the sheets and glare down at her. It feels half-hearted at best. "You're not a witch, you're a succubus."

"Maybe." She drags her lips over my slit. "But last night wasn't enough. If I only get a day or two with you like this, I don't want to waste a moment of it."

There it is, that desperation that's twin to the feeling boiling inside me. I'm not fool enough to think that having sex a few times would allow me to drink my fill of Evelyn. I knew it when I kissed her a few days ago, and last night only drove that truth deeper.

There's no space for self-preservation here, though. We've crossed that bridge and lit it on fire behind us. There is only the pain of losing her, and it will come whether we bolster the time between with pleasure or not.

With that in mind, I force myself to relax. "Very well. Do your worst, witch."

"Oh, Captain, I plan on it."

CHAPTER 20

Evelyn

I SHOULD HAVE CAPPED THIS THING WITH BOWEN AT ONE night. One night can bruise a person, but it shouldn't rock their foundations down to their very core. It shouldn't have them questioning their very reasonable plan to escape a realm they were never meant to wander into. I wasn't built for cities, but that doesn't mean I was built for Threshold.

I don't have to think about any of that now, though. Not with this complicated, lovely man spread out at my mercy. Bowen is . . . stunning. He would argue with me if I said as much, but it's the truth. He has the kind of body meant for work, carved muscles and solid stomach. And his scars. Gods, I'm not one to swoon at signs of violence, but he should be dead a dozen times over if the map of his body is anything to go by.

I suck his cock down as best I can, drinking in his sharp little inhales and the way his thighs flex every time I lick the head of him. For someone so stoic, he holds nothing back from me. It makes me feel powerful and melty. I want to see what else I can do to provoke even more of a response.

I've never been so aware of the time ticking down. We have so little of it. That should be a good thing. This was never going to be permanent. And yet it feels like grains of something priceless slipping right through my hands.

"Come here." Bowen sinks his fingers into my hair and tows me off his cock. I could fight him, but what's the point? He's doing exactly what I want, too. I straddle him and work myself down the length of his cock. It doesn't matter how many times we've had sex; his size means I have to work for it.

I plant my hands on his broad chest and roll my hips. *More. Faster. Harder.* Anything to keep the pending loss at bay. But even as I tell myself to stay silent, I part my lips and words spill out. "It shouldn't be this good. It shouldn't mean this much."

Bowen sits up and pulls me close. He kisses me as if this is our last day living. "It is. It does."

I love him a little bit in that moment for not trying to reassure me. This will hurt him when it ends, just like it'll hurt me. I always was a fool when it came to my heart. Repeatedly tossing it at the feet of people who will hurt me. Literally, in the case of Bowen and Lizzie. I don't want to think about her right now, though. I don't want to think about anything but him and the orgasm barreling down upon me.

It's not love. Not really. But it feels like it could be if I gave in and let myself fall.

I kiss him and ride him faster. At least if his tongue is in my mouth, then I'm not saying things I have no business putting to voice. Except it doesn't seem to matter, because he pulls me even closer, holding me as if I'm the most precious thing in existence. As if he truly is worshiping me like he said last night.

My orgasm crests and there's no peace in it. The pleasure seems to get deeper and stronger with every moment I spend with Bowen.

It scares me. Because there's one rule of Bunny's that was less of a rule and more of a warning. *The women in our family might play at giving their heart away, but the truth is that they only do it once. Guard yours, little bird. Because once you hand it over, you'll never get it back.*

I'm not giving my heart to Bowen. Damn it, I'm not. He might be honorable, and sexy, and protective, but so are a lot of other people. He might kiss me like I mean the world to him, but that's just because he's so devastatingly serious.

He tightens his grip and moves my body over him, fucking up into me. I thought I was done. I should've known better. My thighs are shaking so intensely, I can do nothing but hang on. He doesn't need my help, anyway.

When he comes, it's groaning my name against my throat. He makes it sound like a benediction. Like a prayer.

Bowen scatters kisses along my jawline before taking my mouth again. When he finally leans back, I'm breathless and shaking. He looks just as devastated, which is only a small reassurance. "I can't get enough of you."

The feeling is entirely mutual. I should dredge up some kind of sarcastic, witty response. I have nothing. I just stare at him and shake. "It feels like the world doesn't exist outside this room right now."

He laughs little. "*Does* it exist? Or did time stop the moment we walked through the door?"

"What did I tell you about being charming? It's upsetting." But I smile as I say it. I like him charming. I like him stubborn. I even like him when he's been particularly paladin.

Oh no.

As much to escape my thoughts as anything else, I slide off him and crawl to the edge of the bed. "A bath. What I need is a bath."

Bowen watches me with dark eyes that see too much. "Are you running from me, Evelyn?"

"Of course not. That would be ludicrous. We just had messy sex and I want to clean up. That's all." I don't sound convincing, even to myself. I'm running from the strange feelings in my chest, from the suspicion that's taking root deep inside me. It doesn't matter. It *can't* matter.

I look around the room for something to focus on. It's a rustic kind of cozy, the stone floors covered with a thick hand-woven rug and several macramé pieces of art hanging on the walls in bright colors. The big, sturdy bed dominates the space, but I'm not looking *there* because that bed contains Bowen and the evidence of just how far in over my head I am.

On the opposite side of the room, there's a door to the bathroom—more indoor plumbing, thank the gods—and the large inset stone pool that connects to what I suspect is a system of natural hot springs. Combined with the proximity to the bay and beach, it's no wonder a town sprang into existence here.

The stone pool has steps carved into it, and I wade down them without hesitation. Too fast. The water is hotter than I expected, and while it feels good, it's downright shocking. Not that I let that stop me. Not when I'm too busy being a coward.

"Listen, the sex is amazing, but I think this hot spring might be better than sex."

"Now you're just trying to hurt my feelings."

Even though I know better, I glance back at him. He might accuse me of being a succubus, but it feels like *he's* cast a spell on *me*. One look and I forget why I was running at all. "I'll prove it to you. Come here."

For a beat, I think he might call me on my mixed signals. I see the exact moment he chooses not to. He stretches, and the bastard is definitely putting on a show for me. Then he rises and I watch him with my heart in my throat as he walks naked to the bath. He's so at home in his skin. I don't know why that's a revelation, but it is. Even though I'm sore and tired and exhausted, my pussy pulses.

He eases into the water and moans a little. "I retract my statement. This is better than sex."

I grin. "Now who's trying to hurt someone's feelings?"

"Come here." He holds out his hand but makes no move to close the distance between us. Leaving the choice up to me. But then he always leaves the choice up to me. At least after that first one upon arriving in Threshold.

I should be focusing on ensuring that he understands that this is just sex. And temporary sex at that. I have every intention of finding the portal home and slipping through it back into my life. Or, if not to my life, at least into a realm that's familiar. One where I know the rules. If I have to run, I have a better chance of surviving there. Falling for Bowen means all of that will be so much harder. It's a fool's gamble that I'm destined to lose. Maybe I've already lost.

I slip my hand into his and let him tow me across the distance to situate in his lap. He smooths my hair back from my face. "I feel like my entire world has been turned upside down."

"Sex with me will do that to you." The joke comes out far more strained than I intend.

He smiles, but his eyes remain serious. "We really are the villains, aren't we?"

I can't lie to him. The fact that I would even consider it speaks for itself. I take a breath and cover his wrists with my hands. "I think it might be wise to examine where your laws came from and who they actually serve. I won't pretend there aren't some creatures out there who are dangerous, but the moment we start labeling anything nonhuman as monsters, it becomes a slippery slope." I almost stop there, but I might as well get the rest of my reservations out. "And it's worth asking: Who does it serve that you have a policy where instead of escorting people who are lost back to their home realms, you conscript them into your service? It's almost as if the Council doesn't think people would join of their own volition . . ."

He looks stricken. But he doesn't instantly jump to the defense of the Cŵn Annwn. That's progress. It's a damn shame I won't be around to see him truly break free. Because he will. Bowen is too good a person to continue fighting for a cause that is so clearly evil. He just has to be able to recognize it for the evil it is.

"I feel like a fool," he says. "These are all questions I should've been asking on my own. You shouldn't have had to force me to see the truth."

"What *is* the truth?" I don't know if there needs to be a deeper purpose. Tyrants exist in every realm. Maybe the original Cŵn

Annwn set things up this way so they'd have unquestioned power. Maybe there's some ancient reason for it, but it got twisted by mortals along the way. That sort of thing happens often enough in my realm. Religion and politics exist on a spectrum to be abused by the powerful. If there's a universal truth across all realms, it's probably that.

"I don't know." He slides his hands down to my shoulders and over my arms. It's not a sexual touch, for all that I'm straddling him. He's obviously looking for comfort. "I *should* know."

"Don't beat yourself up too much for not being all-knowing. You were dropped in this world as a child. From the comments you've made, the last captain of the *Crimson Hag* wasn't a terrible person, so it makes sense that you looked up to him and took his word as truth. You never had a reason to question it."

He shakes his head. "Don't go giving me the benefit of the doubt. I've had doubts before now, but I let the laws drown them out. That's on me."

Yeah, it kind of is. But he's already feeling so shitty, I don't want to kick him while he's down. Not when I'm already planning on leaving him to deal with this on his own. Guilt swarms me, but I breathe through it. I am a witch and a thief who likes drinking and fucking in chaos. I am not the person you want at your side if you're starting a revolution. That might not even be something Bowen is doing, but if I stay here, the only choice is the Cŵn Annwn or whatever force rises to oppose them. Which is no choice at all. "What will you do now?" I finally ask.

"I haven't decided. The first step is getting on a ship, and then I'll figure it out as I go. But I don't want to waste the time I have left with you talking about what happens after you leave." His hands find my hips and he jerks me close, eliminating the last few inches between us. "Once more, Evie. Do you think you're up for it?"

Five minutes ago, I would've said there's no possible way I could have sex again without a longer recovery time. Five minutes ago, I would've been a goddamn liar. "I'm only a little sore. Nothing you can't kiss and make better."

He smiles, some of the shadows fleeing from his expression. "You don't have to give me an excuse to get my mouth on your pussy again." He tightens his grip and rises out of the water, turning to set me on the edge. It's much cooler in the room than it was in the hot spring, and my nipples pebble in response.

I prop my hands on the ground behind me and spread my thighs as Bowen sinks into the water until his face is even with my hips. Without him saying a word, I scoot to the very edge. He doesn't fuck around. He covers my pussy with his mouth and kisses me there as if he'll never get another chance. It feels so fucking good, I barely have the presence of mind to mourn the fact that it probably is the last time. If not this time, then maybe the next. The clock on our interlude together ticks faster. This will be over too soon. We just have to make it count.

I've never felt so doomed, even as I'm receiving the best pleasure of my life.

CHAPTER 21

Evelyn

NO ONE HAS EVER TOUCHED ME LIKE BOWEN DOES, AS IF I'll shatter into a million pieces if he holds me too tightly. We come together over and over again, fast and slow and downright lazy at times, but as soon as our bodies cool, one of us will reach for the other and start the process all over again. It's barely been twenty-four hours since we arrived at the inn, but time feels like taffy, stretching into infinity. It won't last.

I want to tell him I'm not breakable, but I'm afraid that I'd be lying. It's good and right that he doesn't cling to me as if he never wants me to leave. He's offering me my freedom, or what passes for it. It's what I wanted. It's *all* I wanted.

Except that doesn't feel quite true anymore.

I don't know what to do with that feeling, so I shove it down deep and work to lose myself in the feeling of his body against mine and his taste on my tongue. It's not enough, but I've long since learned that *nothing* is enough to fill up the void inside me.

It's always been there, for as long as I can remember. Maybe it spawned into existence with my parents' death. I don't know. It was less noticeable then, with Bunny's presence to combat the darkness. But ever since she died, it feels like it's only gotten bigger.

Like it will swallow me whole someday.

A pounding on the door startles us both. Bowen moves before I do, tossing a sheet over my naked body and stalking to the door. It gives me a glorious view of his ass, and, for a moment, I almost forget the potential danger.

He angles his body behind the door and cracks it open. His shoulders drop, which tells me all I need to know.

It's over.

He confirms it when he says, "Dia."

"The *Audacity* just made dock," Dia says. "They'll be here overnight, and then they're headed north to finish up a hunt before they circle back to Lyari. Best that we both be on it when it leaves in the morning."

"Both," he echoes.

I can't see her, but I swear I feel her attention on me all the same. "I haven't survived this long by being a fool, Bowen. That girl is going to take her fate into her own hands, damned or not. I just hope you're not lovestruck enough to do the same. I'll see you in the morning."

Bowen shuts the door and turns around to lean against it. Not even the sight of his glorious cock is enough to combat the sudden weight that settles over me. It's finished. I knew the ending would come at me fast, but this feels too soon. We barely got twenty-four hours. It's nowhere near enough.

Still, he didn't promise me more, and *I'm* the one who's leaving. I'd be an incredible asshole if I held that against him. I try for a bright smile, though it feels painted on. "Please tell me that I heard her correctly and there's a ship named the *Audacity*."

"You heard right." He scrubs a hand over his face. "I'd rather sail on any other vessel. Her quartermaster, Nox, isn't so bad, but the captain is . . ." He sighs. "He's the worst of everything you believe the Cŵn Annwn to be. Everything we *are*. The captain sets the tone for the rest of the crew. If you weren't already headed elsewhere, I'd risk the anger of the Council to wait for the next ship rather than press you to join *that* crew."

I could point out that he's proving my point about the Cŵn Annwn as a whole, but I don't. Bowen knows. Rome wasn't built in a day, and a lifetime of conditioning won't be dismantled in that time, either. He's questioning it now, though. He'll keep questioning it. It might get him killed, but he won't go back to the way he was before. "Bowen—"

"Get dressed." He's still not quite looking at me. "It would be best if they didn't know you were here to question why you aren't coming aboard. Dia won't say anything, but the townsfolk might. I'll get you to the portal tonight. Now."

Now.

Again, I have to bite down on the desire to ask him to come with me. He already gave his answer. He made his choice. I made mine. We both have our own paths to follow, and they diverge as soon as we walk out this door. Simple as that.

It still feels awful to get dressed in silence, my body still sore and singing from our time together. The feeling will fade, no matter how much I wish I could tattoo the memory of his touch on my very skin. I'll escape and the years will eat the little details of my time with Bowen, just like they've devoured so many memories of Bunny. I'll be left with vague impressions and a glossed-over image that lacks the true depth of what I feel right now.

Gods, I am so tired of being left behind. Even if I'm the one doing the leaving this time.

But staying is out of the question. I'm a witch and a thief. I'm not a rebel fighter. The only fights I like are ones that I know I can win, and going to battle against a literal navy is a surefire way to get yourself killed. That's *definitely* against Bunny's rules.

Part of me wants to despite that. It's a small part, but it's there.

Bowen must catch the strange thoughts flickering across my face, because he shakes his head. "You want to go home. That's always what you wanted. As much as I wish you would stay, I don't want you to make that choice for the wrong reasons and end up resenting me."

He's such a damn *paladin*. So self-sacrificing. If he was a little more selfish, he would have fucked me a few more times and entangled my heart completely. Instead, he's ushering me out into the darkness to give me exactly what I want.

Really, he's too good for me. Except, you know, for being a murderer on behalf of elder gods. Tiny detail, really.

Every noble cause loves a martyr, but your name living on as legend won't matter much when you're worm food.

Bunny's right. I *know* she's right. But my steps grow slower as we leave the village and work our way through the forest to the north. There is no cat-sìth here to force us to turn back. Instead, the trees seem to hold their breath as we move through them, as if *they* fear *us*.

And yet they're so familiar that they make my heart ache. I recognize the sight and smell of maple, pine, and hawthorn. If not for the man at my side, I could almost believe that I'm actually back home and this has all been a dream. "Bowen."

"Mmm?"

"If you could find out where you came from and go back, would you?"

He pauses long enough for me to catch up and then matches his stride to mine. "The easy answer is no. This is all I've ever known and suddenly finding out about the first thirteen years of my life doesn't unmake the last twenty. But sometimes I wonder about my mother." He shrugs. "It's possible she was a terrible person and that's how I ended up here, or that she died. But . . . I wonder."

"It's hard not to wonder." I step over a fallen log. "Bunny was my everything, but my mother was her daughter. I think losing her . . . Well, Bunny didn't like to talk about my mother. She died when I was six." My memories of the woman who birthed me are more vague impressions than anything else at this point. The scent of rosemary. Scarlet lips that left their imprint on my cheeks when she kissed me. Green eyes just like mine, just like Bunny's.

"I'm sorry."

"Me, too. For you, I mean." I clear my throat. "Don't get me wrong. I wanted for nothing growing up. Bunny was the best grandmother a person could ask for."

Bowen touches the small of my back, guiding me to the right of a tree. "I'm sorry you lost Bunny. She must have been a wonderful woman to have raised you to be someone equally wonderful."

I miss a step. I can't even focus on that compliment, not with my throat closing and my chest going too tight. Gods, I both love and hate this feeling. I don't want to break down every time I think of my grandmother, but this is *real*. Proof that her fingerprints are on every aspect of my life. That I built myself from the foundation she helped create. "I miss her."

"I know." From his tone, he does. Of course he does. Ezra was his Bunny, come into his life later, but his North Star all the same. Is it any wonder he never questioned the Cŵn Annwn until now when the person he cared most about in the world never questioned them?

Bowen slows. "Here we are."

I peer into the shadows and huff out a laugh. I don't see anything. "Where?"

"Here." He moves forward and carefully steps to the side. "Creek and tree roots. The portal gives off a faint hum that I feel more than I hear. Can't you feel it?"

Not without trying; that's not one of my skills. I send a flicker of my magic and shudder at what it tells me. This is *old*. The tree is an ancient giant of a thing, twisted and crouched over its neighbors. The portal itself is nestled in between two roots as big around as Bowen's biceps. They tunnel down on either side of a creek that's barely a trickle of water.

I never would have found this on my own. There's still no way to know for sure if this portal will take me to my realm or one just like it. "This isn't going to drop me at the bottom of an ocean, is it?"

"No. The portals move regularly, but they're all in a similar atmosphere to where we are now."

Even if I end up back in my realm, I'll likely be stranded in a strange country without money or a passport. My stuff is all on the *Crimson Hag*, which means I'm starting from scratch. I'll have only the spells tattooed into my chest, which *should* be enough to get me home. If I'm not in my realm, there are other complications to consider, but I won't know what I'm facing until I walk through.

I've been worse off. I don't know why I'm hesitating now. This is what I wanted. I should be charging into that portal without looking back.

"Bowen . . ."

He turns to me and pulls me into his arms. "I won't ask you to stay. I'm not that selfish."

"You keep saying that and I'm going to start thinking you want me to stay." My voice is hoarse and, holy fuck, what is this awful feeling in my chest? It's like he's reached a big hand through my rib cage and is squeezing my heart.

He kisses me lightly and then steps back. "Go, Evelyn. Learn to hide yourself from gods. Live a long and happy life. I sincerely hope I never see you again."

This is what I wanted.

I take a breath, square my shoulders, and step toward the portal. Fuck, I'm a fool. It's the only explanation for me turning back toward him. "Give me your hand."

He doesn't argue. He simply holds out his hand and watches as I nick my thumb and trigger one of my lesser-used spells. I press it against his palm. My magic flares violet for a moment and then sinks beneath his skin, forming into a glyph just like the one beneath my right collarbone.

I clear my throat. "If you ever change your mind about staying here, you don't have to go to a strange realm where you don't know anyone, even if it's the one you think you were born in. You can come to this one. If you do, I'll find you with that." I point at his hand.

He shakes it out. "It tingles."

"Yes, dear, it's magic." I grin, but the expression falls away. "I don't care what you say. I hope *I* see *you* again. Don't get killed for your ideals, Captain."

"Keep running, little witch." He swoops down and takes my mouth. The last kiss was a gentle goodbye. This one is filled with all the things we'd be fools to say to each other. *Stay. Don't go. Be with me.*

It ends far too soon. My head is spinning as I take a step back and then another. "Goodbye."

A rumble starts beneath my feet. I stop short and my gaze flies to Bowen, but he looks just as confused as I am. This isn't *his* magic. "What—"

At my back, the portal swells with power. I barely have time to turn when Bowen sweeps me behind him. I peer around his broad shoulders to see the portal shift color, the shadows between the roots growing deeper and darker. Before, I could see through them to the forest beyond. Even as I watch, the shadows deepen until it's pitch-black. And then they deepen further, giving the impression of space bending.

Someone's coming through.

A slim form steps out and it's like my brain blips. I'm seeing things. Surely I'm hallucinating this moment because there's no way Lizzie just stepped through the portal dressed in athleisure and carrying a massive rifle across her back.

Reality snaps into place around me. This isn't a hallucination because of a broken heart. This is happening. Which means we're in serious danger. I grab Bowen's shoulder. "Run."

Her dark eyes snap to mine. "There you are." She sounds so horrifically *normal*. "I thought I was going to have to hunt you down. This is simpler." She swings the rifle around in a smooth, practiced motion, aims down the sight, and pulls the trigger.

CHAPTER 22

Bowen

THERE'S NO TIME TO THINK. I MOVE ON INSTINCT, THROW-ing up a shield with my power. Even so, it's barely in time. The bullet stops close enough for me to see the size of it in perfect detail. If I hadn't shielded, she would have blown off my fucking head. "I take it this is Lizzie."

"Yep." Evelyn sounds strained, and she's not quite huddled against my back, but it's a near thing. "This is bad. We should run."

With my shield in place, I take a moment to study this new enemy. She's lean in the way good predators are, every bit of her geared toward taking down prey in the most efficient way possible. Even if Evelyn hadn't told me she was a vampire, I likely would have guessed. The few vampires I've had cause to meet all have a strange, otherworldly feeling to them. It's too complicated to call it beauty; it's more an energy that draws people—prey—in. Even in the middle of shooting at us, Lizzie has that draw.

She came into Threshold, which means by the law, she should either join the Cŵn Annwn or die. Considering she just tried to kill me, I'm not overly inclined to give her a choice. Except . . . she might be murderous, but she meant something to Evelyn. I can't kill her ex.

How quickly the laws fall apart for me now that I've started questioning them.

I hold up a hand. "Go back to where you came from and we'll pretend this never happened."

Lizzie's face has no expression. No fury. No contempt. No fear. "Cute." She studies me. "Telekinetic. What a pain." Her dark gaze flicks to Evelyn. "He won't be able to save you. Where are my jewels?"

"Funny story—"

"I don't want your story, Evelyn." She pulls the trigger again. Again, I stop the bullet well before it can cause damage. I can't tell if she's honestly trying to murder us or if she's just reminding us that she can. She shifts the rifle to point at Evelyn, raising her brows when I mirror the movement to get between her and the woman at my back.

Evelyn, for her part, is damn near babbling. "I didn't think. You know I don't think when I get mad, Lizzie. You were going to let your mother murder me. I just grabbed them and ran."

"*Evelyn.*"

She grabs the back of my cloak. I can feel her shaking even through the thick fabric. Evelyn clears her throat. "Your jewels are on the *Crimson Hag*. Which is a problem because the ship sailed off with them when the crew left us here."

Lizzie slowly lowers her gun. She looks up at the tree branches overhead. "That's very irritating."

"I'm sorry." Evelyn sounds so small, I want to level this entire forest out of sheer rage.

"Yeah, me too." Lizzie's eyes go crimson.

It's the only warning I get before it feels like every vein in my body rebels. Pain unlike any I've ever known scores through me, sending me to my knees. "Oh *fuck*." I've felt something similar when I fought a water elemental a while back. She tried to force the water in my body out. I was able to deflect that. This is a thousand times stronger. I reach for my power, but it slides through my fingers, my control nonexistent when I can barely draw breath into my shrieking lungs.

"Shit, shit, shit!" Evelyn grabs my shoulders, but her touch is nothing compared to the agony inside me. "Lizzie, stop it!"

Lizzie doesn't stop. If anything, her eyes glow brighter. She reaches out and closes her fist and my whole body jerks forward several feet. I have to do something. She's focusing on me only because she's decided I'm the bigger threat. If she incapacitates me, she'll kill Evelyn.

That thought has my instincts taking over. I don't think. There's no time or energy for finesse. I send out a massive half circle of power. It hits Lizzie and the trees in a wave I can actually see, causing chaos in its wake as she goes flying.

Her control doesn't snap, but the pain eases the tiniest bit. I fall to my hands and knees. "Run."

"Absolutely not. She's going to kill you." Evelyn drops down next to me, her fingers digging into the soft dirt beneath us. "This is all my fault. I'm so fucking sorry."

I open my mouth to reply but the pain flares harsher and I can only grunt. Evelyn isn't running and she's not going to listen to me and fuck, I don't know how to fix this.

Lizzie strides out of the dust of my destruction looking none the worse for wear. Her clothing is a little dirty, but I obviously didn't do any lasting damage with a blast that would have killed a lesser being. Holy fuck, this woman is scary.

"I'm sorry, Lizzie!" Evelyn plants her hands on the ground and a surge of purple magic roars out from the circle we're contained in. Lizzie's eyes go wide as it hits her and then she's gone, tossed away as if by a giant hand. The trees that I damaged crack and crumble in the wake of Evelyn's spell.

Including the portal.

My pain disappears so quickly, it makes me dizzy. I have to focus on drawing in one breath after another. Evelyn slumps against me. "Won't knock her down for long. We have to get out of here. This time, listen to me when I say run."

I turn my head slowly. She's too pale, and her eyes are too wide. Does she realize what she just did? The sacrifice she just made? "The portal."

"I know. I see." She shakes her head and sways. "Worry about it later. We have to go. She heals faster than anyone I've ever met. We have . . . five minutes. Maybe."

Not long at all.

I still feel shaky in the wake of the vampire's attack, but at least my magic comes when I call. I scoop Evelyn up, staggering only a little. "Hold on to me."

"What are you— *Oh shit.*"

I lift us off the ground and, after a beat of concentration, hurl us into the sky. Flying takes a lot of power and a significant amount of concentration. If the vampire attacks now, we'll both fall and we might not survive it. It's still a risk I have to take to get Evelyn away from danger. "What's her range?"

"I don't know. Longer than it should be." She presses her face to my neck and clings to me. "Did I mention I'm scared of heights?"

I tighten my hold on her, even though it's unnecessary. My magic is wrapped around us; we won't fall unless I let us go. *Unless I'm forced to let go.* "You're safe."

"I think you'll find that that's the one thing I'm not." She hiccups a laugh. "Fuck, I destroyed the portal I need to get home. That was a big-brained move if I ever made one. Bunny would be so proud. And Lizzie can't even change her mind and go home—as if that would happen—because there's no open route. She really is going to kill me."

"I won't let that happen." I'm not sure how I'm going to stop it when she defeated me so handily. I could claim I didn't see her coming, but the truth is that I don't know how to combat that kind of power in someone who isn't overly affected by physical attacks. "I thought you said she was a vampire. I don't know any vampire that can do *that*."

"A *bloodline* vampire. Lizzie's family is one of the seven families of born vampires, not turned. She has a whole treasure trove of fun magic powers as a result, but her bread and butter is, well, blood. She can control it in other people, use it to form physical things, and shit like that."

Ah. That explains it. She wasn't manipulating the water in my body, but the blood itself. A crucial difference, apparently. I know how to fight a person with water elemental magic, but this vampire is another beast entirely. I want to say that I'll have something figured out the next time I face her—because at this point, I'd be a fool not to believe Evelyn's claim that she'll keep coming after making her way to Threshold—but I don't even know where to begin.

There's also the problem that I might hesitate to kill Lizzie, but she's obviously intent on murder.

I bring us down as carefully as possible near the docks. Even with all my concentration, we fall the last two feet to the ground. I stagger. "Sorry. Carrying people is more challenging than objects." I look around. After that fight, it feels odd that nothing is amiss here. There's the sounds of people starting their day in the distance and the soft sound of water lapping at the shore, the docks creaking with each small wave. There's only one ship present. The *Audacity*.

I wasn't happy about sailing under Hedd, but there's no choice now. We need to get on that ship and we need to leave Sarvi. Immediately. "We have to get off this island."

"Agreed." She doesn't let go of my neck, though.

That's fine. I'm not feeling the need to set her down right now, either. I hug her closer and press a kiss to her temple. "It will be okay. We'll figure this out."

"I'm in the middle of a mess of my own making. You should drop me on my ass and take off for the horizon. She has no vendetta against *you*."

"No."

Evelyn gives a choked laugh. "You just encountered a trespasser of Threshold and took off instead of offering them a spot in the Cŵn Annwn or killing them. Your Council would probably consider her a monster, too, so that's two laws broken."

She's not wrong. The thought makes me sick to my stomach. "Will she hurt anyone in the village?" If that's even a possibility, then I don't have a choice. I have to put Evelyn on the *Audacity* and stay behind to fight her vampire ex. Even after the last conflict, it brings me no joy to think of killing that woman. If I even can.

"No. It's not impossible, but I really don't see it happening." Evelyn sighs. "She's too smart to go on a killing spree the second she arrives, and she's too much a predator to get enjoyment out of killing people she views as beneath her. She likes a challenge. Plus, she's intent on murdering *me*, which will take priority."

Hard to say if that's a comfort or the worst possible scenario.

"Is that Bowen of the *Crimson Hag* I see?" The question booms over the water and I have to fight the urge to turn around and walk away. If it wasn't for the lethal vampire bearing down on us and my need to get Evelyn to safety, I'd simply wait for another ship.

That's not an option, so I have to put on a good face. Hedd, captain of the *Audacity,* is a blustering asshole, but he's dangerous enough to scent out weakness and exploit it. Better to give him nothing to work with.

I set Evelyn down and tuck her carefully behind me before I turn to face Hedd. He leans on the railing, a massive man with a riot of red hair, a beard that would be impressive if he spent any time taming it, and skin that seems to be perpetually sunburned. He's a berserker, and damn near unkillable. Which is not something I've worried about overmuch in the past, but with my new wariness of all things Cŵn Annwn, I can't help assessing him the way I would an enemy.

"We need a ride, Hedd. I heard you're headed toward Lyari." That's not, strictly speaking, what Dia said, but hope springs eternal.

He eyes Evelyn at my back, but then his attention shifts as Dia moves out of the trees. I can't see his eyes clearly at this distance, but he seems shocked. "What the fuck are *you* doing on land?"

I bristle at his tone, but Dia shrugs it off. "Keep your nose on your face and out of my business, Hedd. Will you give us a ride or not?"

"It wouldn't be right to deny my fellow Cŵn Annwn the sea." He sweeps an arm over his ship. "You're more than welcome aboard. We're heading to Lyari, but we have a hunt to finish first. Three Sisters has a mermaid infestation that needs to be dealt with. If you're on a time crunch, I would recommend waiting a few days for the next ship to come through. You might have better luck with them." From his tone, he doesn't particularly want me on his ship any more than I want to be there.

Unfortunately, we don't have much choice.

I glance at Evelyn, but she's watching the trees Dia just exited as if expecting Lizzie to burst from them at any moment. It took us a few hours to make it to the portal from town, but we weren't moving fast. I don't know the full capabilities of the vampire, but I have to assume she can move at heightened speeds.

No time to waffle on this.

I turn back to Hedd. "One night on land is enough for us. We'll take the long way around. Happy to help with the mermaid issue as well."

"More the merrier and all that." Hedd eyes me dubiously. "We're about to head out, so grab your shit and be quick about it."

"We have everything we need."

His suspicion is a thick thing in the space between us, but he moves back and motions us forward. I catch Evelyn's arm and speak low under my breath. "Don't be caught alone with him if you can help it. He won't . . ." I clear my throat. "He'll just make you uncomfortable, and I'd spare you of that if I can. But the quartermaster, Nox, is good people." I had offered them a spot on my ship a few years ago, with the intention of them serving as quartermaster once they'd earned the crew's trust. They turned me down, saying their brand of chaos would drive me out of my mind in a few short months. They weren't wrong, but I think I still would have preferred them over Miles.

Evelyn's too pale, but at my warning, a familiar glint appears in her green eyes. "I can take care of myself, but thank you for the concern." She slips out of my grip and climbs up onto the ship.

Dia snorts. "She's not as helpless as you keep thinking she is." She lightly smacks my arm. "But love makes fools of us all."

"I'm not—I don't—" I sputter into silence, and it's just as well. Dia isn't listening to me. She follows Evelyn on board, as nimble as someone a fraction of her age.

I cast one last look over my shoulder and then follow. Within a few minutes, the ship is easing into deeper water and the wind fills the sails. I keep my attention on the shore, ready to strike if Lizzie appears. She doesn't.

Somehow, I doubt it's the last we've seen of her.

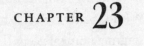

CHAPTER 23

Evelyn

AFTER SAILING ON THE CRIMSON HAG, I THOUGHT I HAD a good handle on what it means to be one of the Cŵn Annwn. It turns out I was wrong. This crew is nothing like the Hag's. Or at least like the Hag's was under Bowen's captaincy.

Hedd, the captain of the *Audacity*, is obviously threatened by Bowen's presence, and he blusters and postures and does everything except pee on the deck to mark it as his. The crew takes their lead from him, giving us snarling comments when they bother to speak to us at all. It's just as well. Most of them are people I would not want to meet in a dark alley.

The sole exception is the quartermaster, Nox. They're a lean but powerfully built white person with platinum-blond hair cut short on the sides and slightly longer on top. Their pale brows give them an almost alien appearance, or that might be their superior bone structure. It's the kind of *strange* one sees on runways back home.

Home.

A place I'll probably never go again. I still haven't processed that. I had barely been willing to hope that the portal actually went to my home realm instead of one that was just similar. With Lizzie's arrival, I have confirmation that it would have sent me home. Except the portal is now gone, demolished by my and Bowen's magic. If Lizzie didn't already want me dead for stealing from her, she'll definitely skin me alive for taking away her route home.

I don't know how to deal with the loss of something I was barely willing to believe I had. I don't know what this means for my future at all, but there's no time to process it while aboard the *Audacity*. Every bit of energy is geared toward avoiding the crew and staring at the horizon behind us, sure that Lizzie somehow found a ship and is already in pursuit. I'm pretty sure she doesn't know how to sail, but it's not as if that will stop her.

I expect the weather to change and grow colder as we sail continually north, but that assumption is a holdover from my realm. I don't even know if they have seasons on Threshold. I guess I should figure it out, since I'll be here for an extended period of time.

I turn to look for Dia, wondering if she'd be willing to share her ever-present joint. Right now, taking the edge off my frantically circling thoughts seems like the only thing I can actually *do*.

"You're new."

I jump and then curse myself for jumping. I've caught Nox watching me a few times, but they haven't approached during the three days we've been sailing . . . until now. "Yeah, pretty new."

"Strange thing, Bowen being left behind by his crew." They're still watching me closely. "He's one of the more upstanding of our number, and while some"—their blue eyes cut to where Hedd lounges against the helm, looking like he's sleeping standing up—"think that's a weakness, he seemed beloved by the *Hag*'s crew."

He was. At least by the crew members that Miles hadn't already coaxed over to his side. Bowen seems to think that Miles would have gained the upper hand eventually, but it's clear that my presence sped that process up. If not for me, he wouldn't have called off the hunt of the dragon and the crew wouldn't have been furious enough to vote him out so quickly.

I feel bad about that . . . kind of. His problems didn't start with me, but getting him to question laws that are obviously corrupt can only be a good thing in the long run. I hope. If Lizzie doesn't kill us both first.

I push that away and give Nox my full attention. "Seems like you have something to say. Might as well stop dancing around the point and spit it out."

They're dressed in the customary color of the Cŵn Annwn, but on them it looks . . . different. Less like a sailor playing dress-up. On Nox, the crimson leather pants, loose shirt, and duster look like part of them. It's a neat trick. Bowen wears his cloak with the same level of comfort and identity, but even he hasn't embraced the color for every bit of his clothing.

They lean on the railing next to me and stare out at the water. "If there's something you aren't telling us that will endanger the ship and crew, I'll kill you myself."

I blink. "That's not very siblinghood of the Cŵn Annwn of you."

They snort. "Only people like Bowen believe that shit. *I*

believe in consequences, and there are consequences for breaking the laws. For the person doing the breaking and for anyone
who helps them, inadvertently or not." Their amusement fades
away. "So answer me truly. Have you broken our laws?"

"No." Not *technically*. Probably.

Nox sighs. "Nothing but trouble, the lot of you."

My nerves threaten to get the best of me. I make a pass at the
metal chain hanging from their slim waist on instinct. I can't
help it. Stealing shit makes me feel more in control. It always has.

Nox grabs my wrist and raises their brows. "What do you
think you're doing?"

Holy shit, they're fast. Faster than Lizzie, even. I blink up
into their perfect face. "What are you?"

"That's a very rude question to ask." They lift up my hand
between us and shake it a little. "If you attempt to steal from me
again, I'll—"

"Kill me. Yeah, I got it."

Their lips curve. They really are beautiful in an otherworldly
kind of way. "Nah, I might just keep you."

"Excuse me?"

They turn my hand over and press their fingers lightly to my
palm. "I like your energy, Evelyn. You're trouble in the best way.
We'd have some fun together."

I . . . Wow. Nothing about this conversation has gone how I
expected it to. I carefully pull my wrist from their grip and
smile. "In another life, I would take you up on it. You seem
like fun."

"I am the very definition of fun, as long as you don't cross
me and mine." Their gaze shifts over my shoulder and their

smile widens. "Oh dear, I do believe I've pissed off your hulking protector. I don't think I've ever seen Bowen this furious. He's normally so stoic." They lean closer. "What do you think he'll do if I—"

They're abruptly lifted into the air and deposited several feet away. The surprise on their face is a perfect match to the feeling rocking me. Did Bowen just use his magic on them?

I get my answer when the man himself appears at my back. His shadow falls over me and he clasps my hips, tugging me back into the curve of his body. But when he speaks, it's not for me. "Keep your hands off her, Nox."

Nox grins, and it's as if they weren't threatening me and then hitting on me in turn a few moments ago. "Never thought I'd see the day. You *like* her."

"Fuck off."

They laugh and turn on their heel, making their duster flare out dramatically around them. "Pass on my message, Evelyn. It's important you don't get in my way." They stride away, their long legs eating up the distance between us and the helm.

Bowen's hands tighten on my hips. "What message?"

"Oh, you know, the usual." I can't decide if I want to step away or snuggle back more firmly against him. He's warm and strong and has been steadfastly ignoring my open invitation to come to my room since we arrived. It probably has something to do with keeping up appearances, but I'm scared and lonely and . . . silly to say I miss him after sharing his bed for only one night, but it's the truth.

"You're angry at me." He turns us toward the railing and shifts so his cloak covers me as well. I wasn't cold before, but I'm instantly warm in a way that curls my toes.

I'm not ready to admit he's right, mostly because I didn't realize I was angry until this very moment. "Nox just wanted to let me know that if we do something to endanger the crew, they'll kill us themself. Simple, really."

"That's not what I'm talking about, Evelyn." His breath ghosts against the curve of my ear. "Were they attempting to seduce you? They're quite good at it."

"Have they seduced you?" I don't mean to ask the question, but I never mean to ask questions when I'm around Bowen. They just . . . pop out.

"They've tried."

Jealousy flashes through me so intensely that I stagger a little. Holy fuck, where did that come from? Bowen and I aren't anything resembling official or exclusive. Three days ago, I was about to leave him behind forever. Not to mention I've hardly been a saint before meeting him, and expecting that of him is really shitty.

But Nox is svelte and charming and dangerous and devastatingly attractive. If they've ever doubted their place in the world, they don't now. Why *wouldn't* Bowen want to be seduced by them?

"Why didn't you let them succeed?"

"Evelyn."

Gods, but I love the way he says my name. Here, in this moment, it might as well be just the two of us. I can hear the crew moving about their business, but they feel very far away. "What?"

"Why are you angry with me? Is this about Lizzie?"

I shudder. I've been trying very hard not to think about Lizzie at all. She should be at a disadvantage since she's in an unfamiliar realm with no transportation, but she shouldn't have been able to find a portal and *me* so quickly, either. Underestimating her is a good way to end up dead.

Even so . . .

I'm so fucking weak, because I'm glad we escaped without killing her. "I don't want her to die. Even after everything. That's very silly, isn't it? I won't say she never cared about me at all, but she's not sentimental enough to let feelings get in the way of her end goals. I wish I could say the same."

"Very few people are that single-minded when there's someone they care about on the other side of the conflict." He settles his arms more firmly around me. "You're not weak for wanting to keep the people you've cared about safe."

Even if they don't give you the same courtesy.

He doesn't say it, but I hear the words all the same. I want to argue that Lizzie shot at *him*, not *me*, but I know better. She's too smart to just straight-up kill me without getting the location of the family jewels first.

I could say all that, but instead what comes out of my mouth is something entirely different. "Why are you avoiding me?"

"What are you talking about?"

"Don't play like you don't know what I'm talking about. They set us up in our own rooms and you could have been in mine this whole time, but you haven't."

His sigh rumbles through his chest and into my back. "I wasn't sure if you wanted it, and I didn't want to put you in a position where you felt like you had to keep sharing my bed to ensure my protection."

Oh, of all the honorable nonsense. "Bowen." I turn around, and he allows it, but he doesn't move back. I have to strain my neck to look into his dark eyes. "If someone tried to pressure their way into my bed, I'd curse them. I'm very good at cursing people, and Bunny had some incredibly creative ones she taught me. How about instead of assuming you know what's best for me, you just ask me what I want?"

He frowns at me as if I'm being ridiculous, when *he's* the one being ridiculous. Finally, he says, "Would you like to share my bed, Evelyn?"

"Yes. Next question—what the fuck are we going to do about Lizzie?"

"I don't know."

It's not the answer I want, but it is the most honest one. That doesn't mean I like it. "Any of the Cŵn Annwn who come across her and try to force a vow will end up dead." I speak slowly, feeling my way. "I suppose that eventually becomes a numbers game. Lizzie is ridiculously powerful but she's not *all*-powerful. She won't survive indefinitely."

I realize that should make me happy—or if not happy, then relieved. She doesn't deserve to die just because she hurt my feelings, but I'm also not going to offer up my throat just because I made the mistake of stealing from her. There are no good options.

"That's the most likely scenario if she won't accept the vow." Bowen lifts his head and looks out to sea. "I suppose the people on Sarvi might take pity on her and fold her into their ranks. There's a small chance she could escape notice that way, though I don't know that it would save her indefinitely. Unless you think it's likely she'll kill them, too."

"No. She's more than happy to slaughter her enemies, and occasionally her family, but she's not one for indiscriminate murder." There is absolutely no possibility of Lizzie giving up the hunt and settling down into some mundane life in a village on Sarvi. Even if there was ... "Do the Cŵn Annwn police the locals?"

Bowen's jaw goes tight. "We're not supposed to interfere with the citizens of Threshold."

Easy enough to read between the lines. It's not even surprising that the Cŵn Annwn would overreach. Anytime there's power to be had, there's power to be misused. Threshold isn't exempt from that rule. Absolute power corrupts absolutely, and all that.

"Then she's still a threat. It won't take her long to figure out she can't kill her way to me or the family jewels on the *Crimson Hag*. She'll take a different route."

"You sound almost relieved."

I am, damn it. Or at least I should be. I shiver. Bowen tucks his cloak more firmly around me. He wraps his arms around me for good measure. As much as I appreciate the comfort, it does little to combat the conflicted feelings inside me. "I won't say I loved her, because that wasn't what we were to each other. But I'm fool enough to give at least part of my heart to the people I sleep with. I don't want her dead. If she comes for me, I'll do whatever it takes to survive, but really I'm going to hope that she never finds me again." If I can find another portal to hop through, it becomes less likely. Threshold is littered with them, so it's just a matter of going through one that she doesn't expect.

Which means leaving Bowen behind. For real this time.

CHAPTER 24

Bowen

AFTER GETTING EVELYN'S THINGS INTO MY CABIN, I leave her to get settled and go in search of Dia. Unsurprisingly, I find her near the stern, smoking. I prop my elbows on the railing next to her and exhale slowly. "You were there when they voted me out. How likely is Miles to pursue branding me a traitor for letting the dragon flee?"

She blows a smoke ring. "He will want to do it for spite, but a brand-new captain is in a precarious position. The crew might not like what you did with the dragon, or how you handled the witch, but you have many years of goodwill built up, even if their confidence in you waned in recent months. When they voted you out, they were very clear in their wishes. They don't want you dead—they just don't want you as captain anymore. Miles is too smart to push something that might turn them against him." She pauses to inhale deeply. "I wouldn't go handing him a knife and turning my back, but I don't think you have anything to worry about."

It's what I wanted to hear, and yet it makes me feel so empty. "They just . . . sailed away."

"Yep." Dia offers me her joint and shrugs when I shake my head. "That's one thing Ezra failed to teach you. The Cŵn Annwn may paint themselves in crimson and importance, but at their heart, they are a fleet of pirates. Pirates look out for themselves, Bowen. It's time you do the same."

I want to push back against what she's saying. But it feels like another set of scales falling from my eyes. How many times have I looked at captains like Hedd and hated how they gave the Cŵn Annwn a bad name? They bully the locals and use the mantle of protectors to take what they think is owed to them. It's not straight-up thievery if it's a gift, even if that *gift* was the result of intimidation and underhanded threats. Sometimes they even hurt people, though any rumors or accusations I've heard have died quiet deaths before reaching the Council.

Or maybe they were snuffed out by the Council themselves.

The growing suspicion makes me sick to my stomach. "There aren't many ships that are run the way Ezra and I ran the *Crimson Hag,* are there?"

"Nope."

I nod. "Thank you for always being honest with me, even when I didn't want to hear what you had to say."

Dia snorts. "There you go again, being the best of us. Return to your witch, Bowen. No matter what course she takes, she's going to need you before the end of this."

I plan on doing exactly that. But I have one more stop to make first.

I find Nox at the helm. They look tired, but then, by my best guess, they've held more shifts on than off. Hedd isn't a good captain, and if he's not careful, he's liable to be voted out. But then again, his crew embraces his awfulness. It paves the way for them to act the same way without recourse. Something that wouldn't be true if Nox held the position.

I can recognize that and appreciate it, even if part of me still wants to wring their neck. "Stay away from Evelyn."

They glance at me. "Just a bit of harmless flirting, Captain. Except I suppose you aren't captain anymore, are you?"

I bite down on my instinctive need to throttle them. "I don't want trouble, but I'll happily wade in it where she's concerned. Do you understand?"

Their amusement never leaves their blue eyes. But their smile does fall away. "I don't go where I'm not wanted. If I'm not mistaken, she just moved into your cabin. That makes her preference clear, don't you think?"

I could stand here talking in circles and get nowhere. Ultimately, they're right. It's not that I think they're an active threat to this thing Evelyn and I have going on, but watching them flirt with her drove home the fact that I truly have no claim. She might have shared my bed, but she's not *mine*. Not in any true way.

Even if she stayed in Threshold, how can I ask her to stay with *me*? I was her captor. I forced her into taking a vow that will cost her life if she tries to reclaim her freedom. Neither of those things is forgivable on its own. Together? We have no chance.

If Evelyn were standing beside me right now, she would point out that I'm making decisions without consulting her. Again.

I leave Nox at the helm and head down to my cabin. Inside,

I find Evelyn with several small bowls emitting colorful smoke and strange scents. I close the door softly behind me. "What's going on here?"

"It's all a little hocus-pocus." She doesn't look up from her mixing. "I have expelled a number of my tattoos, and since they are my heaviest-hitting ones, I don't feel comfortable getting off this boat without having them recharged."

All of my earlier concern and stress falls away, replaced by curiosity. Obviously I knew her tattoos were magic, but getting to witness her set them up feels like the closest sort of intimacy. Or maybe I'm reaching for stars.

She pricks her thumb and holds it over the first bowl. The moment her drop of blood hits the contents, she speaks a single word. My skin prickles at the magic that rises in response. It's gone just as quickly, pulled in by her spell. She quickly repeats the process with the other bowls.

"There." She sits back and puts her thumb in her mouth. Evelyn winces. "That shit always stings more than it has the right to." She holds up a small stick with a needle attached. "Since you're here, how steady is your hand?"

"Steady enough," I say cautiously.

Evelyn smiles. "Then get over here, big boy. Tattoo me!"

I know how it works, but I can't pretend I have any skill at it. "Surely there's someone else who's better suited."

Evelyn waves it at me. "Maybe, but I trust you more than anyone else on the ship. All you have to do is follow the lines that are already there. It'll be fun."

"Fun," I repeat. "You have a strange way of viewing things."

"I would think you'd stop being surprised by that after all

this time." She rolls her eyes. "Look, technically I can do it my-self, but it's a pain in the ass and I need a mirror. It will take me twice as long as it would take you. Please, Bowen."

She's asking me for help. More, she's trusting me to ink her spells onto her skin. The very things to keep her safe and allow her to fight and protect herself. If I was smart, ruthless, I'd force her to drain all of her spells so that she'd stop being a threat.

But that's the Cŵn Annwn way of thinking.

Without Evelyn's magic, the cat-sìth likely would've killed me. Lizzie, too. And her shield gave the necessary time to really think about what we were doing with the dragon. The chain of events might have lost me my ship, but the more time that goes on, the more I wonder if that wasn't a blessing in disguise.

There's no one relying on me right now. No one except Ev-elyn. No crew to weigh in the balance of my decisions. No doz-ens of lives who might pay the price for my questions.

I could no more leave her defenseless than I would toss my sword into the sea.

"Show me how."

Her smile lights up the room. "You're the best." She hands me the first bowl and tattoo instrument, takes off her shirt, and lies down on the bed on her back.

I stop short, all of my attention narrowing on her breasts, shadowed with marks from my beard and mouth, her pretty pink nipples practically begging for another round of pleasure. "Evelyn."

"Oh." She blushes a deep red. "Right. I can cover up if—"

"Absolutely not." I drag the small table over and set the things on it. Then I take the time to kick off my boots and shrug out of my coat. It takes several attempts to find the best position.

After a bit of frustration, I end up straddling her torso. I'm careful to keep the majority of my weight off her, and there's no help for the hard length of my cock making its presence known. Other than raising her brows, she doesn't comment on it. So I don't, either.

It's not until I'm dipping the needles into the ink that I realize what I'm about to do. "This will hurt."

"Tattoos always do." She points to the glyph just under her collarbone. "That bowl goes with this one. We'll have to clean the needles before you switch to the other bowl."

"Okay." I press the needles to her skin. She tenses beneath me, and I almost ask her if she's sure, but she's right; tattoos always hurt. The very least I can do is ensure her pain has purpose—and that it doesn't last longer than necessary. Even so, it's slow going. The glyph is more complicated than it first appears. To distract her, and myself, I ask, "Where did you get all these materials?"

Evelyn carefully sets her hands on my thighs, which would be a distraction all its own if not for concern keeping my thoughts in order. She winks. "I bought it off one of the crew. I don't know if they were a witch, or just had an apothecary worth of supplies, but they had everything I needed to restock."

I consider that as I keep inking. "Do I want to ask where you got the money to make these purchases?"

"Probably not." She somehow manages to laugh without moving. "But I didn't steal from you or Dia, if that's what you're wondering. Or Nox, for that matter. They're too perceptive and their hands are even quicker than mine."

With how often she lifts things off me, I probably should have been wondering if she'd done it again to serve her purposes.

It never crossed my mind, though. I don't know if that's naive . . . or progress. Still, if she's creating enemies on the crew, I need to know. "Tell me."

"Okay, fine. I stole a tiny little ring off the captain. But it's not like I have it anymore, so no one can prove it." She grins. "Easy peasy."

I don't comment that the crew member she sold it to could use that as proof of her thievery. I suspect if they were going to do that, it would've already happened. There is no honor among this crew, and Hedd has no one to blame but himself. "Do you think you can manage to restrain yourself until we get onto another ship? Hedd is a bastard, and he's vicious when he's crossed. I wouldn't lose sleep over killing him—if I'm even capable of it—but it would complicate things and draw further attention to us." Evelyn is silent for so long that I pause and look up to meet her green eyes. "What?"

"Bowen," she says slowly. "Did you just offer to murder the captain for me? How did you know that was my love language?" Before I can come up with a suitable response to that—if there even is one—she points to the second bowl. "Clean that off and then start on the next one."

I finish inking the first glyph and sit back. "I mean to keep you safe. No matter what that requires." I quickly wash off the tool and settle back to start the second glyph. "I know you're joking, but it's the truth."

"I know." She strokes her fingers lightly over my thighs. "I appreciate you and the lengths you're willing to go. I know I came into your life and dropped a bomb. You've been adapting better than I could've expected, and frankly, I'm a little surprised you don't hate me."

I frown, concentrating as I work along a trio of fine dots. "It would be incredibly unfair of me to hate you for asking questions. You didn't create the Cŵn Annwn, and you didn't create their laws. You certainly didn't have anything to do with how Threshold itself is set up."

"Of course not. But there's that old saying about shooting the messenger, and all that."

"I can infer what you're talking about, but I have no idea what you're referencing." I pause. "I think it would be best if you stop stroking my thighs. It's incredibly distracting and I don't want to do this incorrectly."

Evelyn's smile takes on a mischievous lilt. "You're so blunt. I love that. Maybe next time you can practice with paint and we can see just how much distraction you can handle before you start making a mess."

"*Evelyn.*" I have to pause and take a long breath to still my shaking hand. "Please."

Her laugh is music to my ears. She bites her bottom lip. "Okay, okay, fine. I'll be good so you can finish the job. But unless I'm mistaken, we have a few free hours after this. I think we both deserve a reward . . ."

CHAPTER 25

Evelyn

I'VE NEVER CONSIDERED TATTOOS TO BE FOREPLAY. I'M not above a little slap and tickle, but the witch who taught me this trick with prepping my spells was a grizzled older being. They were mean right down to the very bones. Submitting to the first round of tattooing was a trial to be born. Since then, I've mostly done it myself since there are few people I'd trust enough to let them mess with my spells. When you're trying not to fuck up tattooing yourself, the last thing on your mind is sex.

The last thing on my mind right now . . . well, sex is right at the forefront.

I'm only human, and Bowen is too fucking attractive for my state of mind. He's kneeling over my body, a line of concentration between his dark brows as he delicately inks the last tattoo. That would be sexy enough, but his big cock is pressing against his breeches. Right. Fucking. There.

This process is important. It's pretty vital that my tattoos don't get messed up, because without them I'll be next to defenseless. Bowen *is* taking this seriously. I should be doing so as well. But I can't stop myself from giving his thighs little teasing strokes. The third time I do it he reaches over and absently smacks my hand. "Stop that."

The man might as well have waved a red flag in front of a bull. I manage to restrain myself until he's nearly finished. Only then do I set my hands on his hips and run my thumbs up the length of his cock.

Bowen freezes. His expression goes purely forbidding. He sits up and carefully sets the tools aside. I'm already playing with fire, so I stroke his cock through his pants again. His response happens so quickly, I barely have time to process it.

He slaps my breast.

I'm still deciding if I like it or hate it when he cups the same breast with his big, rough hands. *That* feels good. His expression is still purely thunderous. "You are a menace."

"It's not my fault you can't multitask." I undo the front of his breeches and tug on the laces until I mostly free his cock. "I'm sorry, baby. That looks painful. I've got just the thing to help."

His grip tightens on my breast almost compulsively. "We should bandage your tattoos so they don't get infected."

"Mmm. Or, hear me out, we can have sex instead."

"Evelyn."

I wrap my fingers around the head of his cock, just under the crown. He jolts... but he doesn't move me. I squeeze a little. "That's not a no."

"Take off your fucking pants." He removes my hand from his cock and climbs off the bed. Apparently I'm not moving fast enough for him, because his magic wraps around me and lifts me into the air. I can barely process what he's doing when his power hooks my pants and drags them off my body.

It's as if my lust has been jammed up during the tattoo in process and the whole thing exploded. I need him inside me and I need it now. Even so, I notice that he's careful not to rip my clothing. Gods, he's too good to be real sometimes.

Bowen grabs me around the hips and pulls me toward him. He's got such a great way of manhandling me, where he moves me around all while still being so careful. He knows his strength, and he knows how easily he could hurt me. Maybe it's fucked up to get off on that, but I like what I like.

I'm still several feet off the bed, which means I'm perfectly even with his hips as he stands. "This whole magic-while-fucking thing is really useful."

I can't even appreciate his sigh of amused irritation because he chooses that moment to grip my hip and shove two fingers into me. I don't mean to shriek, but even as wet as I am, it's an intrusion. One I welcome. Not that Bowen is giving me time to sink into the sensation. He fucks me roughly with his fingers, wedging a third in before I'm accustomed to the two. I love it. "Give me your cock," I moan.

"I'm. Fucking. Trying."

Trying not to hurt me, even though we're both so desperate that I wouldn't give a shit if he did. I try to lift my hips, but his magic isn't creating a table that I'm lying on; it's wrapped around me. Pinning me in place in midair. I can't stop myself from making a frustrated sound, even as the knowledge that I can't move only drives my need higher. "I can take it, Bowen. Please don't make me wait. I need you."

"Woman, you are going to send me to an early grave." But he

does as I ask. He pulls his fingers out of me and shifts until I feel the press of his broad cock against my entrance. "Taking you at your word," he mutters.

He shoves into me in one long, unrelenting stroke. I shriek again. Bowen pauses, no doubt to ensure I'm okay, but I don't give him a chance to ask. "Don't stop!"

His hesitation doesn't last longer than it takes the words to escape my lips. He grabs my hips and the magic around me shifts my body until I'm at exactly the angle he wants. Then he starts to fuck me properly. He thrusts into me again and again, each time shifting my hips a little bit until he finds the exact alignment that has me screaming and writhing. I can't think. I can't thrust back. I can take only what he gives me.

Again, and again, he pounds against that spot inside me. And then his magic shifts around my body. It's no longer only holding me in place. Little tendrils stroke over my stomach, my thighs, my breasts. Bowen keeps his actual hands on my hips, but the tendrils on my thighs shift down to play with my clit while the others focus on my breasts, squeezing and stroking and toying with my nipples. My lust surges so fucking fast it makes my head spin. My entire world narrows down to his cock inside me and his magic against my skin, stoking my pleasure higher and higher. All while his dark gaze consumes me.

I don't know if I want to hold out or welcome the orgasm bearing down on me. I don't get a choice. I bury my face in the sheets and scream Bowen's name as I orgasm. I come so hard, I don't register that he's pulling out of me until his knees hit the ground behind me, and then his mouth is on my pussy. The motherfucker is still holding me in the air with his magic, still playing with my breasts, though the tendrils move from my clit to make room for his tongue . . . and slide down to press into me. His touch feels seared into my skin, and I wouldn't have it any other way. There's no opportunity to catch my breath. In the time we share together at that inn, he learned what I like and he learned it well.

He fucks me with his magic while he focuses on my clit with his tongue as if he has nowhere else to be. As if he can hold me in this position until the end of days. It's sexy and no little amount of terrifying. So, of course, I promptly come all over his face.

Only then does he rise again, still holding me aloft with his power. He looks like a man possessed, his eyes downright feral and every muscle standing out in his body as he presses my thighs wide and shoves his cock into me again.

I might be out of my mind with pleasure, but that doesn't stop me from raising my head so I can look down to where we're joined. It's so fucking sexy to see my body take him, his broad length spreading my pussy's lips. It's filthy and no small amount of obscene. I love it. "That feels so good."

In response, he presses my thighs even wider until my hips ache. It allows me to take him deeper yet, and we both moan on the next thrust. "Never get enough of you," he mutters. "Can't get deep enough, can't make you come enough times, can't fill you up until you're dripping with me. Barely finish inside you, and all I can think about is starting again."

I couldn't find the words to respond to that even if he wasn't fucking my ability to speak right out of me. I feel the same way. I want to blame it on frenzy, but I've felt frenzy before with past partners. This is different. Even as he is pounding into me as if he wants to imprint himself on my pussy, there's a level of caring that I don't know how to define.

I orgasm again before I have to decide if this is what love feels like. It's just as well. I might be able to recognize it when it comes to family, but I've never felt it romantically. Who's to say this isn't love?

Bowen pulls me to him, careful of my fresh tattoos, and kisses me as he comes deep inside me. He loves to have his mouth on mine as he's pumping me full of him. Truth be told, I love it, too. It's just another in a long list of intimacies that I enjoy experiencing with him.

He gently pulls out of me and we both look down to see evidence of our fucking dripping from my body. I shiver and Bowen kisses me again. Then his fingers are there, pressing back into me slowly. It takes me a second to understand what he's doing.

He's finger fucking his come back into me.

"*Bowen.*"

He brushes a kiss to one side of my mouth and then the other. "Do you want me to stop?"

My active spell ensures I can't get pregnant. This is all for possessive show, not with any endgame in mind. The scary thing is that I'm not sure if it would matter even if I wasn't protected. I kiss him harder and spread my thighs. "Don't let a single drop go to waste."

He groans against my lips and then he takes my mouth as if we both aren't still shaking from coming so hard. As if we're just starting fresh. He gathers up what little come has escaped and shoves it back into me, pressing his fingers deep, as if he can reach a point of no return. He moves down to lick my throat. "You drive me out of my mind, Evie. I don't feel like myself. I know you want to go home, but it's taking everything I am not to haul you off to some island and burn all your clothes. We could spend the rest of our lives just like this, with me worshiping your pretty pussy."

I try to tell myself it's just sex making him say these things, but I don't believe it for a moment. Bowen never says things he doesn't mean, and I highly doubt he's starting now.

He wants to keep me.

And gods help me, but there's a part of me that wants to be kept by him.

I kiss him to stop myself from begging him to do exactly that, to haul me off and take away my ability to leave him. He moves me down to the bed and presses me onto my back, all without removing his fingers from my pussy. "Have you had enough?"

"No. Never." I reach down and grab his wrist, preventing him from withdrawing. "Don't stop until we have to."

Bowen meets my eyes, and I see the same fatalism currently sinking in my chest. This isn't forever. As much as I want to be kept by him, I am no bird to be stuck in a cage. I value my freedom above all else. I might love being trapped for a period of time, but eventually I would grow to resent him. To hate him. And *that* I cannot let happen.

In this moment of perfect understanding between us, I admit to myself this is love. And that sometimes love isn't enough. We're on two separate paths that have overlapped for a short period of time, but it won't last. Eventually, whether it's in a couple days or a couple weeks, or even a couple months, I'll leave him.

And he'll let me go.

He nods, and I can't tell if he's responding to something in my eyes or something in his head. In the end, it doesn't matter. "Okay, Evie. We won't stop until we have to."

CHAPTER 26

Bowen

EVERY SO OFTEN, I'LL BE OUT ON THE DECK AND WITNESS a storm brewing on the horizon. Even with the warning, even knowing it's coming, we still get caught up in it. Sometimes it even kills people despite all our experience, all our preparation.

That's what it feels like having Evelyn in my bed. This moment of safety, of happiness, is only temporary. And it's not because her ex wants to murder her. It's not even because the Council may end up demanding an explanation about the dragon and ruling me a traitor.

It's because she still hasn't changed her mind about leaving Threshold.

I'm not a man of honeyed words. Even if I was, it feels wrong to try to convince her to do something against her nature. She's told me time and time again how important it is for her to be free. I may want to tie her to me, to be the anchor that slows her down, but even I'm self-aware enough to know that it will ruin us eventually. *And if it didn't?*

No, there's no use clinging to useless hope. I know the stories of selkies as well as any sailor. They always go back to the sea, or face the fate of dying of sorrow. I can't stand the thought of the bright parts of Evelyn being leeched away by my love.

It doesn't stop my words from getting away from me every time we have sex. Even as I promise myself that *this* time I won't let my possessiveness take the reins, the moment I'm inside her, I find myself saying the most unforgivable things. I'm nearly certain they make her orgasm harder. Speaking such forbidden words certainly heightens my pleasure.

But once the sweat has cooled on our bodies and our heartbeats have returned to normal, we both pretend that we weren't begging and agreeing to things while in the moment.

There's no reason to think Evelyn will leave me at Three Sisters, but dread takes up residence in my stomach when Nox comes to inform us that land has been sighted. They don't comment on the love bites coloring my upper chest and throat. It's just as well. Nothing I could say in response would be appropriate.

I shut the door and turn to face Evelyn in the bed with the mess of our sheets. "They're hunting mermaids. If you take issue with that—"

"Oh, you don't have to worry about me this time. Mermaids are fucking malevolent and there's no reasoning with them. They're blocking off access to this trio of islands. The people will starve without ships being able to bring in food and goods, and the mermaids will definitely kill anyone who tries to sail past."

I give her a long look. "Someone's been talking with the crew." As much as I would've liked her to stay in my bed the entire time, the reality is we both have shifts to cover and responsibilities that come with being on Hedd's ship. There are no free rides in Threshold. At least not with the Cŵn Annwn.

Evelyn shrugs. "I'll be the first to admit that not every creature in existence is misunderstood. Normally, I would argue for rehabilitation or relocation even with a dangerous being, but the mermaids swarm and they're insatiable. They'll just end up in another place, doing the same thing. Eating all the food and killing all the people."

"There are several kinds of mermaids." I don't know why I say it. She's right. Once the shallow-water hunters show up, the only way to get them out is to kill them. The sole exception I've seen in all my years is Atlantis, the port city that sits out of time and space. It's technically part of Threshold, but a long time ago, they managed to secure a deal that means they govern themselves and the Cŵn Annwn aren't welcome on their shores for unsanctioned hunts. I had to visit a year or so ago while tracking down an unsecured portal that was stolen from one of our people.

I'm not sure how they manage to keep the mermaids contained. Even then, they lose a decent number of ships and crews attempting to sail into the bay and make port there. I clear my throat. "The deep-water ones keep to themselves for obvious reasons. There *is* a swarming season, but no one smart goes near those waters during that time of year. Not even a full crew of Cŵn Annwn are enough to guarantee survival."

"So what you're saying is that you respect the natural rhythm of them and don't murder them for doing something within their nature."

I see her point, but I can't help pushing back. "They kill people."

"So do the Cŵn Annwn," Evelyn says softly.

I open my mouth, but my rebuttal dies before the words can leave my lips. "So do the Cŵn Annwn," I repeat slowly.

She goes up on her toes and kisses me. "I know, baby. It's going to be a long process of unknowing. Go easy on yourself." She moves away to pull on a long coat and slips her dagger—because it *is* her dagger now, it's no longer mine—into the sheath at her waist. That sheath is new, too.

This time, I don't bother to question where it came from. Evelyn has proven herself to be canny with a mostly excellent sense of timing. If she bargained yet more stolen shit, she did it in a smart way. "Stay close. This is Hedd's show, so no big moves on our part. It's my job to ensure no mermaids make it aboard. Try to avoid using fire unless you're aiming it into the water."

"Don't use fire on a ship. Brilliant." Her reply is snarky, but I now know her well enough to detect the nerves under the words.

I take her shoulders and wait for her to look up at me. "I won't let anything happen to you. I promise."

Evelyn wets her lips. "I damn well know that in a fight, there are no guarantees, but when you say that so confidently, I believe you." She shakes her head. "I'll be a good little sailor and obey orders. I'm not trying to be a hero today."

"Good." I lead the way out of the cabin and follow a stream of people up the stairs to the deck. They look haggard, their clothing worn and dirty. It's nothing more than I've noticed before, but it strikes me all over again how much the crew are at the mercy of the captain. It's impossible to know how many of them happily follow Hedd and how many do it out of a dearth of other choices.

You could take captainship. A few months at most to win them over. They'd have to be fools to prefer Hedd to you.

For a moment, I actually consider it. Nox frustrates me to no end, but they're irritating—not a bad person. If we worked together, we could get this ship running like the *Hag* in no time.

And then I'd be right back where I started. Dancing to the tune the Council sets, with no original thoughts of my own. Being . . . the villain.

My brain tries to shy away from that truth, but it *is* a truth. I don't know how I never noticed it before, how it never occurred to me to question it, but now I can't go back to not knowing.

The weather seems to reflect my dark thoughts. Clouds swirl ominously overhead, blocking out the sun and making it nearly impossible to see the trio of islands that compose Three Sisters. I catch sight of Dia leaning against the mast and make my way over to her, Evelyn right behind me. "What are you doing up here?" She's not a fighter. She never has been. Usually, when it comes time to do our duty, she ends up belowdecks.

"Don't have much confidence in this crew." She pulls out a joint, glares at the sky, and tucks it back into her shirt. "I'd rather not go down with the ship if Hedd fucks this up."

"If he fucks things up that badly, the only option will be to swim for shore, and *that* is a death sentence with mermaids in the water."

"Still better than drowning in my cabin when the pocket realm collapses." She shrugs and turns a keen eye on Evelyn. "It would be ill-advised for you to pull another stunt like you did aboard the *Hag*."

"So I've been told." Evelyn cocks her head to the side. "What's that sound?"

The whole crew goes silent. Only the creak of the ship and the soft movement of people shifting can be heard . . . until a faint shriek sounds, so high and wailing that it could almost be the wind itself.

"Incoming," Dia mutters. "Get over here, girl. Stand next to me."

Evelyn glances at me and I nod. "I'll protect you both." I'm powerful, but even I don't know if I could fly both of them and myself to the nearest island. Probably, in a worst-case scenario, fueled by panic and fear and adrenaline, but that would mean abandoning the *Audacity* and its crew.

There's no law against being voted out of the captaincy. Fleeing a fight? That's a different animal altogether.

No, the only option is to keep this damned ship afloat, no matter how badly Hedd mangles the fight. I'm not being fair—the bastard has survived this long, and it's not by avoiding doing his duty—but I don't care.

As if my thoughts summon the man himself, Hedd appears on deck. He holds a great ax that most people wouldn't be able to lift off the ground and his shirtless body is painted in gray symbols.

At my back, Evelyn whistles. "A berserker, huh?"

I glance at her. "You have them in your realm?"

"Yes, though they're rare." She narrows her eyes. "They also don't need the symbols in order to shift into their other form."

"Neither does he. He's just a dramatic fucker."

Hedd hefts his ax. "They're coming! Let's show these monsters what the Cŵn Annwn stand for! Death to all!"

A chill shoots up my spine. That's not what . . . Fuck, I'm going to keep doing this, aren't I? It's like there are ingrained paths in my brain and I can't quite jump the tracks. Another time, I'd remind myself that it took twenty years to make those paths and they won't be undone in a matter of days. Right now, I'm not in the mood to be kind to myself.

I reach back and touch Evelyn. "Stay here."

"You said that already," she murmurs.

"I did." I consider my options and decide there's no reason to pull my sword. Not yet. "And you have a history of ignoring my commands and doing what you want."

"Well . . . yes."

"Don't do it this time."

And then there's no more time for talk because the mermaids arrive. The sea churns as they bound and leap over each other to get to their prey. To us. They're truly monstrous. No one would mistake their top halves for human, though they have a torso and arms and a head. But human fingers don't have that extra knuckle—and they don't end in claws. Human teeth aren't sharp, jagged points designed for ripping and tearing. Even their approximation of hair isn't hair at all. It's closer to tentacles than anything else. Add in powerful tails that allow them to jump well above the surface of the sea and they're every sailor's nightmare.

The shrieking noise becomes almost too much to take. There are more of them than I anticipated, but that makes sense. We're rarely called out for small infestations.

They surge up in a wave almost as a single unit, intent on breaching the deck. I grit my teeth and throw up a wall of power, breaking them against it. The impact shudders through me. Those monsters hit harder than the dragon.

As soon as my magic drops, the crew is there with harpoons and fire and various magical attacks. The shrieking takes on an agonizing tone as those attacks find their victims. The water churns violently, dark purple blood coloring the blue.

And then they turn on their injured counterparts. They're equal opportunity predators, and a little cannibalism doesn't bother them in the least. I knew it was coming, and it still makes me sick to my stomach. It's not enough to stop the next attack, though. They're insatiable, bottomless destroyers.

"That's it! Send them to a watery grave!"

The mermaids shouldn't gather themselves for a singular attack again—not when a portion of their number are eating their injured comrades—but I still keep an eye out for the possibility as I bat individual creatures from the air before they can make contact with the deck. It takes nearly as much effort as the wall did because there's an element of precision involved. If I'm not careful, I'll sweep the crew members into the water, and that's a death sentence.

In the chaos, I catch sight of Nox on the other side of the ship, their crimson duster flaring out behind them as they send streams of fire and air in turn against the mermaids. Very few people with elemental-based powers have access to more than one element. Nox can tap into all four.

Hedd appears next to me, his form shifting and growing. It's not a pretty sight, but once he's in his berserker rage, he can go for hours and he's damn near unstoppable. There's not a lot of room left for coherent thought, though. "Let them on board!"

I frown. "Excuse me?"

"Is this a fight or is it a *fight*?" He smacks my shoulder hard enough to stagger me. "Let them come. That's an order."

"People will die!"

"*You* will fucking die if you disobey a direct order. Let. Them. Come!" He raises his ax menacingly. "Or I kill that little witch cowering behind you."

CHAPTER 27

Evelyn

I KNEW THAT THE CAPTAIN HAD A BAD VIBE, BUT EVEN I hadn't anticipated this level of recklessness. Bowen is the only thing keeping those shrieking mermaids off the deck. Even from where I stand next to the mast, I can see how sharp their claws are, how vicious their teeth. Bowen is doing his best, but they've dragged no less than three crew members down into the deep.

And now the captain wants to make it worse.

"Don't do it." I don't mean to speak, but Hedd immediately turns his vicious attention in my direction. It's too late to back down. The only way through is *through*. I lift my chin, trying not to flinch as someone screams far too close. "It's the wrong call."

Hedd looks at me for a moment and then dismisses me just as quickly. "I'll pretend I didn't hear that mutiny."

"Someone questioning a dangerous order is not mutiny!"

Bowen answers without looking at me. "That's enough,

Evelyn." He nods slowly. "Of course we'll follow your orders, Captain."

Hedd grins and rushes toward the railing. I waste no time grabbing Bowen's arm. "You can't seriously mean to obey. I thought we were past this."

"He's a berserker." Bowen speak so softly, I can barely hear him over the sounds of fighting. "If he attacks you, even with all my power, it will be a battle of attrition. While we're fighting, the mermaids will kill too many of the crew. There's no choice. Set up a shield around you and Dia. Don't argue with me, Evelyn."

He considered all that in the span of seconds? I don't want to admit that he's right, but I can't find a fault in logic with what he just said. I lick my lips. "What about you?"

"I'll be able to function better if I'm not worried about you and Dia."

There's no time left to argue. I grab his shirt and pull him down for a desperate kiss. "Don't you dare die."

"And lose out on even a moment with you? Never." He guides me back to the mast. "Shield. Now."

I pull my chalk out of my shirt with a shaking hand. Dia watches with interest as I draw a circle just large enough to encompass both of us. I hesitate to close it, but Bowen is already moving away. He's trusting me to do what I said I would. I have to trust that he'll do the same. I press my hands to the deck and speak the words that bring the shield into being. It snaps into place with the strength that makes me shudder.

Dia carefully presses a hand into the air in front of her. "Neat trick. Most folks I've seen make shields do it with a bit more pizzazz."

"I don't know about other types of magic, but if a witch is using a bunch of song and dance to cast a spell, it's likely for the benefit of those watching." I don't rise. I can see clearly enough from my position where I'm crouched. Besides, if I need to break the shield, it will spare me a second or two. "Why is he doing this?"

"Hedd?" Dia shrugs. "He likes a fight, and berserkers aren't built for long range."

I have nothing to say in response to that. This man's selfish desire to commit violence is going to get people killed. *His* people. And there isn't a damn thing anyone can do about it. I'm so furious, I can barely breathe past it. Or maybe that's fear. It's hard to tell the difference right now.

I don't know if it makes things better or worse to be able to watch Bowen in action. It's the first time I've seen him truly fight, aside from the cat-sìth. It's never been clearer that he's in his element.

Instead of using a wall, he moves through the fight with targeted attacks that send the mermaids hurtling back to water. I can't tell if we're making headway with their numbers, or if they are truly unending. It certainly feels like it. In reality, judging from the frothing waves around us, there are . . . maybe a hundred? It's hard to estimate when they move so chaotically.

Hedd swings his ax wildly at a knot of the creatures. I might hate the man, but even I can admit that I'm glad he's not fighting us. He's cutting through the mermaids as if they're paper. I shudder. "He's a monster."

The sweet scent of pot reaches me. "So are most of the Cŵn Annwn. You haven't been around long enough to notice, but the ones they pick up who are gentle folk don't last long." Dia's tone is neutral enough, but when I look up at her, her dark eyes contain sorrow. She's lost someone she cares about. Maybe several someones.

I'm trying to come up with a response when a roar makes me whip around. A mermaid has latched on to Bowen's back, its teeth ripping into the spot where his shoulder meets his neck. I scream and lurch forward to break the shield on instinct. I don't know what the fuck I can do to help, but I can't just sit here and watch him die.

I never get a chance.

A burst of power surges from him, so strong that I can feel it even through the shield. It sweeps the deck, and for a moment I swear nothing actually happens.

Then the mermaid on Bowen's back slumps to the deck, boneless in a way that makes my stomach queasy. Then it happens again, and again, and again. Everyone goes still and silent, shock written across all their features. But not just shock. They stare down at what's left of the mermaids on the ship with disgust and fear—and those emotions aren't directed at the dead monsters at their feet. They shift away from Bowen as if that will do anything when he just killed every single mermaid on deck.

Nox steps onto the railing, one hand clinging to a line of rope, and leans over. They whistle in the sudden silence. "Best I can tell, every single mermaid is dead, Captain."

Bowen collapses to the deck, unconscious.

No.

I don't make a conscious decision to move. One moment I'm screaming in my head as I watch Bowen fall and the next I'm at his side. I barely register breaking the shield to get to him. "No, no, no, oh, you fucker, don't you dare die. You promised me!" I never thought it was even a possibility. From the moment I met him, Bowen has been larger than life. Untouchable.

As I fall to my knees next to him, he looks all too human. Too pale. Too still. "Bowen!" *I can't lose you. Oh gods, please let him be okay.*

"What the fuck did I tell you?"

I glance up to find Hedd standing over us, cursing and spitting. He hardly looks like the captain I've come to dislike so intensely, his form twisted and strangely out of proportion. He's also still holding his giant ax, its double blades dripping deep purple blood.

He's a threat, but I can't focus on him right now. Bowen is losing too much blood with no sign of stopping. I press my hands to his wound, but it does nothing. Right. What the fuck am I doing? I have magic. I'm not as good at healing spells as Bunny was, but I can keep him alive until we can get to a proper healer. I trigger the glyph over my heart and press my hand to the wound again. For a moment, nothing seems to be happening, but then the flow of blood begins to slow. The skin doesn't knit back together, but I'm pretty sure I see several veins reforming.

Now I have to deal with the captain.

I very much do not want to put any distance between me and Bowen, but this motherfucker seems to respond only to strength, and I have to get us out of this alive. There's no way I can win a fight against a berserker, but I'm not thinking about that when I slap my hand to my chest and summon violet fire in a ring around me and Bowen. It takes more power than I want to admit to keep it from actually making contact with the deck.

I rise to my feet. Hedd looks downright demonic in the flickering light of the fire. I can only hope I look half as intimidating. "You're welcome. How many of your crew are down? Bowen just saved us all." I fling my hand out to encompass the various fallen forms. I don't know how many of them are alive or dead, and later I'll feel guilty for the fact that I was only worried about Bowen and no one else. But not yet.

"He disobeyed a direct order." He's not backing down. In fact, Hedd grins at me as if he can't wait to see what I'm capable of.

Fuck. I might have just made a fatal mistake. I look around again, frantically searching for something that will stop this fight before it starts. My fire is fearsome, but it's draining my magic as an astonishing rate. I normally use it only for concentrated blasts—not to create barriers.

My only hope is the crew themselves. I lift my voice. "Is your desire for a fight worth your entire crew? We did what we came to do. We eliminated the mermaid infestation."

He lifts his ax like he wants to cleave my head from my shoulders. I don't know what the fuck I'm going to do if he attacks. In his berserker form, I don't think my fire will kill him. It might not even slow him down.

"I will brook no disobedience." Nox appears at Hedd's back. "Bowen was given an order and he failed to obey. You're challenging your captain as we speak." They cross their arms over their chest and jerk their chin at the island in the distance. "We can't have you on the crew, so we'll leave you on the shore of First Sister. You can find your own way from there."

Hedd turns a mottled purple, but he doesn't counter his quartermaster, not with the crew slowly gathering around and murmuring about what a close one that was. Not everyone made it out alive. I see the exact moment he realizes that Nox has allowed him a graceful way out. "Nox, get them off my fucking ship."

Things happen quickly after that.

Dia appears and helps me heft Bowen's unconscious form to the side of the ship and then into a smaller boat. She grabs my hands before I can follow. "Take care of him." I open my mouth to ask her to come with us, but she shakes her head before I can. "I have my own path to follow, Evelyn. We'll see each other again."

I'm not so sure.

Not a single member of the rest of the crew tries to help us. They go out of their way to avoid my gaze as I give the ship one last sweeping look. Their apathy is more or less what I expected, but it's still really fucking shitty considering Bowen just saved all their lives.

We came on board with only the clothes on our backs, and that's how we leave. Considering Bowen had a crisis when he was left behind by the *Crimson Hag*, I'm not looking forward to how he reacts when he wakes up and realizes that we are yet again stranded, this time on a different island.

We sail the distance in record time, propelled long by some strange combination of water and air magic, courtesy of Nox. They stop us about ten yards off the beach. "This is as far as I go."

I examine the distance. "That's not going to work. If you toss us out here, he's going to drown before I can drag him to shore." I glare at them. "This is a really shitty thing to do after how he saved everyone. You would've lost more people if he hadn't released that blast of magic." I'm still not ready to examine the sheer delicacy and power required to do what Bowen did. I'm pretty sure if I think about it too hard, I might actually pee my pants in fear. The man is a fucking monster, and he's been in my bed for the best part of the week. I don't want to examine the truth that the same power that brought me so much pleasure is also responsible for so much death.

Nox props their elbows on their knees. "I'm in a particularly precarious position. I don't expect you to understand, but as long as Hedd is captain, things will be done a certain way. Yes, Bowen saved a lot of the crew's lives. But I just saved both of yours."

I want to argue . . . but the truth is they're right. Hedd was going to kill me right there. I might have held him off for a few moments, but I was going to lose that fight. Then he would've finished Bowen off, and there's not a goddamn thing I could've done. Still. "You're clearly the better captain and the better person. Why aren't you in charge?"

"You were on the ship long enough to know the answer to that. I don't have the votes. There are plenty of the crew who are happy with how he runs things. Until that changes, the only thing I can do is counteract his more extreme impulses." They sigh. "Get moving, Evelyn. I'm not so ungrateful as to let him drown. Trust me."

After the fight with the mermaids, the very last thing I want to do is slip into the inky water surrounding our boat. Anything could be below the surface and I would have no idea until it was far too late. Not to mention I'm not entirely certain I trust Nox enough not to let us drown. It would be a convenient way to take care of a problem.

Unfortunately, I don't have a choice.

I take a deep breath that does nothing to fortify me and slip over the boat's edge into the water. It's colder than I expected, significantly more so than two islands ago. I'm still trying to figure out how I'm supposed to get Bowen in the water with me when Nox rolls him over the side.

I curse and make a grab for him. I can't touch the bottom of the shallows, and it's everything I can do to shove his bigger body over me so he doesn't drown. For a moment, I think this is it. What a pathetic way to go out after everything I've survived. Bunny will be so disappointed when I meet her in the afterlife.

But then the water around me changes and seems to grow almost solid. It lifts me up to the surface, making Bowen's weight less significant. I sputter and cough and look up into Nox's amused face. "Told you I wouldn't let you drown. There's a safe house about thirty minutes' walk north up the coast. It's hidden in a crevasse that looks like an X. You can find food and clothes there. Stay safe, little witch."

The water around us shifts again and then we're being ferried away from the boat and the elemental sitting in it. Within seconds we're spit out onto the rocky beach. It's one of the more surreal moments of my life. I've known people who can harness the elements, of course, but Nox is on another level. They might be helping us right now, but I can't stop the shiver of fear at the thought of ever being on the opposite side of a fight. With their control, they could stall the air in my lungs or pull a move like Lizzie and rip the blood right out of my body. Or, rather, the water in my blood. Semantics won't matter when I'm dead.

They aren't on our side, but at least they don't want us dead.

This is the moment when Bowen chooses to wake up. He coughs a little, so I turn him onto his side to keep him from choking. His neck still looks pretty gnarly, but he hasn't started bleeding again. At least my spell's holding. It should continue to do so until his body heals enough that he won't die when the spell fades.

"Evelyn."

"I'm here." I move around so he can see me without straining. He's too pale, his dark eyes standing out. Worry worms through me, but I swallow it down as best I can. "Do you want the good news or the bad news first?"

He curses and slumps onto his back. "Good news."

"Rookie mistake. You always ask for the bad news first. It makes the good news feel more optimistic."

His lips curve, but that's the only hint of amusement I get. "Give me the good news, Evelyn."

"Suit yourself." I sink onto the rocks next to him and try not to shiver in my cold, wet clothes. "We're alive. Hedd was going to kill us both after you collapsed, but Nox stepped in—very cleverly, I might add—and saved us."

He shudders out a long breath. "Okay. And the bad news?"

"Funny story. Really, you're going to laugh." Damn it, I'm stalling, and not even in a clever way. "It seems we're stranded again, and about to watch another one of the Cŵn Annwn ships sail away."

"About what I expected." He presses his hand to his wound and winces. "What happened? The last thing I remember is a mermaid on my back."

I swallow hard. I really don't want to revisit the events that ended that fight, but he has a right to know. The sooner we finish this conversation, the sooner we can find somewhere warm and dry. Hopefully. "It bit you. Quite badly. You sent out a wave of power that, as best I can tell, turned every bone in every mermaid body to liquid and made their bodies flesh sacks. It was really impressive in a horrifying, nightmarish kind of way."

Bowen is silent for several beats too long. "Did I kill anyone else?"

CHAPTER 28

Bowen

MY CHEST TURNS TO ICE AS I WAIT FOR EVELYN'S RE-
sponse to my question. It's been so long since I've lost
control, and I don't know that it's ever happened to this degree.
Except . . . there's something that almost feels like an echo of a
memory lingering in the back of my mind, a surety that I *have*
lost control and someone I cared about died when I did. It
must've happened before I came to Threshold. It's the only explanation for the bone-deep fear that rises in response.

"I don't think so." Her expression is troubled. "I would really
like to promise you didn't hurt any of the crew, but it was pure
chaos in that moment and right afterward. I didn't see any of
them taken out by your magic, but I'm not willing to lie to you
just because I'm not sure."

I exhale in something that's almost like relief. My body
hardly feels like my own. My throat and shoulder are pulsing in
agony. I'm not sure I have the strength to move right now.

Which is a fucking problem, because we have to get off this beach. "Let's get going."

"Nox said there was a safe house thirty minutes up the coast from us. If you don't have a better idea, I think we should head for it."

A safe house? What are they talking about? That's not something the Cŵn Annwn possesses. There are permanent locations where our people can rest or recover, but they are public knowledge, at least among the crews and captains. A safe house is a secret.

Kanghri on First Sister is to the west, a port town nestled across the strait from its twin, Mairi on Second Sister. Together, they form one of the largest communities in this part of Threshold. It's not quite as large as Lyari, but no other city in this realm is as large as the capital.

I've stopped in Kanghri often enough to know some of the locals. That's where we have to go if we want to find a ship sailing south to Lyari . . . but I don't know if I'm thinking clearly. The size of Kanghri means there's plenty of danger there, and being a Cŵn Annwn has been enough protection previously, but I've never come to the city on foot, without a crew behind me. Weak. It might be fine, but I can't guarantee it.

On the other hand, Nox saved us. Maybe we should trust them.

"Let's go see the safe house. Kanghri is farther away, and Hedd and his crew will likely make port there tonight before they head back south. It would be best if we don't run into them."

"I'm not about to argue in favor of seeing that jackass again."

The walk to the safe house might be thirty minutes for a healthy, able-bodied person, but it takes us the better part of two hours to make our staggering way along the coast. Even then, we almost miss the sign Evelyn was told to look for. The crevasse leads through a narrow canyon and into an open area that houses the . . . Honestly, calling it a shack might be too generous.

I stare at the rotted boards and walls that I'm nearly certain would collapse if they weren't shoved into the narrow space between canyon walls. The roof sags precariously and there's no way it doesn't leak when it rains. If I'd happened across this place by accident, I would turn around and walk away. I certainly wouldn't risk life and limb walking through the door that's held up by a hope and some creative patching.

"For something Nox called a safe house, this doesn't seem very safe." It's a good thing it's blocked in on all sides, because a mild wind would cause it to collapse.

"Took the words . . . right out of . . . my mouth." Evelyn is propped under my arm, doing her best to keep me upright. It shames me how weak I am, but no amount of stubbornness can override my physical limitations. I can't even use my magic, either, because it's drained to dangerous levels. I'm shaking in a way that has nothing to do with my wound and everything to do with overextending myself.

We don't have any other options. We can't turn around and make the trek back to Kanghri. As much as I don't want to walk through that door, it's got to be better than sleeping in the open in damp clothes. "Let's check it out."

Pushing through the creaking door, I expect to be met with cobwebs and maybe a few mice. Instead, we walk into a cozy little living room. The furniture is all faded, but clean. Same with the floor underfoot, and the maritime paintings on the walls.

"Another pocket realm?" Evelyn gives a pained laugh. "I always thought this kind of thing was more myth than anything else, and you have them just lying around all over the place."

"They're not as common as all that," I say absently, still jarred by my expectations coming up against the reality of the room we stand in. "They're incredibly expensive, because there are only so many people who can create them. This isn't a pocket realm, though. It's clever construction and a bit of theatrics." This place doesn't seem abandoned. It almost feels like someone just stepped out, like the room is holding its breath waiting for its occupant to return. "Hello?"

"It's empty. Can you feel it?"

"All I feel is exhausted."

Evelyn gives a tired laugh. "Why don't you sit down and I'll do a little magic to make sure we're truly alone." She pauses. "But maybe you should take off your wet clothes before you do."

I don't want to admit that I don't have the strength to undress, but Evelyn senses it all the same. She slips out from under my arm and in a few minutes has divested me of all my clothes and wrapped me in a knitted blanket. She presses me down onto the couch and frowns at my throat. "Maybe we should have taken the route to the city and gotten you to a healer."

We'll have to get me properly patched up before we try to leave Three Sisters, but even if we managed to make it to the city, I don't currently have the strength to deal with Cato, the only healer I trust in Kanghri. "Do your sweep and then we'll talk."

It pains me to sit in place and wait for her to return. This building is larger that I would've guessed; several rooms seeming to be carved out of the cliff itself. It's cleverly done. Everything about this house's exterior is designed to prevent people from paying too much attention. In that, it serves its purpose as a safe house . . . but who is it a safe house for? The Cŵn Annwn don't utilize such things. They—we—operate out in the open. There's no group more powerful in Threshold, so we don't need to hide to be safe.

Evelyn returns several minutes later with another blanket. She strips with shaking hands and dumps her wet clothes in a pile next to mine. "I'll clean that up in a minute, but—"

"Come here."

Again, she doesn't argue. She slips carefully into my lap and wraps her blanket over the space mine doesn't reach. Her skin is clammy and cold and I hold her close as our temperatures start to readjust. I don't know that we're in a worse position than we were back on Sarvi, but it's certainly not better. "Once we've warmed up a little, I'll start a fire."

She points a shaking finger at the fireplace and a violet flame erupts among the wood stacked there. "Got it."

I pull her closer. "That was unnecessary. Save your strength."

"No, *you* save *your* strength." She buries her face in my chest. "There's a full working kitchen through that door. The pantry is completely stocked. I don't recognize all the food, but most of it seems to be nonperishable. There's also an ice chest filled with different prepared soups. I don't think anyone's been through here in the last couple days, but it hasn't been longer than a few weeks, either."

We aren't technically on the run. Yes, I disobeyed an order, but it was in the pursuit of doing what the Council commanded us to do. Kill the mermaids. I'm nearly certain that's not enough to get me branded as a traitor, but that's two ships turning me out in less than a week. Someone is bound to take notice if it keeps happening, and I can't see a scenario where it *doesn't* keep happening. I no longer have the ability to mindlessly obey without pushing back.

No, there has to be some other way. Some other route. Something. Because every time I misstep, I put Evelyn in danger. *Unacceptable.* "I don't know how to get you home yet, but we'll figure it out."

She lifts her head and glares at me. "Is that what you think I'm worried about right now? You almost *died.* Several times. In a very short sequence of events. If I leave now, I'm going to spend the rest of my life worried that you charged nobly into the next conflict you came across and got your silly honorable head chopped right off your shoulders." Her lower lip quivers. "Don't ask me to do that, Bowen. Either come with me ... or ..."

I can't stand to see her sad. Something almost akin to panic rises inside me, and I speak the first thing that comes to mind. "Do you know, I think there's a good chance I came from the portal on the first island where you tried to escape." I don't intend to voice the suspicion that's been growing inside me. "I knew too much about the cat-sìth. Even its name. That knowledge didn't come from being one of the Cŵn Annwn. It came from the time before."

She stares at me. "If that's true ... do you want to go through the portal? To figure out what you left behind?"

"No," I say slowly. "There's something bad lingering in the back of my mind. I suspect I'll have to deal with it eventually, but I'm not in a hurry to face it. I don't think what happened aboard the *Audacity* is the first time I lost control like that. I think last time it happened, I hurt people I didn't mean to."

"But it would be a familiar realm. That's more than we can say for most of the others. If we escape there—"

"Then nothing changes." I speak the words softly and yet they still feel like a giant boulder dropped in the middle of a still pool. It's the truth I've been working toward, the one I wasn't ready to face. What's the point of going back to the first thirteen years of my life when all I'll be able to focus on is the evil I've perpetuated through the last twenty? Because that's what it is. *Evil.*

Even now, there's a part of me that pushes back against that word. It doesn't matter. It's the truth. "I never wanted to hurt anyone. I only wanted to protect them. But what the fuck do my intentions matter when I'm serving an unjust system? I have been a tool used for reasons I don't understand yet." I look at her, knowing that my next words will be the ones that end things with her for good. "I can't change what I've done. But I can change what I do next. I want answers. More than that, I want to set things right."

Her eyes shine with unshed tears. "You're going to get yourself killed. You're only one man against how many fucking Cŵn Annwn? And that's not even getting into the Council or the elder gods that may or may not still be lurking around somewhere. What can you possibly do against those odds?"

"I don't know." I brush her hair back from her face and cup her jaw. "But if they're going to hunt me, then I'm going to give them a damn good reason to do it. Not by running away. By fighting."

The trembling in her lower lip gets more pronounced. "That is the most foolish, self-sacrificing, paladin thing you've ever said." A single tear escapes the corner of her eye. "Bunny is probably doing backflips of glee in the afterlife. She has to be, because I've never loved you more. I guess that makes me just as much a noble fool as you."

Is she saying what I think she's saying? Surely not. "But you want to go home."

"Of course I do. That realm is the only one I've ever known. It's the only one that contains places I spent time with Bunny." She takes deep breath. "But unless there's another portal home lying around . . ."

I wish I could tell her something positive. I slowly shake my head. "As far as I've experienced, there's a single portal on each island."

"A portal that's now destroyed. I have no one to blame for that but myself. But even if it was still open, I find myself in the same position that you are. I can spend the rest of my life chasing my past . . . or I can move into the future."

"Threshold is a realm of magic beyond knowing. There's nothing to say that portal was your only way home. There might be others. It's not as if I know every secret about this place."

"There's nothing to say it isn't." She shakes her head. "No. I'm not going to keep chasing a fool's dream when there's a very real fight to be had here. One that maybe I can help with. One where I might have a future."

Hope is a horrible, nebulous thing. If I don't ask the question then I can stay in this moment of not knowing. There's magic in ignorance; haven't I learned that lesson several times over by now? But if I'm going to start being brave and searching for answers, that needs to start now. "A future with me?"

It's hard to tell in the growing shadows, but I'm nearly certain that Evelyn blushes crimson. She won't quite meet my gaze. "I don't know that you want me on your side if you're starting a revolution. I'm just a witch who also happens to be good at picking pockets."

The hope in my chest unfurls with a strength that makes me want to howl at the moon. She's really saying what I didn't dare wish she'd say. She's *staying*. In Threshold. With me.

I gently urge her to face me. "There's no 'just' about it. I want you by my side. No stipulations. No conditions. No caveats. But you are a value, Evie. You ask questions that need asking, and that's worth its weight in gold. People like you, too. They're scared of me, but they instantly warm up to you." She opens her mouth, no doubt to argue some more, and I press my finger to her lips. "I understand if you don't want to fight. This isn't your battle. But never say that you're not valuable. You are to me."

"There you go again, saying all the right things."

"I never say the right things." My laugh feels choked. "Or at least you're the only one who thinks so."

She wraps her hand around my wrist and squeezes a little. "Bowen, this feels really big. Like *really* big."

"I know." In the space of a single conversation everything has changed. My heart doesn't know whether it wants to twist itself up in knots or beat right out of my chest. I can't catch my breath. "But if you change your mind—at any point—I will help you find a way home. I promise."

"I know you will." She releases my hand and slowly stands.

"It's absolute foolishness to fall in love with you, and yet here I am."

I shake my head sharply. Did she just say what I think—hope, gods, I *hope*—she said? "Say it again."

"Bowen."

"Say it again, Evie. Please."

She wets her lips, her blush a fearsome thing. "I'm falling in love with you. I'm feeling very awkward with the realization, so please don't make a big deal about it."

A big deal about it. Gods, I really do love this woman. Only she would confess something so world-shattering and ask me to pretend like it's just a normal thing to confess. When I finally manage to speak, my voice is rough. "I'm falling with you. Never think you're alone in this."

"Oh. Well. Good. Um. Yes, okay." She drags her hands through her hair and winces. "Look, I know this isn't romantic, but I'm kind of freaking out a little and we're about to embark on a freaking war against the most powerful faction in Threshold and my ex still wants to kill us, so maybe we just let this simmer for a little while?"

It's everything I can do to keep from lunging to my feet, picking her up, and spinning us around until we're both dizzy. "Okay."

"Okay. Great." She backs away slowly. "I'm going to take a shower and put on some clothes. Don't touch your wound. I don't have magic to accelerate the healing beyond whatever has already been done. That spell won't prevent you from reopening it if you fuck with it."

It's only when she walks out of the room that I collapse back against the couch. I've never been weaker in my life, more help-less, and yet I find myself grinning like a fool. *Hope*. Is that the thing I've been missing my entire life? Well, hope and Evelyn. Even a perspective change wouldn't have been enough to put me on this path without her at my shoulder, asking me questions I didn't have answers for.

Now we'll find the answers together.

CHAPTER 29

Evelyn

I CAN'T PINPOINT THE EXACT MOMENT I DECIDED TO STAY in Threshold. To stay with Bowen. Maybe it happened even before I realized I had access to a portal that would take me to a realm similar to mine. I think I started to love him when he went into the village to question the people instead of shutting me down and going after the dragon to finish the job. The feeling has only grown in the days since. Too fast. People aren't supposed to fall in love in a matter of weeks.

The people in our family fall fast, little bird. Make sure you choose someone who's worth it.

I've chosen well. I may not have known Bowen long, but I know enough to be sure of that.

I duck my head under the spray and shampoo my hair a second time. Everything about this safe house has been a surprise. After finding the magic icebox packed with food, I discovered the closets filled with clothing in a wide variety of sizes. As if they expect people coming here to show up with nothing. To be on the run. Food and clothes and shelter, just like Nox promised.

It's a shame that the *Audacity* has sailed away by now. I have some questions for the quartermaster. They saved our lives, and that would've been enough. But directing us here? It's another journey in waiting. Another mystery tempting me to unravel it.

This isn't a safe house for the Cŵn Annwn. Which leads me to wonder if it's a safe house *from* the Cŵn Annwn.

It makes sense. Not that Nox would be connected to it, but that there would be an underground rebellion of sorts. It's interesting how Bowen doesn't seem to recognize this for what it is, which means he's never come in contact with any kind of pushback. So maybe that's not what this rebellion is doing. Maybe they're secreting people out of Threshold. If Bowen's belief about the vow being linked to tracking is true—and at this point, I question everything—then the people who come through here must have been found by the resistance before the Cŵn Annwn got ahold of them and forced the vow.

Do they send them home? Or do they shift them to places on Threshold where they can be folded into the community without having to become monster hunters?

Too many questions, but at least these ones give me hope. It's much easier to join with an already established resistance than it is to build one from the ground up. Infrastructure is invaluable. Based on the readiness of this safe house, Nox's people have it.

I turn off the water and get dressed in the borrowed clothes I found in a dresser in the bedroom. They don't fit in a particularly flattering way, but that's just as well. The muted browns and grays and greens available suggest they were picked for their ability to blend in.

I braid my hair and return to find Bowen dozing on the couch. His big body is sprawled out, legs hanging over the edge. He's still too pale, but the steady rise and fall of his chest is reassuring. Tenderness nearly takes me out at the knees. He's so fucking fearsome and powerful, but right now he's vulnerable and trusting me enough to not bother to hide it. It makes me want to wrap him up and take him somewhere safe where he doesn't have to fight anymore. It makes me want to stand at his back and support him while he does what's necessary to balance the scales in his head.

I clear my throat, announcing my presence. "Shower's open. Be very careful with your neck." He doesn't look too good. When he stands up, he moves with the careful way of someone devastatingly injured. "If you need help—"

"If you help me in the shower, I'll be tempted to help you out of those clothes."

I blink. "There you go, being charming again. You have a terrible sense of timing. Don't look at me like that. With all the blood you lost, if you get an erection right now, you're going to die. Do you really want *that* on my conscience?"

He huffs out a laugh. "I wouldn't dream of burdening you like that, Evie. Why don't you get us some food started instead?"

"Now you have me playing little wife." I grin, but my amusement falls away at the hungry expression on his face. Oh, yeah, he wants *that*. Very much. "Go shower before you get us into trouble." To prevent myself from indulging in temptation, I head into the small kitchen.

Much like the bathroom, the more I snoop, the more questions I have about the magic required to keep this running. It's not cheap, and it would require someone to maintain it. Which supports my suspicion that the safe house is being used regularly. I was too tired to pay much attention to the terrain we walked through to get here, but it was mostly rocks and cliffs and dirt. Nothing particularly foreign to my realm, but nothing easily identifiable, either. As a result, I can't say much about the realm this island must have a portal to.

In the icebox, there is food in packages in neat little rows, each labeled with a painstakingly neat hand. I don't recognize the language on sight, but the letters form into squiggles and then morph into English. Translation spell. As I found out earlier, it's a bunch of different kinds of soup, all precooked and just needing to be heated. I grab the beef stew and find a pot to cook it in.

Then I go hunting.

I don't expect to find much; no safe house is perfectly safe. If the Cŵn Annwn were to find this place, whoever owns it wouldn't want to give them a list of clues. But people are people, and people like to leave their mark. I hit pay dirt in the second bedroom. The top drawer is empty, and when I start tapping on it, I find a false bottom. "Ha. Oldest trick in the book."

Inside is an old, weathered book. A book filled with writing from one hundred different hands in dozens of different languages, though there must be a translation spell on this as well because they morph into English before my eyes. I carefully turn the pages. I don't know how they mark time here in Threshold, but it's clear that this goes back decades, at least.

I turn to the most recent entry and settle down to read.

I'll keep this short, because the last thing I want to do is cause harm to those who have helped me. If this book is any indication, I'm not the first, and I likely won't be the last. I knew better than to be drinking on the night of the new moon, and I was surely taught not to wander the woods. A fairy circle. What a fucking joke. I thought they were myth, and yet I ended up here. In a place where none of the rules make sense. It's sheer dumb luck that one of them found me instead of the Cŵn Annwn. If it had been the latter, I don't think I would've lasted the fortnight. I'm not a warrior. I have little magic to speak of.

And now I'm going home. Tomorrow, I will follow the instructions I was given, and hike to the north side of the island. There, I will hope with everything I have that I am being steered by benevolent instructions, and I will walk into the red-capped fairy circle. If everything goes as I was promised, it will take me back to my realm.

If you're reading this, they must've helped you, too. I hope you're able to return home.

Safe travels.

—Tom

"I *knew* it."

"Knew what?"

I look up to find Bowen leaning against the doorframe. He seems a little better now that he's showered, but he's still too pale. I also highly suspect the reason he's leaning is because he can't stand straight on his own reliably. I pat the bed next to me. "Come look at this."

He joins me and peers over my shoulder as I read through a few other entries. Some of them are long. Some are short. All are from people relieved to be heading through a portal and out of Threshold before the Cŵn Annwn can coerce them into making a vow. Considering who sent us here, I have to believe that at least a few of the Cŵn Annwn are part of this network. Nox is more than proof of that, but there have to be more.

Bowen trails his finger down one page. "A couple weeks ago, I would have called this treason."

"I know."

He's silent for quite some time. I let him think as I continue reading through the entries. My curiosity about these people, about how they got here, about how they're getting home . . . it's like a live thing inside me. I won't pretend that I've been altruistic for any part of my life. Bunny had a strange way of looking at that sort of thing. Or maybe not so strange at all. She charged through the nose for her services, but more than once, I caught her slipping spells to people who never could've afforded her prices. I've done the same.

This is different.

This is . . . *purpose*.

"As a former captain, no one helping these people will believe that I genuinely want to be part of this group out of the goodness of my soul. They'll assume I'm a plant."

I carefully close the book and give him my full attention. "For a lot of people, they'll look at your actions over the last twenty years. It will take time for you to prove that you're something more than that man." I make a face. "Though I'm not exactly sure how to handle that without getting us both killed by the Cŵn Annwn."

"Yes . . . that's something I'm considering, as well." He frowns. "But then again, Nox is part of the Cŵn Annwn. It appears that they're also part of this movement. I'm not sure how they manage that while being quartermaster to Hedd. There's no way that *he's* aware of this."

"Agreed." I shudder. From what I know of that man, he's more likely to behead someone seeking sanctuary than to give them the means to return to their realm. "But if Nox is managing to pull it off, then I bet there are others, too. There have to be for this to work. They can't be operating alone. This is too organized for a single person to be behind it. Maybe there's a way to look like we're fulfilling our vows, but to work against the Cŵn Annwn."

He stabs a single finger against the cover of the book. "Perhaps. But I find that I no longer have the stomach for monster killing. We'll have to find another way. One that doesn't paint a target on our backs in the process."

I lean against his shoulder carefully. "What if we're just very bad at what we do? We'll try really hard, but those wily monsters will slip through our fingers again and again. Except mermaids. Fuck those mermaids."

Bowen chuckles. "We don't have to have all the answers right now. We'll stay the night here and then head into the city tomorrow."

I don't want to go into town. I want to stay in this strange, magical place where possibilities seem endless and we don't have to make hard decisions. It's a silly dream. Life is full of hard decisions, and if we mean to work against the Cŵn Annwn, then we have to figure out how to thread the needle. But he's right; we don't have to figure it out tonight.

"Let's eat." I stand and offer my hand. It's a testament to how shaky Bowen is that he accepts it and allows me to tug him gently to his feet. Worry is a physical thing inside me. He needs to see a healer. A proper one. The wound isn't infected or actively bleeding, but now that he's clean, we definitely need to bandage it at least. "But first, I'm going to play nurse."

I lead him to the kitchen and urge him into the chair. A quick stir of the stew reveals it's almost ready. I have just enough time to slap a bandage on this man. In my initial search, I found first aid kits—or at least Threshold's version of them—in every single room. I can appreciate the level of preparedness, but it does make me wonder how many times people end up here while bleeding out.

It's not a comforting thought.

Bowen holds still as I carefully apply the bandage to his neck. The only nurse I've ever played is the sexy kind, but it's a fucking bandage. It's not rocket science. Even so, I can't help being afraid that I'm messing this up. If he dies because of my ineptitude, I don't know how I'll live with myself.

"Evie." He covers my hands with his and gently guides them away from the bandage. "It's okay. I'll be okay."

I worry at my bottom lip. "All my magic did was stop the bleeding. Those mermaid teeth looked vicious. Even if they're not poisonous, there's no way you didn't get some gross ocean bacteria into the wound. Maybe we should head into town tonight. I don't know if it's a good idea to wait."

"Evie," he says my name again, and I don't think I really registered that he'd started shortening my name. It just sort of happened—kind of like falling for him.

"Bowen." My voice is a little wobbly, but my world is a little wobbly right now. "I'm worried about you."

"I know." There's so much satisfaction in his tone, my knees go a little weak. He smiles. "This is not the first mermaid bite I've lived through. The previous ones didn't get infected, and I doubt this one will, either. Even so, it will hold until we go to Cato tomorrow. Ze's good at zir job, and ze'll put me back together again without a problem."

The way he says that makes me think that this Cato has healed him from significantly worse, which does little to help my blood pressure. I've seen the map of scars across his body. I know he's lived through a lot of horrific injuries, but that isn't reason enough to get careless now. "It would be very foolish of you to die over something incredibly preventable."

"I'm not going to die. At least not yet." He turns my hands over and presses a kiss to each palm. "You saved my life, and you've bandaged me up. The wound is clean. Let's eat and sleep; that will do more to help than anything else."

I highly suspect that he's being a bit patronizing right now, but it comforts me all the same. If he feels well enough to be high and mighty, then he's not knocking on death's door.

The trick is keeping him from doing something foolish.

CHAPTER 30

Bowen

THE BED IS SMALLER THAN I WOULD PREFER, BUT THE UP-side is that Evelyn ends up sprawled across my chest. She falls asleep within minutes, her body loose with exhaustion and her breathing steady. Her presence is almost enough to combat the fears that come in the dark.

Nothing about this world is what I thought it was.

Not the Cŵn Annwn. Not the people. Not even the monsters.

There's only one person who might be able to give me answers, and they are currently sailing away on the *Audacity*. Sometimes it's months before we see the same ship again. Sometimes even longer. The only regularity among the Cŵn Annwn is the requirement to visit Lyari on an annual basis to present ourselves to the Council.

I always thought those annual visits were a waste of time, an unnecessary presentation of everything we've accomplished since we last stood before the Council. They already know the details of each hunt we embark on, courtesy of the required reports we submit through the magical relay system in each captain's desk.

Now I wonder.

Are those visits meant to reinforce the authority of the Council, to remind us who we answer to—and the consequences of betrayal? I've heard of captains being stripped of their position, but I've never heard of anyone being put to death because they were part of a resistance against the Cŵn Annwn. Which doesn't mean it never happened . . . only that the Council didn't want to advertise that a resistance exists in the first place.

Nox would know, I bet.

I have no idea where Hedd is headed next, which means I have no idea where his quartermaster will be next. And they are the only person who can tell me what the fuck is going on. If they knew the location of this safe house, knew to send us here, then they have sent others. I don't know if this underground organization has a leader, but if it does then I need to find them.

The problem is that they're not going to allow themselves to be found by someone like me. Not until I prove I'm not a danger to them. I don't know how to go about doing that without Nox. If I can convince *them*, then maybe they can vouch for me.

Evelyn lets out a cute little snore, and I cuddle her closer. No matter what else is true, I have her. She's choosing me, the same way I'm choosing her. I just have to work hard to ensure I'm not signing her death warrant. This journey we're on won't be safe. But then, what about life *is* safe?

When Evelyn said she'd spend the rest of her days worried about me getting myself killed . . . I feel the same. If she left, I would spend the rest of my years wondering if she had many decades filled with joy and happiness before going out at the end of a life well-lived. It would drive me mad. I'd made my peace with that knowledge that I would always feel like I was missing part of myself once she walked out of my life.

I haven't had a chance to really process that she's staying. That she's here in my arms with no intention of leaving.

I want to be worthy of this woman's love. No matter what she says or thinks, I'm not there yet. Maybe I never will be. But that just means I'll fight all the harder to honor her.

Her steady heartbeat soothes my racing thoughts and I find myself matching her slow inhales and exhales, my body getting heavy. I wrap my arms more firmly around her, letting the feel of her tempt me into closing my eyes. I fall asleep without any concrete answers, only the assurance that I'll never get used to sleeping with Evelyn.

To waking up with the scent of her surrounding me.

When I open my eyes, the woman herself, however, is gone.

Moving hurts. I take stock as I sit up, but there's no sharp pain. Just general bruises and exhaustion from the fight yesterday. My neck is the worst of it, throbbing in time with my heartbeat. I meant what I said, that I've been bitten by mermaids before and I've never seen an infection as a result. But Evelyn is right that we need to see a healer. Just in case. It would be unforgivable to let arrogance be my downfall.

It's time to make the trek to Kanghri and throw ourselves on Cato's nebulous mercy.

I find Evelyn in the kitchen, reheating another soup. When I raise my brows, she shrugs. "There's not much in the way of perishables, and I don't recognize most of the stuff in the pantry. So soup for breakfast it is."

"I'm not complaining."

"That's because you're a very smart man with good survival instincts." She barely lets me take a spoonful of the soup before she says, "I understand if you don't want to talk about it, but I just want to put this out there. It's okay to be conflicted about your past. Both the past with the Cŵn Annwn and what came before. If there ever comes a time when you want to take a break from fighting for the greater good to find answers, I support that. I support whatever you need to do."

"I love you." Three simple words, and yet they shift my entire world on its axis. I hold her gaze. "I appreciate the offer and the support, but I meant what I said last night. Whatever answers my home realm offers, it ultimately doesn't matter."

"Maybe it doesn't matter now, but that might change. You're too paladin not to feel guilty if your personal questions override your cause. I'm just preemptively telling you that there's nothing to be guilty about. No matter where you land on it."

It's tempting to brush off the statement again, but she's right. "Thank you for preemptively absolving me of my guilt." I grin.

"Oh, don't play with me like that. You seem the type to adore your guilt. You find it highly motivating. It's okay. It's part of what makes you so lovable." She pokes at her soup. "But don't think you can distract me with all the love talk, even though I will never get tired of hearing those three words on your lips. You are seeing a healer today. End of story."

I like how concerned she is about me. I don't want her to worry, but it warms me all the same. It's far too tempting to tease her over it, but I resist the urge. Barely. "Agreed. It's been some time since I've traveled up this way, but if Cato is still in Kanghri, ze can finish patching me up."

She gives me a long look as if I'm trying to trick her. "No arguments?"

"I'm a smart man, Evelyn, despite recent evidence to the contrary. Arguing for the sake of arguing is silly in this situation. We need me at full health to face our next steps."

"Uh-huh." She shakes her head. "Hurry up and eat, and let's get moving."

It's not quite as quick as all that. Before we leave, we take the extra effort to ensure the safe house is exactly as we found it. I find a rack of wood tucked against the back of the building. There isn't much in the way of trees on First Sister, so they have to haul the wood in with the other supplies. More indication of care and planning going into keeping this place ready for unexpected travelers. I bring some in to replenish the stack by the fire. It's time that we could spend traveling, but it feels important to do this.

I find Evelyn sitting on the bed, holding the book again. "Do you want to write an entry of your own?"

"No." She sets the book back in the drawer and replaces the false bottom. "This is for people going home. We're going to be the ones helping those people. It's better that there's no evidence of us here."

She's right. That doesn't mean I like the bittersweet look on her face. "Are you sure?"

"Yes." She rises and brushes off her pants. "I'm not going to pretend that I won't miss things about my realm. But ultimately, it's like yours—in my past. Threshold. You. This rebellion, or whatever the fuck it is. That's my future."

I do her the courtesy of not commenting on the bruised look in her green eyes when she speaks. This, at least, I understand. We've both lost quite a bit to get to this point. Having a direction to head, a place to dig in and fight . . . it doesn't make that loss go away.

Instead, I hold out my hand. "Let's go."

"Lead on, Captain."

It takes longer than I would like to hike to Kanghri. After some debate, we decided not to take the most direct route. The location of the safe house isn't exactly hard to find if someone is searching for it, but there's no reason to advertise its presence—or that it's in active use. Most of First Sister is deserted cliffside, with the majority of the population of Three Sisters residing on Second Sister. The sole exception is Kanghri, but it exists only because Mairi essentially overflowed its banks and needed somewhere to shove all the people who couldn't afford to live on Second Sister. As a result, Kanghri is filled with tradespeople, rather than what passes for nobility in this part of Threshold.

Personally, I prefer Kanghri to Mairi for that very reason. It's less pretentious for the sake of appearances. A waste of time and resources in my opinion.

We follow the coast to the south and then west toward the strait that runs between First and Second Sister. The sun is just starting its descent as we reach the edges of town. I reach out and grab Evelyn's elbow. "Stay close to me."

She raises her brows. "Is this place more dangerous than the ones we've been to so far?"

"In some ways." For all that I prefer Kanghri to Mairi, I am not oblivious to its faults. Most of the tradespeople who work in Mairi live in this town, but there are a number of less than reputable businesses that run here as well. Each community in

Threshold is technically self-governed, but the local authority in Kanghri is mostly for show. The true power runs behind the scenes and prefers to deal in the shadows. As Cŵn Annwn, it was not my domain to worry about local crime lords, but it still makes my skin prickle to walk down the streets of Kanghri. Today is no exception.

The sensation has nothing to do with the eclectic group of beings already out and about currently. The population of Kanghri is more diverse than anywhere else on Threshold. It's not just people who are local to the realm on the other side of the island's portal who reside here. They're tall and gaunt to the point of being eerie, their skin various shades of gray that match the rocks that create most of the island of First Sister. Their fingers have several more digits than humans and their joints bend both ways, the better to climb with.

Intermixed with them are people who look human enough that they could have come from half a dozen different realms. There are also small populations of minotaurs, satyrs, and Aadi's people. The name for the latter is a series of clicks and whistles that is incredibly difficult to replicate without a beak.

No, what makes my instincts spring to alert is the feeling of being watched that plagues me from the moment I pass into the town limits. I've never actually seen someone watching me— and I certainly don't today—but the sensation is there, pressing uncomfortably against my skin. "Just stay near me and don't steal anything."

"Okay, look, I know I stole from you the moment we met, and yes, I did lift a few things off Hedd when we were on his ship, but . . ."

I take several steps, only to realize that she's not at my side. I curse. "Evelyn—"

"Oh *fuck*."

I spin around, responding to the fear in her voice. She's not looking at me. She's not even looking in the direction we are headed. She's half turned to where we can see the docks. This late in the day, the space is filled with people coming back from work in Mairi. The crowds are quiet and orderly, no one pushing or shoving. There's nothing there that should put *that* tone in her voice. Except . . . On my second look, I realize what caused her fear. Or, rather, who.

Lizzie.

As if she can hear my very thoughts, the dark-haired vampire pivots in our direction. She's wearing different clothing than the last time we saw her—her fitted pants and shirt obviously sourced from somewhere on Threshold—but she still has that damned rifle over her shoulder. I can't see her eyes clearly at this distance, but there's no mistaking the way the hair on the back of my neck stands on end. She's seen us. *Fuck.* "If we go into town—"

"It won't work. We can't be sure she won't cause a scene. And if she does, other people will get hurt." Evelyn takes several steps back, heading toward the cliffs we just came from. "We have to eliminate the possibility of collateral damage. Which means we have to run. Now."

There's no time to argue. Not when Lizzie is heading in our direction, her long legs eating up the distance. Even the crowd isn't enough to slow her down. People scatter in front of her, minnows before a shark.

I'm right on Evelyn's heels as we race out of town. This feels like a mistake, but she's right. We can't afford a massacre. Both for the loss of life, and for the attention it would attract from both local authorities and the Cŵn Annwn. The problem is that I am nowhere near full strength; not magically, and sure as fuck not physically.

Lizzie almost killed me last time. As much as I would like to blame that fight on a similar level of exhaustion, the truth is that the more I think about it, the more I am certain that she could take me even at full strength. Her concentration is too good, and her powers are too fearsome.

If she can take me, then she will certainly kill Evelyn.

We careen around the corner, breaking the line of sight. I hook Evelyn around the waist and steer her toward a narrow canyon that's almost invisible from this angle. "Go in there. Hide. Create a shield. I'll lead her off and handle this."

Her breath comes just as harshly as mine. We haven't even run that long, but after the fight yesterday and the long trek to town today, our stamina is at an all-time low. That doesn't stop Evelyn from glaring at me fiercely enough that I actually take a step back. She points a finger in my direction. "You did not give me all those honorable speeches last night and this morning only to kill yourself by way of my ex-girlfriend."

"I thought you said she wasn't your girlfriend."

Her jaw drops. "Of all the silly, useless things to focus on right now. I swear to the gods, Bowen—"

She never gets a chance to finish that sentence. A wave of agony hits me so hard that I stagger. It doesn't stop. Instead my body lifts and flies several feet to slam against the cliff wall. I grunt in pain as I crumple to the ground.

"No more running, Evelyn." The vampire is barely out of breath, and even in my current state, I have the presence of mind to wonder if she has to breathe at all. I suppose it doesn't matter; she doesn't need breath to kill me. She's doing a damn good job of it.

"Stop it, Lizzie!"

I can't make my eyes focus. I get the sense of movement and when the vampire speaks next, she's significantly closer. "That's not going to protect you. You're wasting your time."

"It's not to protect me, you stubborn bitch." Evelyn snarls out several words and her magic snaps around me. Between one beat and the next, she breaks Lizzie's hold on me. The pain fades to a horrible throbbing, but at least it's no longer acute. A shield. My brilliant witch put up a shield to protect us. But when I roll onto my side, my relief drains away into horror. She put up a shield, all right.

Around me. Only me.

On the other side of her pulsing magic, Evelyn climbs slowly to her feet and walks to meet the vampire.

CHAPTER 31

Evelyn

I'VE DONE A LOT OF FOOLISH THINGS SINCE ARRIVING AT Threshold, but this has to top the list. I can't take Lizzie in a fair fight, and I probably can't even take her in a dirty fight. She's too fucking powerful.

And the worst part is that she's never looked better than she does right now.

Back in our realm, the only time she let down her hair, figuratively and otherwise, was in bed. The rest of the time she was perfectly polished and put together. Not so right now. She's wearing tight leather breeches and a shirt that clings to her lean form. Her dark hair, normally pulled back from her face, whips around her in the wind coming off the sea.

"This ends here."

She shrugs off her rifle and tosses it to the ground next to her. "Give me one good reason why I shouldn't skin you alive and carve you up into little pieces."

Fear shorts out what little logical thought I have. It's the only explanation for running my mouth at a time like this. "Oh, I don't know, maybe because I was the best sex you've ever had. Maybe because the main reason you're so pissed right now is because I left you, instead of the other way around. How about that?"

She makes a sound like an angry teakettle and then her power is in my blood, freezing me in place as she stalks closer. She stops a few inches away and her dark gaze flicks over my shoulder to where Bowen is yelling something incomprehensible. "Maybe I won't kill you. Perhaps I'll just finish the job I started with that little worm. And then you can live the rest of your life knowing that you're the reason he's dead. You have too much heart for *that* not to eat you alive."

I have no idea why she hasn't killed me yet. It doesn't make any fucking sense, and my bravado once again has me speaking without thinking. "Oh, baby, are you jealous? It's not like you wanted to keep me when you had me."

She grabs my chin, her grip so tight that I make a pained sound before I can stop myself. She doesn't relent. Of course she doesn't relent; Lizzie has never been one to show mercy. Her nails prick my skin. "Where are my jewels, Evelyn?"

Right. She hasn't killed me because she still needs me around. Her vengeance matters less to her than retrieving the things I stole. There's absolutely no reason for that to sting as much as it does. It's nothing more than I expected. But, damn it, it *does* sting. "Did the missing heirlooms anger Mommy dearest? Poor thing. Always dancing to her tune. I should've known that being in another realm entirely wouldn't be enough to break the leash she has on you."

Lizzie gives me a shake that makes my spine scream in protest. "Always. So. Difficult."

Honestly, it's kind of amazing that she hasn't broken my jaw with her hand. I know she's capable of it. Her hold hurts, but it's not doing permanent damage. I'm a fool for letting that knowledge feed my bravado. "What can I say? You bring out my perverse side. You used to like that about me."

She snarls in my face, more animalistic than I've ever seen her. "I will fucking rip your heart out and eat it, Evelyn. Don't test me."

I almost point out that she's very nearly quoting one of my favorite movies, but she's distracted and I'm not going to get another chance like this again. I slice my nail across my palm and slap it to my chest. She barely has a chance to tense when I snap out the words to trigger the spell.

It's the same one I used the first day on the *Crimson Hag* and again back on the island that contained my portal home. My magic hits her in the center of her body and sends her hurtling away. She takes a bit of my skin with her, her claws scratching my face in the process. It's not going to be enough to kill her, and fool that I am, even with the threat of her right in front of me, I can't bring myself to summon fire.

I don't know what the fuck is wrong with me. Normally I'm not one to let something like being sentimental color my actions. But this is *Lizzie*, and she . . . "You were going to let your mother kill me! You didn't even give me a way out! And now you're pissed that I found an escape and took a little something with me to *survive*? Fuck you very much, Lizzie!"

Nearly fifty feet away, she staggers to her feet. She's bleeding from several long cuts on her arms and face. I watched in horror as she draws the blood from her skin and forms it into a knife.

Within seconds, the cuts themselves vanish, courtesy of her accelerated healing.

I am so fucked.

I draw Bowen's dagger from its sheath at my hip. Bunny made sure I had plenty of self-defense training, but in the years since she passed, I've forgotten to practice more often than I've remembered. A good thief doesn't need to defend themselves; they're there and gone before anyone knows the valuables are missing. The last fight I had was a drunken brawl in a bar, and very few people are actually trying to kill each other in drunken brawls. It's just a bit of fun to let off some steam.

I can't say the same for *this* fight. If I don't win, she'll kill Bowen. That, I can't allow. I take a breath and brace myself, and then she's on me.

Fast. Lizzie is so fucking fast. I barely manage to deflect her strikes, and even then, I am nearly certain she's pulling her punches. I'm not this good. It's just reality. She could have killed me several times over, and I'm starting to think her holding back has nothing to do with keeping me alive to find her jewels.

Which doesn't make any fucking sense. She didn't care about my life when I was in her bed. Why the hell would she care about it now? "You were going to let me *die*," I repeat. My breath is fire in my lungs. Gods, I would've thought my stamina would be better after all the time working on the ship, but I've never been a match for Lizzie. No human is.

"You really believe I was going to let you die?" She slips under my guard and draws a shallow, fiery line over my stomach. "Why do you think I was there to catch you stealing my family heirlooms, Evelyn? Because I came back to get you out!"

"Don't lie to me!" I stumble back. "You were in that room for the jewels. Not for me."

Bowen is still banging on the shield, which is draining my magical reserves faster than I would like. I can't keep this up indefinitely. If I hit her with fire, it might be enough to override her healing magic. Again, I hesitate even as the little voice in the back of my mind screams at me to finish this.

"I knew you'd get out. You're too smart not to." Her eyes are glowing crimson. "I didn't think you'd steal from me in the process."

I shuffle back a few more steps and give a half-hearted stab. Suddenly I'm not so sure I'm right. She *was* in that room when I went through the portal, and even if she was there for her family heirlooms, that meant she went back to her bedroom.

It means she went back for me.

"Why didn't you just fucking *say* that, Lizzie? For someone who normally acts like they're charged by the word, you sure as shit have a lot to say today."

She gives another of those snarls that make my skin prickle in terror. She's losing her temper in a way I've never seen. Normally, when Lizzie is angry, she goes cold. There's nothing cold about her now—she's all frenzy. She comes at me far faster than I can meet, leaving a trail of tiny cuts in her wake. "You are the most aggravating person I've ever met. Impulsive, reckless, and downright suicidal at times."

"You sure did like the things I do with my tongue, though."

She hisses. "The jewels. Where the fuck are my jewels? Don't make me torture you, Evelyn. I'll do it."

That's the thing . . . I'm starting to think she won't. She could have ended this fight dozens of times since it started. Gods, she could have ended it *before* it started if she'd used her magic on me. She didn't. I might be bleeding from a dozen places, but they're nothing a quick bandage can't fix. Even my jaw is only slightly sore. She's been holding back. She doesn't want to kill me any more than I want to kill her.

The trick is getting her to admit it.

I slap my bleeding hand to my chest again, triggering the second attack. It's the last one I have of this nature. She curses as she goes spinning into the air. This time, she hits a tree hard enough to make me wince. It doesn't matter. She'll be fine.

She limps to her feet, her hair matted to her face with blood. "I'm going to fucking *kill* you." She charges me.

"No, you're not." I drop my dagger to the ground and spread my arms. My body is shaking from the fight and the use of magic and Bowen's renewed attack on my shield, but I manage to keep my feet as she skids to a stop in front of me.

She lifts her blood dagger, expression murderous. "I'm not bluffing."

"Neither am I." I move slowly and grip the front of my already gaping shirt, tugging until one of the buttons pops. "Here's a nice open target for you."

She grabs the back of my neck and drags me to her blade, forcing me closer until it pierces my skin over my heart. "I'm very good at finding things, Evelyn." She speaks softly, intimately. "I found you twice in as many weeks. You don't think I can find my family heirlooms without you? Don't tempt me."

She's still threatening instead of killing. I'm right. At least, I hope I'm right. "How long do you think you can avoid the Cŵn Annwn in the search of yours? The fact that you managed to do it this long is a small miracle."

She curses and shoves me down. I land on my ass hard enough to knock the breath from my lungs. I'm slightly gratified when Lizzie drops down next to me. She throws her blood blade to the ground, and it shifts back to liquid almost instantly. "There's nothing to keep me from killing my way through the lot of them. It might be fun."

I snort. This is the Lizzie I know. I'm still not entirely certain the threat has passed, but if she's willing to talk, I'll do my best not to incite her further. Probably. "You would take a lot of them down before they finally cut you to pieces, but it's a game of numbers, and you don't have the advantage. Not to mention, this whole damn realm is water. Your chance of stealing a ship and remaining undetected is almost nonexistent." I watch her out of the corner of my eye. "But you already knew that, didn't you?"

"Just tell me where, Evelyn."

At this point, there's no advantage in keeping the information from her. "You know, if you'd ask questions instead of coming through the portal ready to blow our heads off, we could have saved a lot of time and energy. I didn't even mean to steal them. I was just so angry at you, and you know how comforting I find stealing when I'm upset."

She lifts a brow, the imperious expression on her face all the more horrifying because she's covered in blood. "It's a terrible coping skill."

"I'm not arguing that." I very carefully don't look over my shoulder to where Bowen has gone quiet. Thank the gods he has the wherewithal to realize we're poised on the knife's edge. One wrong move starts the fight again. "Your jewels are on the *Crimson Hag*. They tossed me off the crew after I interfered with them killing a dragon. I didn't have a chance to collect my things in the process."

She exhales a soft curse. "That's convenient. How do I know you're not lying?"

"Easy." I almost slump against her shoulder before I remember we aren't not-girlfriends anymore, and she's been definitely trying to kill me for the last couple weeks. "You know how much shit I took. Do you really think I have it hidden on my body?"

"It would be simpler if you did." She pinches the bridge of her nose. "I guess it's time to steal a ship, then."

I blink. "That is a huge leap of logic. How the fuck are you going to get anywhere? And did you forget about the entire realm of hostile motherfuckers who don't take kindly to trespassers?" A tug on my magic makes me turn my head to find Bowen leaning with one arm braced over his head against the shield. His expression is thunderous, and it's aimed directly at me. *Fuck.*

"If I let him out, do you think you can resist the urge to attempt to murder him?"

"Evelyn, I am still fighting the urge to murder you. I make no promises."

Not the most optimistic statement, but I don't think it's going to get better. I take in a slow breath and concentrate on breaking the circle. In seconds, Bowen is at my side. His hands clench as if he wants to grab me and drag me away from Lizzie, to put as much distance between us as possible.

Instead, he drops down next to me. "If you ever do that again, I'm going to put you over my knee and paddle your ass until it's purple."

Lizzie lets out a musical laugh. "Oh, you're obviously new to this. Adorable." Her tone says that she finds him anything but.

If I don't rein this in, we're going to end up in a bloodbath. Again. "You can't just go around stealing ships, Lizzie. Someone will report it to the Cŵn Annwn, and then this only ends with your death."

"Perhaps." She shrugs a single shoulder. "But if the ship I steal is one of the Cŵn Annwn ships with those distinctive crimson sails . . ."

"Hard to sell it as one of ours—theirs—without a crew," Bowen rumbles.

"Don't need much of a crew. With the amount of magic seeped into those boards, I'd wager those fucking ships practically sail themselves—at least long enough to get me where I need to go." She pushes to her feet, and my pride doesn't hate the fact that she stumbles a little. "There's one of the crimson-sailed motherfuckers just off the coast right now. The gossip says they had a rough go of it fighting some mermaids. I just need to kill enough of the crew for the rest of them to agree to work with me. Simple."

She pauses and looks at us. "Well?"

"Well, what?"

"Are you coming or what?"

CHAPTER 32

Bowen

I DON'T KNOW IF MY HEARTBEAT IS EVER GOING TO RE-
turn to normal. Watching Evelyn attempt to fight this monster of a vampire, knowing she's willing to sacrifice her life to
save me? I've never experienced fear like that. I still don't quite
understand how the fight turned from verbal to physical to
verbal again, but it's increasingly clear that these two have an
incredibly complicated relationship. There's a part of me that
wonders if Evelyn will want to take things up with her ex now
that they're no longer literally at each other's throats, but she
slumps against me and leaves her head on my shoulder as we
watch the vampire pace.

"That's a terrible plan, Lizzie," Evelyn says conversationally.
"The crew you don't kill will just wait until you sleep and then
slit your throat. You might survive it, but if they toss you into
the water and start pelting magic at your head, even you would
have a hard time walking that off."

It's just starting to register what ship the vampire's talking about. The *Audacity*. She hasn't sailed away, and it's impossible to say if it's because the losses were greater than I realized, or if Hedd is having some kind of drunken binge in victory. With him, he could go either way.

But it means they're not out of reach.

It means *Nox* isn't out of reach.

I clear my throat. "It would be challenging to pull off by yourself, but with three of us, as long as we can deal with Hedd, it's an all-but-guaranteed victory. At least with *that* ship, and *that* crew."

Evelyn straightens and gives me a long look. "What are you saying?"

"I don't know why Nox has allowed themself to remain as quartermaster. Maybe it's like they told you and they don't have the votes, or maybe they have other reasons. But if we kill Hedd—and his most loyal supporters—then we're looking at a very different crew. One that can give us answers." I glance at Lizzie. "One that should be able to chase down the *Crimson Hag* to retrieve your stolen goods."

Evelyn looks unconvinced, her mouth tight. "You don't think killing half a Cŵn Annwn crew *and* the captain will bring attention to us? I thought that's the last thing we wanted."

Normally, I would agree wholeheartedly. But there's one specific detail working in our favor right now. One that gives us a chance of pulling this off when we'd never be able to otherwise. "You heard the vampire."

"I have a name," Lizzie snaps.

I ignore her. "The only thing known on First Sister is that the crew of the *Audacity* sustained enough losses when fighting the mermaids to prevent them from coming ashore or leaving immediately. It's not inconceivable that a large part of the crew would die. It's happened before. More times than I would like to think about. If the remaining crew is ... motivated ... to embrace that as truth, who's to say any different?" It would require Nox massaging the report a little, but I suspect that wouldn't take much convincing.

If Hedd was anyone else, he'd have already filed his write-up of the end of the hunt, but he's notorious for being late on such things. His laziness is our boon right now.

Not to mention, if we have Nox in close quarters, they can't dodge our questions forever. We can find out more about the network of safe houses used to send people home. We can find the best place in the underground organization to be the most helpful.

And we have the best chance of staying alive while doing it.

Lizzie crosses her arms over her chest and glares down at us. "This plan—*my* plan—is all well and good, but neither of you is at full health currently. You're dead weight. You're about to pass out, Evelyn. And you." She turns her cold shark eyes on me. "All it would take is one good hit to put you in the grave. Maybe I should put you out of your misery and take care of it right now." She flashes her fangs.

"Lizzie, we're past the point of threats. If you could do this on your own, you would've already done it and you wouldn't practically be rolling out the welcome mat inviting us on to be part of your murder party. You want your jewels. They're on the *Crimson Hag*, and you need our help to get them back without bringing the whole of the Cŵn Annwn down on you." Evelyn uses my shoulder to push to her feet. "We're going to town right now to get patched up, and then we'll board the ship under the cover of darkness."

The vampire's lips thin, but something almost like amusement flickers over her face. "I see that you've embraced the pirate life."

"Of course I have. Swashbuckling, thieving, and looking good while doing it? It's like it was made for me."

"Mm-hmm. And I'm sure the fact that the Cŵn Annwn murders all nonhuman beings while calling them monsters doesn't offend your soft, beating heart."

"Oh, that?" Evelyn waves that away. "We're just going to have to bring down the Cŵn Annwn. Easy peasy."

The vampire laughs, and I find it upsetting that the sound is particularly pleasing. I suppose it makes sense though. Vampires are predators, through and through. It makes sense that everything about them is designed to draw in unsuspecting humans. My power shifts around me, but I make an effort to calm it. Our plan isn't foolproof, but it's also not the worst I've come up with. However, if Evelyn and I try to do it without the help of the vampire, we'll have a significantly more difficult time.

Besides, there's nothing to stop me from tossing Lizzie in the ocean if she becomes too much of a threat.

I stagger to my feet, ignoring Evelyn trying to step in and take my arm. Perhaps it's foolish, but I don't like the way the vampire's looking at me. There's no reason to show more weakness than I absolutely have to. "Cato should be able to get us all patched up in short order. Then we'll see about the best way to reach the ship." If the *Audacity* hasn't left by now, I highly doubt they'll sail off before morning. We have a little time.

As we retrace our steps toward Kanghri, I can't help wondering if I'm really going to go through with this. It's one thing to passively disobey the laws, but what we're talking about is treason. There's no two ways about it. Even if we're successful at installing Nox as the captain, there's nothing to stop them from turning us over. Even if they really *are* part of some rebel group, it would be a clever way to ensure suspicion never lands on them. It's ruthless, but they haven't gotten to their position by being a bleeding heart.

Still, it's the best plan we have. We need answers, and Nox is the one who has them.

Once we reach the edges of town—again—I lead the way down to a little storefront tucked in an alley near the docks. In all the years we've been coming through this route, Cato has never moved locations, even though ze definitely has the funds to do it. I think ze gives away all large number of zir services for free, and the best place to be able to do that is here in Kanghri.

Not over the strait with the rich in Mairi.

"Let me do the talking," I say softly. I'm not too worried about Evelyn making a smart comment because I have a feeling that Cato will find her incredibly amusing. The vampire, on the other hand? Less so.

I knock on the door. It's only a minute or two before it opens, revealing Cato. Ze looks much the same as ze did the last time I saw zir. Short and round, with close-cropped curls and dark brown skin. Ze frowns at me. "What are you doing here? I didn't get word that the *Crimson Hag* had made port." Zir gaze lands on my bandaged neck. "Hounds' tits, what did you do to yourself? Come in, come in." Ze moves back and motions me with flapping hands into the depths of zir home.

Evelyn sticks close to me, and I can sense the vampire

behind her, doing the same. It's just as well. Cato keeps a chaotic household. Ze is a collector of sorts, acquiring trinkets and treasures from every corner of Threshold and beyond. And every single piece of it seems to be stacked in this room alone. There is a narrow pathway that I have to concentrate to follow, ensuring that my shoulders don't knock into any of the towering piles on either side. It looks like the worst kind of disorganization, but I know from experience that Cato knows the location of every single item. It upsets zir when people mess with it, so I take great pains not to disturb anything with my passing.

By contrast, zir workshop is practically bare of everything except the tools of zir trade. Cato all but shoves me down onto the chair in the center of the room. It's at that moment that ze seems to realize I have company with me. Ze narrows zir eyes. "You both look nearly as bad as he does. Sit your asses down and I will see to you after I deal with this one."

They sit without argument.

For the next fifteen minutes I am the object of Cato's tender mercies. Ze curses me quietly under zir breath as ze examines my wound. "Well, at least someone had the insight to see to you before you bled to death. That's about the only thing you've done right since you acquired this injury."

Over zir shoulder, I see Evelyn stiffen in outrage, but I meet her gaze and try to convey the need for patience. Most medics I deal with have terrible bedside manner, Aadi being the sole exception. And even then, she gets plenty snippy when her patients ignore her medical advice. Not that I have to worry about that now that I'm no longer sailing on the *Hag*. There will come a day when that realization doesn't feel like a bucket of cold water in my face, but today isn't that day.

As grateful as I am that Evelyn asked the questions that shone the light of truth on the situation in Threshold, I miss my crew. Not all of them, of course. I could go the rest of my life without seeing Miles again. But some of the others. Kit and Aadi and even Lucky, though that one is a bit of a reach.

Cato finishes sewing me up and then administers a magical patch that should seal the wound completely within a couple hours. I know from experience that it will be sensitive and prone to reinjury for a little while, but it's better than walking around with an open wound.

"Thank you."

"I'm not doing this out of the goodness of my heart. You're not as bad as the rest of them, most of the time, but your gold keeps this place running, Bowen. So best believe I will be charging you extravagantly for my services."

Like any good seafarer, I have a number of gold coins sewn into my cloak. If I had access to my cabin before we were kicked off the *Hag*, I would have more. As such, I expect that this will bankrupt me. Which begs the question of how the fuck I'm going to pay for things going forward.

A problem for another day.

I'm certainly not going to short Cato for zir work. Ze moves to Lizzie next, and it takes only a few minutes before ze pronounces her perfectly healthy, if covered in filth. Evelyn receives a few small bandages for her cuts, but none of them require stitches. That's a relief. I still haven't fully addressed that stunt she pulled, and I don't have the words to do it properly without threatening to throttle her again. She scared the shit out of me, and I don't know how to deal with that.

Cato leaves us alone after pointing to the door that leads to

the shower for patients, with clear instructions to clean up before we leave to avoid bringing attention ze isn't interested in
dealing with. I barely wait for the door to close before I turn to
Evelyn. "What can I say to convince you to stay here with Cato
until this is finished?"

Lizzie snorts and stands, stretching her arms over her head.
"Good luck with that. I'm going to bathe while you two fight."
She disappears through the door, leaving us staring at each
other.

"I'm going to pretend you didn't just ask me that." Evelyn
moves around the room, poking at the various tinctures and
equipment Cato keeps here. "I have as much a stake in this as
you do. Either we're full partners, or we're not. You can't shuffle
me to the side every time there's a hint of danger. That's not how
I work, Bowen. I realize that I am not a badass telekinetic like
you, but I would think after my saving your ass several times,
you would finally understand that I can defend myself. Just because I don't want to kill unnecessarily doesn't mean I'm weak."

"I would never dream of calling you weak."

She crosses to me and makes a show of glaring. "Besides, if I
don't go with you, I'm sure you're going to find a sword to fall
on in the most paladin way possible. You're too self-sacrificing
for anyone's sake, and I won't have you dying just because it
seemed like a good idea at the time."

That draws a reluctant laugh out of me. "Very well. I won't
ask you to stay behind again." Or at least I'll do my best not to.
At this point, I can't make any guarantees. Worry for her is a live
thing inside of me. It was bad enough when I was concerned for
my crew in their safety and their future. I'm beginning to understand that I didn't love them, at least not in the way that I

love Evelyn. Not as this all-consuming thing that drives me out of my mind and makes me act against type.

She leans down and examines my bandage. "You were right. Cato is very good. Ze patched you up in half the time I expected it to take."

"Yes." I stand and shrug out of my cloak. "Now grab your stolen dagger and help me cut these coins out of the lining. Time is of the essence."

CHAPTER 33

Evelyn

THERE'S A TICKING CLOCK PLAYING IN EVERYONE'S MIND, but like any plan worth having, it takes longer than anyone expects to get the pieces into place. By the time Bowen acquires a small boat similar to the one Nox used to drop us off, the moon is high in the sky. He glares up at it as he rows. "It's practically a spotlight announcing our presence."

"If the light doesn't announce us, your incessant bitching certainly will."

The other thing I didn't anticipate about this plan: my ex and my current paramour, both more than capable of murder, trapped in a close space. They keep making little snarling comments at each other, and while they haven't exploded into violence yet, I can't discount it as a possibility. It's incredibly irritating. And stressful. Which makes me bitchy, which only aggravates the issue, because they both respond to my bitchiness.

We all fall silent, though, as we leave the relative safety of the enclosed strait between First Sister and Second Sister. Even with the light of the full moon, I can barely see the *Audacity* bobbing gently in the distance. Surely they must have just as much difficulty seeing us.

The truth is that we might climb aboard to find a murderous crew waiting to slit our throats and toss us right back into the sea. We won't know until it's far too late to do anything about it. Not that I'm nervous or anything. I'm definitely not. I'm sitting here, cool and composed and perfectly at ease with the thought of what we're about to do.

We have no choice. This is our only option. We're putting a lot of faith in the fact that Nox apparently doesn't actively want us dead. And a lot of hope in the crew members who are loyal to them. It's a leap of faith to assume they'll understand what we're trying to do. We're taking a gamble and not even a good one.

We sit in tense silence as Bowen continues to row us closer to the ship. Cato did one hell of a job on him. He's not quite moving as if he was never injured in the first place, but the exhaustion and pain that seemed to be weighing him down is no longer in evidence. I'm feeling pretty fresh, too. All of my cuts have healed; aside from my used spells and slightly shallower magic reserves, I'd barely believe I was in a fight earlier today. And yesterday. Lizzie, of course, looks pristine.

"You should probably be the one rowing," I say under my breath. "You were less beat up than him, and you're not human. You have vampire stamina."

"And deprive the big, strong man of showing us how big and

strong he is?" She doesn't look at me as she says it, matching my tone in a way that is designed not to carry. "I wouldn't dream of it."

Petty until the bitter end. But Bowen wouldn't even consider the possibility of someone else taking the job. He snapped and snarled until we sat in the places he indicated. It serves him right to do all the work. Not that *I'm* interested in rowing.

If I'm going to stay in Threshold, I'm going to have to take up some kind of strength training and cardio just to keep up. *Gross.* But as little as I like the idea, I like getting bested in combat even less. If my time here so far is any indication, I'm going to see a lot of combat. As formidable as my magic is, Bunny was right when she said we shouldn't rely on it at the expense of the other tools in our toolbox. It was one subject we always argued about, mostly because I was a lazy teenager.

Now I see the wisdom in her words ... but that doesn't mean I like it any more now than I did at sixteen.

Soon enough, we're too close to the ship to risk snide comments. Bowen gives one last strong pull, sending us coasting over the surface until we nearly bump into the ship itself. Only Lizzie throwing out a hand to stop our momentum prevents it.

"I'll take care of Hedd, as we discussed. Keep the crew off me. Whoever keeps fighting after he's dead needs to be removed."

My stomach twists in upon itself. There's no going back now; truth be told, there was no going back the moment we reached that safe house and understood its implications. I'm not supportive of wholesale slaughter, but all it took was a couple days on the *Audacity* to realize that plenty of the crew members mimic their captain in his values ... or lack thereof. They're not good people. They're gleeful murderers, and they don't much care if the creature on the other side of their sword is truly a monster or not. The night before the fight with the mermaids, I overheard two of them laughing about killing a selkie. A fucking *selkie*.

Without their seal skins, they're practically human. But that didn't stop those two crew members from ending this one's life.

No, I won't show mercy. Not to people who would gladly cut me down just for questioning an order. Not to monsters in men's skins.

Bowen slips past us, light on his feet as he scales the side of the ship faster than anyone has a right to. Lizzie watches him go with an unreadable look. "You next, Evelyn."

"If you wanted to stare at my ass, all you have to do is ask." It's a testament of how freaked out I am that I'm flirting with her. There's certainly no intent behind it.

She snorts. "I'm concerned about those weak little arms of yours. If you take a tumble, I'll have to catch you before your splash alerts everyone that we're here."

"Bitch."

"I'm not wrong, and you know it." She motions for me to precede her up the side of the ship.

I'm embarrassed to admit how right she is as I climb. Even with the solid rest I got last night, I'm exhausted. I want a cozy blanket, a racy romance novel, and maybe some hot sex in between naps and reading. I don't want to be damn near ripping my fingernails off as I search for a handhold on the side of a ship in the middle of the night.

Bowen is a bastard for making the climb look so easy.

Knowing Lizzie is behind me, judging, keeps me moving. By

the time I reach the top, my arms are shaking and I'm not sure I'm strong enough to pull myself over. I don't get a chance. Bowen leans over the railing and then his magic wraps around me like a gentle hug. He lifts me up and deposits me next to him. I almost snap that he could've done that to begin with and saved us a lot of trouble. But he presses a single finger to my lips.

I realize why a moment later. There are three people hovering in the air, Their limbs plastered to their sides, and their mouths closed. It takes a moment to realize how they're gagged. "Bowen," I whisper. "Are you holding their jaws shut?"

"Yes." He barely waits for Lizzie to land on the deck before he's moving again. "As we discussed."

It's not a very good plan. Or maybe it's brilliant in its simplicity. He's going after Hedd, and Lizzie is to take care of anyone who attacks us. And I am supposed to find Nox and somehow convince them to see things our way. Like I said, easy peasy.

Before I can move away, Bowen grabs the back of my neck and pulls me in for a rough kiss. "Be safe, Evie. You can't afford to hesitate. Not tonight. Promise me."

I might hate this, but I'll do anything to get back to his side. I want all three of us to survive to see the dawn, and I refuse to be the reason one of the people I care about falls. "I promise."

He releases me slowly, as if it pains him to do so. And then he's gone, striding toward the captain's cabin. Technically, I'm supposed to be headed down to the crew's quarters, but I follow my instincts and circle around to the helm instead. In the time that we were aboard the *Audacity*, I saw Nox there more often than Hedd. If the captain spent the last day partying like Bowen suspects, I bet he put them in charge.

Sure enough, I find them leaning against the wall with their eyes closed. Sleeping? Not sleeping? I've seen what they can do with their elemental magic, and I have no desire to be on the other end of that. "Nox."

Their eyes fly open and the breath is jerked from my lungs. It happens so fast, I don't have time to even make a choked sound. I claw at my throat, but it's not my body betraying me. It's Nox's magic.

"What the fuck are you doing here?" They grab me by the throat and spin around to pin me to the wall. Only then do they allow me to breathe. Barely. "You should be at the safe house recovering. I expected Bowen to have a death wish, but you seemed much more practical. It's a pity I was wrong."

"I think so, too." My voice is so raspy, it's nearly incomprehensible.

"I'll ask you one last time." Menace radiates off them in waves. "What are you doing here?" This is not the charming, flirty pirate I interacted with a handful of times on the trip here. This person is dangerous. If I don't find the right words, I have no doubt that they'll kill me.

I spent a lot of time on the ride over considering all the charming, manipulative things I can say to get them on our side. They all fail me now. There's only the truth. "We came to kill Hedd and his supporters. We want to know who's running the network of safe houses, because there is a network; don't tell me there isn't. We want to help—by serving on a crew that's loyal to the cause, not the Cŵn Annwn. Like you. Like the people on *this* crew."

Nox's face gives nothing away. "Not all of them."

"Not all of them," I agree. My lungs finally feel like they're fully expanding again. It's everything I can do not to suck in great inhales. "But those loyal to the Cŵn Annwn aren't the reason you haven't taken over, are they? It's Hedd." If Bowen wasn't entirely sure he could take the captain in a fight without losses, then there's no way Nox can do it.

They all but confirm my suspicion when they lean in close, pressing harder on my throat. "Regardless of what you think you know, that motherfucker is damn near unkillable. As long as he is captain of the *Audacity*, things will remain the same." They push me away with a disgusted sound. "You came back here for nothing. All you're going to do is die."

I really fucking hope they're wrong. "And if we don't die? If we succeed, will you help us?"

Whatever response they may have had is lost in a roar that I swear shakes the very boards beneath my feet. It's the only warning I get before the door to the captain's cabin blows off its hinges and crashes into the sea. A body flies through the air and hits the railing hard enough to splinter it. He staggers to his feet, and I have to press my hands to my mouth to stop myself from crying out.

Bowen.

He looks like shit. Hedd obviously got off a few good punches, because one of his eyes is already swelling shut, and he's bleeding from the mouth. He's steady on his feet, though. That has to mean something. It *has* to.

The being that comes through the door is barely recognizable as human. I thought we saw the full transformation into berserker in the fight against the mermaids, but that obviously wasn't true. Hedd is easily seven and a half feet tall, and broad enough that he has to come through the door sideways. Each of his meaty arms have doubled in size, but they're not perfectly proportioned. He looks like a clay doll that a child molded into the approximation of a warrior. That lack of grace should slow him down, at least in theory, but he's fast on his feet. Too fast.

He charges Bowen, and even as I scream, it's already too late. They collide in a crash of limbs and topple through the splintered railing and into the water.

CHAPTER 34

Bowen

I EXPECTED HEDD TO BE DAMN NEAR COMATOSE FROM PAR-
tying. That's what made me hesitate. Even now, even hating
him as much as I do, the thought of murdering a man in cold
blood was one step too far. That moment of hesitation cost me.

Now I'm sinking to the bottom of the fucking sea with
Hedd's hands around my throat in an unbreakable grip. I pum-
mel him in his face, but I might as well be punching the tide. He
doesn't feel it. If I'm doing any damage, it's so minuscule as to be
nonexistent.

The fucker doesn't care that he's drowning alongside me. Or
maybe he's not. I always suspected that in his berserker form, he
can hold his breath for significantly longer than a normal human. It's the only reason I can think of that Nox hasn't killed
him yet.

None of that is helping me right now, though.

Even with the thin shield of my power protecting him from
crushing my throat, he's doing a damn good job strangling me.

Black spots dance across my vision. A handy trick, that, considering we're surrounded by blackness at this depth.

Desperation is a live thing inside my chest. I can't afford to lose control. We're too close to the ship. I may not have killed the crew last time, but there's no guarantee I can avoid it if it happens again. Even with my weakness, I could slaughter the lot of them on accident. I could slaughter *Evie*.

I have to . . . I need to . . .

The cold pressure of the depths presses against me as hard as Hedd's hands. And we just keep sinking. His body is denser than a human's. He's acting the part of an anchor, pulling me down. He can survive this pressure. I don't think I can. Not for much longer.

There's no help for it. I have to strike now.

I press my hands to his chest and give a soundless roar of my own. I channeled my power into his ribs and sternum and heart, wave after wave after wave. It's like fighting a mountain. But even mountains crumble eventually. On my fifth blast of power, Hedd's grip weakens on my throat. I hit him again twice more for good measure. The final blast since his body is spinning away from me into the depths. I don't have time to make sure I finished the job.

My lungs shriek for oxygen and my limbs feel leaden and slow as I start to fight my way to the surface. In desperation, I use my magic to propel me, but I'm once again dancing too close to my limits. It sputters in fits and starts. Or maybe that's my brain slowly losing control.

Fuck. I always knew there was a possibility I would die by drowning. It's a reality for anyone who lives their life at sea. But I don't want to go out like this, not so soon after finding Evelyn.

For all that she holds half my heart, there's so much about her I don't know. A lifetime of little details, each a treasure to unveil and discover. I'll never get a chance now.

The water shifts around me. I tense, sure that Hedd has somehow come back from the dead to finish the job. But there's no one around me. Only the water moving under my body and pushing me upward. Faster and faster until my upper body breeches the surface. I choke and gasp and frantically fight to ensure I don't go back under, but the water is solid beneath my feet.

"Bowen!"

I look up to find Evelyn leaning over the railing, her gorgeous face a mask of fear. At her side, Nox stands with their hands outstretched, their eyes narrowed in concentration. They snarl when they see me. "I can't hold you forever, you fool. Get up here."

They saved me.

It takes twice as long to climb up the side of the ship as it did the last time. My lungs are on fire and every muscle in my body shakes. I can't help looking over my shoulder again and again, half certain that Hedd somehow survived after all that. But he never surfaces. No matter how extended his ability to hold his breath is, he doesn't have gills. He can't do it indefinitely. He's dead. He has to be.

Evelyn practically tackles me as I haul myself over the railing. Her hands are everywhere, checking me for injuries. She makes a pained sound when she reaches my throat and brushes her fingers over the tender skin there. "Oh, Bowen."

I look over her head to find the deck filled with absolute carnage. There are easily twenty dead bodies. At first glance I'm not entirely certain how they died, only that there's a lot of blood.

And there, leaning against the mast as if she has nowhere better to be, is the vampire. This is *her* work. I don't know that I'll ever be comfortable in her presence, but I can't deny that she is a useful ally to have on our side.

Nox crouches in front of me, their expression serious. "I think it's time we talked."

"Yes," I rasp.

"Give me two minutes." They stand and turn to face the few crew members left living. Nox projects their voice. "We have to move fast. These poor souls were victims of the mermaid attack gone wrong. We eliminated the pests, but lost them in the process. Give them a sea burial and get this deck cleaned up. We sail at first light. I'll file the report as soon as we put some distance between ourselves and Three Sisters."

The surviving crew leaps into motion. There are no questions and no challenges to Nox's order. We were right. The people here who follow them, follow *them*, not the Cŵn Annwn.

Evelyn helps me to my feet and slips under my arm. As we stagger after Nox in the direction of the captain's cabin, I catch sight of Dia. She seems unharmed, and even gives me a saucy wink as I pass. Thank the gods she's okay. I didn't realize how worried I was about her until I see her alive and well.

Lizzie joins us in the cabin, still looking bored. Evelyn urges me into a chair, and I can't help staring at the vampire and wondering at her complete lack of concern over murdering nearly two dozen people. If it affected her at all, there's no evidence of it on her face. There's still a coiled tension to her body that I suspect means she can burst into violence at any time. I don't know why that surprises me. Evelyn has told me time and time again how dangerous Lizzie is.

But she pulled her punches in her fight with Evelyn. It gave me a false sense of security. I can't afford to underestimate her, for all that she appears to be on our side. For now. There's no telling how long that will last. It's become clear she doesn't actually want to kill Evelyn, but that doesn't mean she's safe for anyone else to be around. At least there's some assurance that she will cooperate until we find the *Crimson Hag* and she gets her family heirlooms back.

What happens after that is anyone's guess.

Nox looks around the room in disgust. It's not particularly filthy, but there is evidence of Hedd everywhere. His clothes strewn about on the floor. Several racks of weapons leaned haphazardly against the wall. His desk piled high with bottles of liquor, to the point where it's almost impossible to see the surface. A quick glance at the small open space reveals several notifications of tardy reports.

Nox sighs and crosses their arms over their chest. "I don't know whether to thank you or cut your throats and be done with it."

"I highly suggest you go with the former option considering we just secured you the captaincy." Lizzie speaks mildly as she examines her nails, which only makes her threat more pronounced. "You're welcome, by the way."

Nox is completely unfazed. They turn to the vampire. "I don't know you."

"You don't need to know me. You know her." Lizzie flicks her fingers at Evelyn. "So let's stop pussyfooting around and get to the point. Like Evelyn said, we helped you out. In return, they want information. I want a ride until we cross paths with the *Crimson Hag*. A small price to pay for your new promotion. If you don't cooperate, I'm sure there's someone else among the crew we can convince to see things our way."

I tense, ready to jump in if things escalate, but Nox just laughs. "I can see that you're going to be a pain in my ass. Great." They turn to me and Evelyn. "If I tell you this, there's no going back. You're either with us, or you don't leave the ship alive."

"We've already gone too far." I take Evelyn's hand and squeeze. She's still hovering close, as if she's certain I'm going to slide it right out of my chair. "Tell us."

"Suit yourself." They lean on the edge of the desk. "There's a number of people who don't agree with the way the laws are set up in Threshold. The Cŵn Annwn are more than capable of transporting people back to the portals that will lead to their home realms. There's no reason that we don't do so—except for control. It's a power grab that ensures the Council won't be questioned, and that the ranks of their hunters are always filled."

It's the conclusion Evelyn and I already came to. She saw the cracks in the system immediately. It took her practically smacking me over the head with them in order for me to see them, too. It still doesn't explain how this rebellion is happening, and how they've gone this long without anyone noticing. "So someone decided to do something about it?"

"So someone decided to do something about it," Nox agrees. They shrug. "I suspect sympathetic people among the Cŵn Annwn have been allowing trespassers to slip through their fingers for generations. It wasn't until . . ." They hesitate and seem to have an internal battle with themself. Finally, they continue.

"Our leader is someone uniquely situated to create a proper network. They are able to manage communications, and ensure that we are able to move more effectively toward our goals."

"What goal is that? Getting people home . . . or something more?" Again, I'm nearly certain I know what Nox will say before they speak, but I want to hear them say it. There's a feeling in my chest, a bubble growing that I'm terrified will pop. Evelyn is mostly joking when she calls me a paladin—at least I think she is. But the truth is that the label fits far better than I'll ever want to admit aloud.

I need a cause to believe in. I don't know if I'll ever follow on faith alone again or without question, but maybe my loyalty means more that way. I don't know. It's something to think about later.

Again, Nox hesitates. It strikes me that they've had to be so careful with their words and how they carry themselves while serving on this crew. It must be strange to be asked to speak plainly. To be *able* to. "When's the last time the Cŵn Annwn actually hunted? I don't mean all of us sailing around on crimson-sailed ships, and I sure as fuck don't mean those peacocks in the Council. I'm talking about the originals. I'm not certain they exist anymore. The only proof we have is the Council's say-so." They shrug, but the move is far too tense. "It's above my pay grade. All I've ever wanted is freedom, and the life we live isn't free. It just looks that way from the outside."

At my side, Evelyn shifts a little. "You're talking in circles. If you really want to be free, we need to remove the Council and hope the originals aren't around anymore to take interest in the goings-on in Threshold."

"Yes." They look at each of us in turn. "It's not time to make that move. There are too many captains like Hedd out there, too many crews who are happy to misuse the power that comes with flying crimson sails. If we remove the current Council, a new one will pop up in its place. They might not be in a place to make real change for years, or even longer. Making a public move is a huge risk and we'll get a single shot at it. This won't be a dramatic, quick battle. If you're signing on with us, you're signing on for the drudgery of a long-haul voyage."

"Speak. Plainly," Evelyn snaps. "We're facing a choice just like we were facing when we first came to Threshold—join up, or die. The difference is that we're going to sail around, pretending to be the Cŵn Annwn, occasionally killing actual monsters and saving people."

Nox smiles thinly. "It seems I don't have to speak plainly, after all. You understand me well enough."

If we're found out, we'll be executed in a truly spectacular way. This goes beyond making a vow and running, or disobeying a direct order. This is out-and-out rebellion. I wrap my arm around Evelyn's shoulders. "And this leader? Who are they?"

"Very few people know their identity, and you'll probably live and die without finding out." They meet my gaze steadily. "Can you handle that?"

"As long as you—and they—don't require unquestioning obedience. I won't spend the rest of my life moving about with my eyes closed. If I don't agree with an order, I'm going to question it, and if I still don't agree with it, I will not be obeying. Can *you* handle that?"

"I wouldn't have it any other way." They swivel to face Lizzie. "You. Vampire. You've been awfully quiet since mouthing off a few minutes ago."

"And interrupt this rousing speech?" She sounds absolutely bored. "As I said, the only reason I'm here is to get my family heirlooms. I'm hunting the *Crimson Hag*. As soon as I find that ship, I'm returning to my realm. Expect no vows from me, but I'm more than capable of pulling my weight and playing nice in the meantime."

It's hardly a binding promise, but I'm beginning to understand that it's as close to one as Lizzie will get. I tuck Evelyn tighter against my body and look down at her. "Well? What do you think?"

She's a little pale, a little scared. But her smile is genuine. "I do believe that your paladin ways are rubbing off on me. Let's be the good guys."

CHAPTER **35**

Evelyn

BEING ONE OF THE GOOD GUYS IS A LOT OF FUCKING work. It takes nearly a full day to clean up the bloodbath caused by Lizzie and Bowen. Apparently a burial at sea just means tossing the bodies over the railing. I'd assume they'd wash ashore in short order, but when I say as much to Nox, they get a strange look on their face and say, "They won't have a chance to."

I don't know what that means, but I suspect it has to do with sea monsters, and in that case I'm better off not knowing. I maintain that eliminating the mermaids was a service to the people of Three Sisters. I'm glad that I forced the issue with the dragon; I really hope she and her youngling escaped okay. But that doesn't mean I want to know about every predator that hunts beneath the surface.

Not when I'm sailing on what amounts to a tiny boat. Yes, the ship is plenty huge, but compared to a kraken or some other beastie that I've never heard of? The thought makes my skin prickle, so I very intentionally don't let myself linger on it.

Bowen and I are assigned the same cabin as before, but there's no time or energy to do anything but sleep in the bed. We work all day, then collapse into a state not unlike unconsciousness at nightfall. Even so, the change in Bowen is marked.

He's lighter on his feet. Smiles more often. Even his shoulders seem straighter, as if he set down a burden he's been carrying for far too long. And when he holds me, he holds me closely, as if he believes I might slip away at any moment.

On the fourth day, Lizzie finds me hiding in the pantry. She leans against the door and crosses her arms over her chest. "What are you doing?"

"Just taking an unsanctioned break."

"I see." Instead of letting the awkwardness grow or walking away, she steps into the pantry and drops down on the faded wooden box next to me. "The portal to our home realm is destroyed."

"Yeah." Guilt tries to wrap around my throat, but it took two of us to make that happen. I was reckless with my magic, and she wasn't exactly slowing down to ask questions before she attacked. "I'd say we both share the blame with that."

She shakes her head. "You're always so eager to look for someone to blame. It was an accident, and beyond that, it's not the only way home. Threshold might be the space that connects all realms, but that doesn't mean the rest of them aren't also connected in some way. It will take some time, but there's no proof that it's impossible."

She's not saying anything that I hadn't already considered

myself, but that raises the question of *why* she's saying it. I twist to face her. "If anyone can do it, you can."

"Of that, I have no doubt." She taps her fingers on her knee. "What I'm trying to say is that I realize I may share part of the responsibility for us coming to this place and getting into this situation. As such, I'm offering to escort you home. After I retrieve my family heirlooms."

Shock steals my words for several long moments. She hasn't tried to murder me lately, but a removal of active animosity is not quite the same thing as forgiveness. Neither is this, technically. Still, it's more than I could have dreamed of being offered. "You're serious."

"I see how you light up around him, Evelyn. You might think it's love, but what happens when the lust wears off? You'll realize that you're stuck in a life you never wanted. You like to party, steal things, and embrace every moment of life to its fullest. If you stay here and take part in some revolution, you're likely to end up dead." She stares at her fingers. "It . . . upsets me . . . to think you might die for a cause that's not yours."

Maybe it should hurt that she wasn't willing to give even the slightest indication of caring until I was well beyond her reach. There was a moment in the past when I could've given my heart to this vampire. I don't know if it would've worked out, but it doesn't matter anymore. That moment is gone. I still care about her, but it will never be what I feel for Bowen.

Still, the fact that she's offering this option at all warms my chest. I bump my shoulder against hers. "I care about you, too, you know. But what I feel for Bowen is entirely different. It's more than just caring, and certainly more than just lust. I love him."

She sighs. "I thought you might say that."

"You're right that I've never had a cause to fight for before now, but this one is noble. It's one that Bunny would approve of." It's true, but it's not the full truth. "But even if she wouldn't have . . . it's time I start making my own decisions. *I* believe in this cause. What the Cŵn Annwn are doing in Threshold is wrong, and I might not be a great warrior, but I can help right the wrongs they've committed. It's dangerous, but it's the right thing to do and I feel strongly about being part of it."

"If you change your mind—"

"I won't." I make an effort to gentle my tone. "But I appreciate the offer. Really, I do." I stand, my sore muscles groaning in protest. "I better get back to work."

I leave Lizzie alone in the pantry, her expression unreadable. I didn't realize I needed to have that conversation as much as she apparently did, but I feel lighter for having done it. As if I really gave us proper closure, instead of running from the discomfort of something ending. *How novel.*

I want to seek Bowen out, to talk to him about the new confidence settling inside me, but I make myself wait until our shift is over. Nox runs a tight ship and they don't take kindly to someone shirking their duties—especially since we're sailing with a much lighter crew than the *Audacity* really needs to perform at capacity. Nox said something about picking up more people soon, but they've been incredibly vague about what that means—or what happens after.

They still don't trust us. That's fine. We'll earn their trust with time.

I find Bowen in our cabin, standing in the shower with his hands braced against the tile. It's the most natural thing in the world to strip and join him in the small space. I slip between him and the wall and wrap my arms around his waist. "Hey."

"Hey." He kisses my temple. "I'm ashamed to say it, but being captain for so long means I'm out of shape. I thought I knew what hard work was, but this is kicking my ass."

"Mine too." I don't want to let go of this moment of peace, but it's important that I share what happened today. "Lizzie came to see me earlier."

It's only because I'm holding him close that I feel him tense. "Oh?"

"She offered to take me home, after she reclaims what I stole, of course." I lean back until I can see his face. "I told her no. I hope she's right and there is a path back to our realm; for her sake, at least. But I meant it when I said I love you, Bowen. Not just because you fuck like a god, and not just because you hold me like I'm the most priceless thing in existence. I love you for your stubbornness and your honor and your willingness to do whatever it takes to right the wrongs you have inadvertently caused. You're stuck with me, at least for as long as you'll have me."

He smooths my hair back and searches my expression. "You mean it."

It's not a question, but I answer him all the same. "I mean it."

"I love you, too, you know." He traces his thumbs over my cheek bones and down my jaw to the corners of my mouth. "I think I started falling in love with you the moment you stole my flask." He brushes a kiss to my lips. "I guess you stole my heart at the same time."

"That is so corny and I love it." I love him. Gods, we aren't on an easy path, but it's still one worth traveling. The one I'm *choosing*. That's the only thing that matters.

Warmth suffuses me, and for a moment, I'm certain I can feel Bunny's approval, the sensation as familiar as her hugs. It's a strange thing to experience while naked in the shower with Bowen, and I actually look at the door as if expecting her to be standing there. She's not. Of course she's not. But the feeling takes several long moments to fade.

"Is something wrong?"

"No." I turn back to him. "I was just thinking that my grandmother would have liked you quite a bit."

His smile is soft and achingly sweet. "Considering she's responsible for raising the woman you've become, I think I'd have liked her quite a bit, too." He grabs the shampoo and starts working it into my hair. "It's going to be a while before they trust us enough to allow us to meet the leader of this movement. We're looking at a long road and a lot of work."

"Does that bother you? Being on a ship and not being captain? Of losing that prestige?"

He shakes his head. "It feels a little like penance, but I'm happy to pay it. I have a lot to learn."

"That's so *paladin* of you." I go onto my tiptoes and kiss him. "I won't promise that I'll always be graceful and happy about the process, but I'm not afraid of hard work when it means something. And *this* means something." I press my body to his. "Now, if we hurry up and exchange orgasms, we can still get like six hours of sleep before our next shift."

Bowen's power wraps around me, sliding against my wet skin and hooking the back of my thighs to lift me into the air. I relax into the hold, loving the way his dark eyes have gone intense and hot. His magic guides my head back to rinse the soap from my hair even as two tendrils of it start playing with my breasts.

"Evie."

"Hmmm?"

He chuckles. "For us to only have six hours of sleep left, that still leaves four hours of fucking."

"Does it?" I ask innocently.

"Yes." His voice is low and amused. "Barely enough time. We might have the rest of our lives, no matter how long or short that time may be, but it will never be enough. Eternity with you would never be enough."

I kiss him. "Then we better make it count."

ACKNOWLEDGMENTS

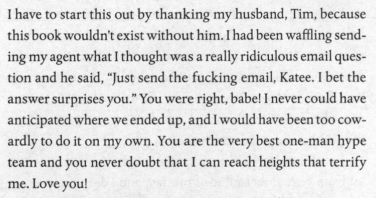

I have to start this out by thanking my husband, Tim, because this book wouldn't exist without him. I had been waffling sending my agent what I thought was a really ridiculous email question and he said, "Just send the fucking email, Katee. I bet the answer surprises you." You were right, babe! I never could have anticipated where we ended up, and I would have been too cowardly to do it on my own. You are the very best one-man hype team and you never doubt that I can reach heights that terrify me. Love you!

Biggest thanks to my agent, Laura Bradford, for taking my "Hey, I had this thought" email and saying, "Let me put out some feelers." I think things may have happened faster than either of us expected, but look at us now! We finally sold a pirate book!

Huge appreciation to Cindy Hwang and Kristine Swartz for helping me polish this bonkers little book to perfection. The story is a thousand times better for your comments and suggestions. I'm so excited to write pirates for you and for the journey to continue!

Many thanks to the team at Berkley! Thanks to Kristin Ci-polla, Jessica Mangicaro, and Kim-Salina I for getting this book into so many hands and onto so many shelves! Drafting a book may be done in a vacuum, but getting it formatted, beautified, and printed isn't. Thanks to Mary Baker, Christine Legon, Me-gan Elmore, Janine Barlow, Courtney Vincento, and Rakhee Bhatt. Thank you to Rita Frangie Batour for the *phenomenal* cover!

Big hugs to my friends for holding down the fort through this whole process. To Jenny Nordbak for constantly being there while I go "OMG WTF" while drafting, promoing, and just generally existing. Your "KATEE YES" gives me so much energy to keep going, and I appreciate you. To Melody Carlisle for being such a force of positivity that it makes ME be positive even when I'm at my most cynical. To Asa Maria Bradley for never once doubting that I could do this. To Hilary Brady for only being a Marco Polo away for the days when life got too overwhelming. To Melissa Taylor for being in the trenches with me, through the good and the bad.

Last, but never least, thanks to my kids. You put up with a lot from your absent-minded mother, and I deeply appreciate your patience when deadlines make me more forgetful than normal. Love you!

LOOK OUT FOR

Blood on the Tide

THE NEXT BOOK IN THE CRIMSON SAILS SERIES

Author photo by Bethany Chamberlin

KATEE ROBERT (she/they) is a *New York Times* and *USA Today* bestselling author of spicy romance. *Entertainment Weekly* calls their writing "unspeakably hot." Their books have sold over two million copies. They live in the Pacific Northwest with their husband, children, a cat who thinks he's a dog, and two Great Danes who think they're lapdogs.

Ready to find
your next great read?

Let us help.

Visit prh.com/nextread